HUMBUG

HUMBUG

THE UNWINDING OF EBENEZER SCROOGE

TONY BERTAUSKI

Copyright © 2019 by Tony Bertauski

All rights reserved.

No part of this book may be reproduced in any form or by any electronic or mechanical means, including information storage and retrieval systems, without written permission from the author, except for the use of brief quotations in a book review.

❦ Created with Vellum

CHANGE

It does not happen in a single night.

PART I

THE GHOST OF CHRISTMAS EVE

10:32 A.M.

I'm running two minutes behind, so I'll keep this entry short.

Jacob died this morning.

A massive coronary. Can't say I'm surprised, the idiot doctors he trusted. A man with money should live to a hundred. To die before seventy?

Ridiculous.

The world does not know what it lost today. Not just a man, but a visionary. A force that could change worlds. A will that could move mountains. A mind that could transform dreams.

Tragic.

Listen, I loved the man. He was my brother in every sense of the word. We didn't share a mother or father, but we were brothers nonetheless. We didn't always see eye to eye, but who does?

But he wanted to help the world, period. That was it. That's not a bad thing. He always said, "Ebenezer, I want to help the world. I want to help you."

I don't need help. On that account he was quite wrong. I am rich. But the world needs help, that's a fact. So I am sad today. Very sad. The world should be, too.

And that's it. Okay?
Good.

1

Ebenezer Scrooge watched the rain bead on the mahogany lid. *A nice coat of wax*, he thought. *Well done. Fitting.*

The rails were platinum, the inside lined with maroon velvet and a luxurious five-star mattress. No expense spared. Eb would've preferred something more reasonable—Jacob Marley wasn't going to see it, after all—but his dead friend's estate paid for the final resting place, so why sweat the details?

Waste of money, that's why.

The attendees were crowded beneath the tent, hugging each other for warmth and comfort. Rain pooled on the sagging canvas roof, dripping over the edge.

Outside the tent, a flock of black umbrellas protected the attendees gathered beneath the gray sky. They wiped their cheeks with tissues, holding each other close. Eb had shed one tear that morning. Considering he hadn't shed one since he was in diapers, a single tear was quite an episode.

If you asked him.

"We gather here today..." the preacher began.

The attendees wore black suits, black dresses. They wore pearls and furs, shiny shoes and sparkling earrings. Black veils and black hats. Eb wore a shiny tracksuit with two white stripes down the sleeves and legs and a round pair of spectacles that slid down the oily slope of his nose.

Very few in attendance were family because Jacob Marley had none. Except Eb. And he wasn't family, really. Not by blood, anyway.

These people were members of the Southern California community, representatives of charities that had received Jacob's goodwill; they were business associates and politicians.

Jim Thompson, CEO of Medicine Today, his unnatural tan defiant beneath the pallor of a wet umbrella. Marianne Clark, editor of *Wired Brain*, looking stylishly gaunt with a touch of gray in her bangs, heels spiking the soft earth. John Pendergrass, director of Body and Technology Research, with his age-appropriate wife touching the corners of her mascara-rich eyes.

They were all there.

They mourned the loss of a man that was "taken from his earthy vehicle too soon," the preacher preached. The crowd agreed and praised the Lord.

They were phonies.

They stole glances in his direction. He didn't praise the Lord out loud, oh heavens no. They looked at him because they were curious, judgmental. None of them consoled *him* for the loss of Jacob, his brother. Well, *like* his brother, the media corrected, often.

They were curious and unsympathetic because of the unusual figure that stood among them. It stood six feet tall, its skinwrap dull gray. Its trench coat, black and unusual for an android, was cinched at the waist. A top hat covered its head, quite silly. But that wasn't the worst part. The worst part was the face.

It wasn't the requisite eye holes and bump of a nose; there was no slot for a mouth where someone might insert a coin. That was last year's model. Eb had the most current servant droid, one that looked almost human.

He'd invented the droid, after all. Well, it was mostly Jacob. Eb helped.

Eb was at the funeral, but not in California. He was in Colorado.

It was absolutely unacceptable, in any culture or social status, to bring a servant droid *to* the burial. Eb didn't bring it, he sent the droid in his stead.

The newsfeeds were going to have a fit. They were going to skewer his callousness and question the poor decision-making, but he had his reasons. Not that anyone would understand. He had mourned that morning, shed that tear. They didn't see that.

In an attempt to appease the inevitable gossip, the dull gray droid projected Eb's features on its face rather than its own, as if Eb was standing at the foot of the casket, a tanned, square-jawed man. Unshaven. Grief-stricken.

Eb was neither unshaven nor grief-stricken. He didn't have a square jaw. If he did, it was hidden beneath multiple chins and a blotchy complexion. While the servant droid endured the rainy, cold season, Eb stood quite still in the dry, toasty projection room as the events unfolded around him as if he were actually there. Only dry. And warm.

He wasn't just there in spirit. He was there in every sense of the word. Just not in the flesh. The newsfeeds could debate all they wanted whether flesh or presence was more important at a funeral.

It was presence.

Eb raised his hands and rubbed his cheeks. The droid, connected to his actions through the sync suit, echoed his movements, patting away tear-streaked cheeks. Eb squeezed his eyes shut and practiced crying. It came so easily that morning, but lasted less than a minute. Now his sobs were dry and rehearsed, thick with sarcasm. He couldn't remember the last time he cried.

Maybe he forgot how.

Crying was for little kids and weak-minded individuals. Eb was neither. It didn't matter that his attempts were disingenuous. His projected expression would be altered. The attendees would see a sincere expression of grief on the servant droid's face, where tears rolled as plump as rain, where he wiped them away and blew his nose in a white, embroidered handkerchief.

Sandy Kaufman, CFO of St. Mary's Children's Hospital, was

outdoing him with the wailing. Eb brought up the volume of his grief, including sniffling and sudden, "Why, Lord? Why, why, why?"

It only drew more stares.

How do they do it? I'm dying to sit down and they keep standing and standing and the preacher keeps preaching. How many times do we have to praise him? Jacob Marley was my brother, but come on, people. Just because he's going in the ground doesn't qualify him for sainthood. He lived quite an unselfish life, okay. Honestly, it was remarkable. But you don't rise to the top of the technology world without splitting a few lips.

Jacob wasn't shrewd, but he could be ruthless. Only Eb saw that side of him. But Eb saw a lot of things other people didn't see.

When the service ended, some of the attendees shook the droid's hand. Eb reached out. The pressure was simulated inside his glove as they embraced. They were offering condolences to a dull gray droid with his face projected at them. And it wasn't really *his* face.

Hilarious.

A door opened twenty feet to Eb's right. The edges of the doorway curved along the domed projection wall, a squarish space carved from the dreary scene. A dull gray droid—an exact duplicate of the one shaking hands with the preacher now—walked into the room. This androgynoid wore a tracksuit similar to Eb's, the sleeves pushed up to the elbows.

As far as Eb was concerned, all droids were mindless servants that followed their programming. Tell them what to do and they did it because they were idiots. Jacob had begged to differ, arguing they had a personality that closely mimicked human behavior. They were still morons, simple as that.

Dum-dums.

"Auto," Eb muttered.

Disconnected from Eb's sync suit, the mourning droid continued to run the grieving program, freeing Eb to walk around the projection room.

"The news," Eb said. "Give it to me good."

"I don't feel good about this, sir."

"First of all, you don't feel. Second, that wasn't the question. So go, now. Give it to me."

"This was not Jacob's wish, sir."

Eb clawed the air, tendons stretching. "Did you or did you not do what I asked? And let me remind you the wrong answer gets you a one-way trip down the tumbler."

"But—"

"Zip." Eb snapped his fingers at him.

He really didn't want to recycle him. Servant droids were insanely expensive. Eb had more money than half the world, but there was no need to be frivolous. *Unless someone deserves it.*

"Yes?" Eb said. "Or no?"

"Yes, sir."

"You're sure?"

"I am, sir." The droid cocked his head to the side. "I am here to help you."

"I won't turn on the feeds and hear Jacob Marley willed his ownership to the Boy Scouts of Antarctica, will I?"

"No, sir."

"Complete and total and one hundred percent of Avocado, Incorporated, now rests in the name of Ebenezer Lennox Scrooge?"

The droid paused. "Yes, sir."

"What? Why'd you just pause?"

"I didn't use your middle name, sir."

"Why would you do that?"

"Because you don't use your middle name, sir."

Maybe a ride down the tumbler was in order. But then he'd have the same conversation with the same droid personality in a different body. There were seven of them, a hive mind sort of personality that would one day cause all of his hair to fall out.

"Never mind." Eb propped his elbow on his protruding gut and tapped his spongy chin like he was hammering a finishing nail into place. "Jacob wouldn't use my middle name, either. The lawyers will make it right."

A smile dug into the droid's flexible cheeks.

Eb tapped his jelly chin, never once reaching above the space where a dimple might reside. He rarely touched his face without washing. But in a rare lapse of judgment, he removed his round glasses and rubbed his eyes.

"Are you crying, sir?"

"No."

But he was, sort of.

Joy gushed from his stomach, a geyser of warm emotions that had reached his face, almost leaking from his eyes. *Almost*. Avocado, Inc., was his now. He couldn't remember crying twice in one day.

To be fair, he couldn't remember much about his childhood.

A line of grieving attendees was still waiting to shake the droid's hand, a few standing at the coffin with their heads bowed in hopes this unfortunate event wouldn't change their altruistic relationship with Avocado, Inc., once owned by Jacob Marley and Ebenezer Scrooge but now owned by Eb and Eb only.

A crocodile smile crept over his face.

He twisted the obsidian ring on his right hand, something that could be mistaken for a wedding band. An identical ring was on his left hand. He swiped his hands like a magician.

The funeral scene winked out.

The dome-shaped projection room went to sleep, the generic walls arching overhead. These were the moments Eb felt like a cooked goose beneath a serving dome.

"Avocado!" he shouted. "Come on down!"

The curved wall shimmered. A giant avocado appeared; a thick stem curved at the top, the word *avocado*—all lowercase letters in off-white—situated in the Buddha belly of the leathery fruit.

Colorful furniture appeared, original designs that conformed to every position the body could imagine. Jacob had insisted the kooky chairs and couches be arranged in an open office environment, a feng shui thingy that promoted progress by failure, thinking outside of the box. Eb was only interested in the progress part. The rest of it was stupid.

And failure was the wrong direction.

"Where is everyone?" Eb said.

"Many are attending Jacob's funeral, sir."

"Not all of them."

"It's also Christmas Eve, sir."

Eb glanced at his wrist, pretending to see a watch. "It's not even lunch!"

"The holiday has begun, sir."

"Bah!" Eb couldn't think of a word to express his contempt for such excessive year-end celebration. What could capture the guttural disgust he felt when employees—people he was paying, for crying out loud—flaunted excess in his face?

"Bah, unacceptable!" *That's not it.* "Call them back. They're paid to work till five o'clock."

"Many have left town, sir."

"They have laptops, right? It's kind of what we do; have them log in and work. Text them or message them or call the police, I don't care. I want every minute accounted for. You think I'm an ATM machine?"

"That's redundant, sir."

"What?"

"ATM machine is like saying automated teller machine *machine*, sir."

"You think this is a joke? That it's funny?"

Eb snapped his fingers and pointed in the droid's face. He walked the perimeter of the room, the spongy floor oozing between his toes. *Tap, tap, tap* on his chin. He passed projections of pumpkin orange loungers and seaweed green coffee stations and eggplant purple treadmill desks. Empty, all of them.

The avocado logo dimly lit the far wall.

"We're not an art studio," Eb muttered.

"Jacob felt this environment fostered innovation, sir."

"I'll tell you what it fostered—Peter Pan syndrome. There's a child-sitting room over there if you don't have a babysitter. Over there is a coffee bar for lattes and smoothies. And there!" Eb pointed at the back room. "Ping-Pong. I mean, come on! Is this a joke?"

There were times when the projection room wasn't big enough to contain his rants. The illusion of space seemed endless. He often forgot he wasn't actually in the Avocado plant and banged his head on the curved wall. But that was the point—to be there without actually being there. To believe he was outside when he was inside. It was all the beauty of living life in the safety of his home.

He adjusted his round spectacles.

"I want it out," he said. "All of it."

"Sir?"

"This ridiculous furniture! Burn it, drop it off a bridge, I don't care. Get it out!"

"But, sir, this work environment has proven effective. Avocado was ranked Fortune 500's number one innovative technology company."

"We can be better."

"What is better than number one, sir?"

"Number one A, just do it. All of this touch-feely weirdness is embarrassing. I look at it and just want to unzip my skin. Don't even sell it, just throw it out. Wait, scratch that. Put it on eBay, all of it. Use reserve pricing."

"I suggest we run your requests through predictive modeling, sir. These sweeping changes will greatly affect morale. I would expect widespread defection of some top-shelf talent."

The droid stepped next to Eb. The musculature writhed in his calves and flexed across his shoulders. His tracksuit was unzipped between the shapely pecs. Tension rippled his forehead as he cocked his head, a bird searching for a worm.

"Gone, Dum-dum. All of it."

"And replaced with what, sir?"

"Good old-fashioned desks in straight lines, not one of them crooked. I don't want to hear about freethinking. We run this company like a watch from now on. This is a business now. We do it my way."

"Why would you make their environment so unpleasant, sir?"

"It's all about the message."

Confusion wrinkled the droid's nose. "The message, sir?"

"Get in line."

The droid cocked his head, expecting more.

"That's it, get in line. Gets to the point, doesn't it? And that is the point. You know, it's time to rethink the slogan. I see it now, the avocado logo with a label stamped across the midsection. *Avocado... Get In Line.*" He swiped an open hand across an imaginary banner.

"Jacob would be disappointed, sir."

"Jacob is dead. Rest his soul, he was a good man, a great man." Eb sniffed. It was a little easier admitting to Jacob's altruistic greatness now that he was no more. It still stung, just a little. "He was my brother and I loved him. He also turned over all his shares to me. How nice of him."

"I did that, sir. Not Jacob."

"What? I'm sorry, I couldn't understand... aren't you supposed to erase that bit of information?"

The droid frowned. Moments later, a slight downturn of his lips indicated he had erased that information from his database and all traces of it.

"Jacob Marley is indeed dead, sir," he muttered.

"As a doornail," Eb said. "Now bring on the hammer."

The droid's shoulders slumped, the lower lip out and pouting. Eb ignored the tantrum on his way to the open door. When the droid didn't follow, he turned.

"What now?" Eb said.

"The stockings, sir."

"What are you talking about?"

Eb knew very well what he meant; he saw them hanging from a cherry-red pipe above the company kitchenette, one for every employee with a name stitched along the white, fuzzy collar.

"The employees, sir. They will be disappointed when they return from holiday."

"Becaaaaause...?"

"They will be empty, sir."

"And there should beeeee...?"

"Candy in them, sir. Sometimes little toys for their children or memorabilia."

"Are you saying Santa won't visit if I take them down?" A delicious smile licked his lips.

"It was Jacob that filled these stockings, sir. Not Santa."

Eb narrowed his eyes. The droid's shoulders slumped further, a loud sigh passing more oxygen than lungs could possibly hold. He didn't need to breathe, obviously. The sigh was purely a display.

Where did he learn such things?

Eb left the door open. "Remove the stockings. And the tinsel and the garland and all those trees. Christmas is over at Avocado, Inc. It's dead, just like Jacob. Let hard work reign."

He pumped his fist.

Bah!

If only there was a better word.

2

Steam obscured the far side of the shower.
Eb felt his way along the slippery wall. His James Perse micro twill robe was just outside the shower room. He slipped into it and cinched the belt and carefully dried his knees, calves and feet before stepping onto the self-propelled hoverboard.

Electric motors whirred as he leaned forward, grippy rubber wheels gliding past the bidet and squatty potty, the Jacuzzi and sauna, the jet-stream bathtub and massage table. A broad display of sinks and mirrors greeted him. Padded slippers awaited his supple, dry feet.

He twisted the black ring onto his right hand, the second one onto his left, but not before thoroughly drying his splayed fingers beneath a high-capacity vent. His hands tingled; a ticklish sensation travelled across his palms, up his arms and rang his head.

Connected.

He flicked his hands at the mirrors, his thoughts distributed to the house system. Newsfeeds streamed around the mirror, everything from liberal chatfests to conservative outlets, financial reports, world news and technology insider. Gossip, too. Oh, the guilty pleasure of gossip, sitting back and judging whoever stepped into the public crosshairs. He liked to stay current, stay on top of what the kids were doing these days. Follow the kids, find the money.

The revised mission statement.

He propped the round glasses on his nose and dialed the lens tinting to clear. The time was in the upper left lens. 11:40 p.m. He liked to be out of the shower by 11:30 p.m. He could shave ten minutes off his post-shower routine.

Three tiny flashes in the upper right signaled the glasses were fully charged and recording. The life of Ebenezer Scrooge was uploaded to a cloud daily. One day the world would see what he saw, know what motivated him, how he ran his life; they would place his thoughts in some technology hall of fame, displaying them like gems.

He'd be long gone before that happened. Last thing he wanted was someone judging him the way he judged them. Besides, people loved others more when they were dead. Weird.

With twenty-five voices talking over each other, he began his post-shower ritual. Some newsfeeds were reporting on Santa's progress from the North Pole to deliver all his free stuff to children on the nice list. Not the naughty, though.

They got diddly.

Eb inspected his nose hairs. Next, ear hairs. Stragglers were plucked, long ones trimmed. Then there was lotion for the feet and hands, cream for loose skin on his elbows, jojoba oil beneath his eyes, rosehip oil over all his chins, and tamanu oil behind the ears and across the forehead. He combed a sharp white part on the left side of his scalp; his ink-black hair lay perfectly in place.

Lathered up and fresh, he downed a heaping dose of melatonin.

The Avocado logo appeared in one of the newsfeeds, a black ribbon tied to the stem. Eb dragged it to the center mirror. Palm up, he increased the volume.

"A bit of somber news this Christmas Eve," the putty-faced reporter said, "Jacob Marley was laid to rest this morning. He was sixty years old and died of an apparent heart defect. Considered a leader in technology, Marley was co-founder of Avocado, Inc., a company that first investigated artificial stem cells. Mired in ethical debates and legal battles, the company struggled to bring its discoveries to the general public, but Marley never lost hope."

"We will prevail." Jacob's face filled the mirror, displaying that casual smile that put enemies and advocates at ease. Eb jumped a tiny bit, seeing the ghost of Jacob in his mirror. He preferred his longtime friend's eyes closed. The man had a way of looking into your soul.

That was the last thing Eb needed.

"Avocado stayed financially solvent through the development of artificial intelligence and gaming," the reporter said. "His breakthrough algorithms regarding artificial intelligence spawned an entire generation of computer programmers and subsequently the success of servant droids. However, Marley often stated the mission of Avocado was helping humankind, not entertaining it."

"Fool," Eb said.

They never got the story right. So many details of failure swept under the rug of obscurity, dusty tidbits that would otherwise muddle a good story. The artificial intelligence, they got that part right. Eb was there to see it. That was all Jacob. But Avocado's medical research was financial quicksand.

"A very private man, Marley's inheritance will be closely watched by the technology sector. The company was preparing to go public at the time of his death. That decision now rests with the surviving co-founder of Avocado, Ebenezer Scrooge, who was a no-show at his late partner's funeral."

"Wrong!" Eb shouted. "I was there in spirit. You know I was. You media... always with the story."

The funeral scene appeared—the tent and the rain, the preacher and the coffin. The dull gray droid stood out among the dour crowd like a clown at a... well, like a clown at a funeral.

"Some speculate Scrooge's surrogate was a shameless plug for the company's development of droid technology, while many of the Marley faithful saw it as a sign of respect."

"There we go," Eb said. "Respect."

"Concern for Scrooge's mental health has been a talking point for years," the reporter continued. "A well-known introvert, insiders suggest the public-shy genius has been heading toward Howard Hughes infamy for years now."

A flyover of Colorado replaced the reporter's smug grin, a white landscape of rolling hills. Perched on the side of a craggy mountain face was a sick mansion, an architectural feat unrivaled anywhere in the world, as if a titan crammed a Frank Lloyd Wright into solid granite.

"How'd you get that shot?" Eb said.

He owned that mountain and the one next to it. Those were no-fly zones, including drones. *Someone's getting sued*, Eb thought. But he was soon distracted by the awesomeness that was named by the media as Castle Scrooge, later to be shortened to just the Castle. Anyone that talked about the Castle knew it was Scrooge. And once you got popular with one name, well, that meant you made it to the top. The media made that happen.

They weren't always bad.

"It's been several years since the introvert has been seen in public"—smug-face was back—"but his people did release a statement following the funeral."

My people.

Scrooge had a small army of droids, not people. People were emotional and irrational and had bad breath. He was an introvert by choice. A logical decision. He wasn't some helpless emotional invalid that couldn't tie his shoes in public. He was smart. That was why he'd built Castle Scrooge.

The newsfeed showed the released statement. In fact, several of the feeds were covering it. Scrooge's silky, confident voice overlapped in *row, row, row your boat* fashion. His masculine, square-jawed image looked nothing like the saggy flesh bag standing in front of the mirror. Except for the eyes, he had the signature eyes.

One green, one blue.

A genetic flaw, some said. Eb considered it an honor to be so unique. He was one of a kind.

His sculpted image spoke words of sorrow and regret concerning his childhood friend; the sudden passing had taken everyone by surprise.

Right on cue, he sniffed back emotion and pinched his nose, his eyes red and glassy. The round spectacles were clear so the public could see his sorrow in hi-def. Scrooge would have to pass along his compliments to the droids. They doctored the emotional display wonderfully before passing the projection along to the media.

Kudos.

Someone was laughing.

There was nothing funny about this. Eb's statement clearly demonstrated sadness and mourning and everything that was appropriate. He grabbed the laughter in the lower left mirror.

"This is hilarious," one of three hosts said. "Nothing could be faker. I mean, look at that chin."

The host, a twentysomething fashionista, piercings all around her ear, grabbed a still frame from Eb's statement. A bright red line circled his beautifully sculpted chin, dotted the Hollywood dimple and underlined the square powerful jaw.

"Did he pull this from a comic book?" Earrings said.

"I think *Hell Boy*," the one in the middle said, this one with a pink stripe down the middle of her face.

"And what about the hair?" She scribbled a mop of red lines over the well-groomed coif. "Did he come from Milan men's fashion week?"

"Seriously," Pink Stripe said.

"*Seriously*," Eb mimed. "Did a cartoon drive down your face? I'm suing."

"You know what he is?" the third one, a middle-aged man with a shiny scalp and tiny glasses, said. "Captain America."

"Oh. My God." Earrings covered her mouth. "You are so right. Without the shield and the mask and the muscles and brain. And good intentions."

"Of course," the other two weirdos said.

"And the green eye and blue eye thing," Earrings said. "He's trying too hard to be memorable."

"Real!" Eb announced. "Real, you idiots. Take a look—"

"I'll bet he's fat," Pink Stripe said. "Not obese, but sort of middling fat, you know the kind of belly that's hiding a basketball with a toupee of chest hair."

Eb gasped.

He didn't need to open his insanely expensive robe to know she was spot-on. His round belly was stretched tight. And indeed there was a patch of thinning chest hair above the top fold.

"And hair plugs, the doll kind," Pink Stripe continued. "He parts it with a ruler."

Eb worked his fingers through his beautiful black hair then quickly combed it back into place.

"I bet his teeth are super white," Bald Tiny Glasses said. "The kind of white that could blind pilots.

They took turns drawing electronic graffiti on the still, scrawling the word LOSER over a fake crown. Eb pulled his robe shut, his reflection grimacing in the holographic newsfeed.

"And toenail fungus," Pink Stripe added. "I'll bet he's got big, thick yellow toenails that could chop wood."

"Suing! I'm suing, I'm suing. All of you! Dum-dum!"

"He's going to run that company into the ground," Bald Tiny Glasses said. "You watch."

The avocado logo teetered over Eb's still-frame image like plump mistletoe dancing on the graffiti crown. And then a big bite fell out of it.

"Dum-dum!" He waved off the newsfeeds. "Dum-dum!"

The droid's gray face appeared in the mirror. "Yes, sir?"

"Get their names, all of them." Eb's cheeks were flush and steamy. "And their family names, too."

"We are not the mafia, sir."

"Just do what I say."

"May I suggest not watching the newsfeeds, sir? It only raises your blood pressure."

"They can't say things about me, not like that."

"It is the freedom of the press, sir."

"I don't like it and I have a lot of money. Get their names and send them up. I want them sued for slander and bigotry. We'll give the proceeds to charity."

"You will, sir?"

"I'll think about it." He wouldn't.

He rested his left arm on his belly and propped his right elbow to tap his chin. All right, so he was fat. That wasn't slander. But he could still sue.

"Anything else, sir?"

"Maybe we should, I don't know, tone down the... you know, the projection of me a little bit."

"You think, sir?"

"Yes, I think. A little less, you know..."

"Greek god, sir?"

"Yes."

The droid nodded, his eyes snicking closed for a moment. His face began to fade.

"And get the exercise room ready for the morning," Eb called.

He would get in shape. It was a new year. A new life. Jacob had passed. No more holding back Eb's vision for what the company could do. Or how much money it could make. Eb would hit the equipment and get super ripped. Next time the public would see him in the flesh, not some projected image of a top-shelf athlete turned Oscar-award-winning actor turned trillionaire. And he'd laugh right in the fashionistas' faces.

After he sued them.

Eb rode the hoverboard into the bedroom and changed into his silk pajamas. Twisting the black ring off his right hand, he slid it under the cool pillow. The left ring remained on his hand. The next night he would alternate so as not to start a rash.

With a thick, padded blindfold in hand, he lay on his side, with the blankets tucked under his armpit, left arm on top. It was almost midnight. Right on schedule, he was ready to sleep on his side, arm out. Because that was how he did it.

His head sank into the pillow, the scents of his various lotions and oils filling his head. He would fall into a black sleep and wake refreshed in the morning.

He tapped his glasses. The record went off. It was exactly midnight when it did. He would remember that detail for the rest of his life.

"Hello, Eb," Jacob Marley said.

3

Jacob was seated across the room, legs crossed. Eb sat up, stripping his glasses off. "Dum-dum," he muttered. "Come here, Dum-dum."

"Why do you call him that?" Jacob said.

"Ah!" Eb crawled behind his pillow.

Jacob's laughter was uproarious, a sound Eb had heard many times during his life, a laugh that others described as infectious and uplifting. For Eb, it was more like fingernails in his ears.

Eb swallowed. "You're a ghost."

"Do you believe in ghosts?"

"I do not. But, Jacob." Eb swallowed again. "You're dead."

"Yes, Eb. I know."

"I had nothing to do with your death."

Jacob chuckled. "Of course you didn't, my friend."

Was Eb sort of happy that his childhood friend had died? Yes and no. He didn't want Jacob to be dead, that was the truth, scout's honor. But Avocado was Eb's now. Not exactly a bummer.

Jacob brushed his thighs. He always had cat hair on his slacks, always brushing it away. His black skin blended into the dark corner, but the knitted beany he insisted on always wearing was evident. He wasn't see-through, not hovering near the ceiling or wearing chains.

It was Jacob.

"If you're not a ghost, then what are you?"

Jacob bobbed his head, pensive, searching for words. Before he could find them, the droid burst into the room.

"What is that?" Eb jumped from the bed. "You see it, too. Tell me you see it, too."

The droid's eyes widened, gears turning, processor processing. He looked up. "It appears an image of Jacob is projecting into the room, sir."

"You see?" Jacob pointed. "He's not so dumb, Ebenezer."

"I can see the projection," Eb said, sounding a bit insulted because of course it was a projection, he knew that. "I want to know what it's doing in my bedroom."

The droid initiated a silent investigation, connecting with the networked computer system that integrated the Castle with the Avocado plant in California to become an adaptive, intuitive learning program that anticipated Eb's wants and needs, a network that adjusted the shower to the right temperature, that brewed coffee to the right bitterness, that adjusted the furnace to fit his mood, all without Eb having to ask for it.

Butler superpowers.

"It appears Jacob has uploaded his personality in the network, sir."

Jacob pointed a finger. *Bingo.*

"It was part of his alternate reality program, sir. He's been wearing electrodes along his scalp for the past year to upload thoughts and memories."

"You mean, like the ones…" Eb stammered.

"Like the ones you wore the year before, sir."

Eb had considered the wireless upload technology Jacob was proposing, but they already had enough controversial projects in the cooker. First the synthetic stem cells, then the unfettered artificial intelligence, and now memory upload? Too complicated, too risky.

They'd run out of money before these innovations saw the light of profit.

That was why Eb opted for the glasses. Simplicity without a drop of risk.

"The extracted memories have been assembled into a comprehensive likeness of Jacob Marley, sir."

That explains the stupid beany. Eb's eyes widened, wondering if Jacob could hear his thoughts. *Don't be silly. He's not magic.*

Jacob smiled.

"How'd he get into the Castle?" Eb asked.

"I'm data," Jacob said.

"Shhh for a second. You're not real. Dum-dum, how'd he get in the Castle?"

"Um, he's data, sir."

Jacob punctuated the zinger with knee-whacking laughter. Eb ground his teeth, turning his back on his former best friend. Eb didn't dream often—actually, hardly at all—but when he did, it was a doozy.

"I'm dead, Eb. I know that. I died suddenly of a heart defect, and you had nothing to do with it."

"And how would you know it was a heart attack if the memories were uploaded before you died?"

"Newsfeeds, sir," the droid interrupted. "His personality is an adaptive program."

"Okay, all right. Enough," Eb said.

"I know what you did, Eb." Jacob's voice turned very grave. He only did that when he disciplined employees or intimidated bullies. A chill dripped into Eb's knees.

"I don't know what you're talking about."

"You changed my will, Eb."

"I did... *whaaat*? Dum-dum, do you know what he's—"

"You had our friend here change it during the funeral."

Eb tapped his chin. This was serious. And not fair, really. When you died, you were supposed to stay dead, not come back and catch people doing things. Kind of crappy of him. What kind of dead friend did that?

"How do you know that?" Eb asked.

"The same way I knew of my death, simply watching the newsfeeds, monitoring the data. I know you converted my share of the company into your name."

"Well, you had it going into some trust that would handcuff me, Jacob. What did you expect me to do, sit around and let someone run the company? That's not what we had in mind." Eb drew courage from his misplaced outrage and crossed the room. "I only did what's right, Jacob."

Jacob hummed.

When the lights came on, his body appeared no less solid than the lounger he was seated upon. His eyes twinkled in narrow, joyful slots, a gentle smile resting in the corners. He watched Eb approach warily, chuckling when he poked at him, his hand passing through the apparition.

Eb yanked his finger back. "You're going to make me change?"

"No, Eb," Jacob answered. "Only you can do that."

"Do what?"

"Change."

"Change what, Jacob? Be specific."

"This isn't a contract, Eb. You need to change. You know what I'm talking about."

"Okay, good." That didn't make a lick of sense. Jacob was projecting into the room, clearly he was in the system. What was stopping him from changing a few ones and zeroes? What if he took all the shares away from Eb and put them all in a trust fund to help starving elephants or something?

"What do mean by 'only *you* can do that'?" Eb said slowly.

"You're going to change."

Eb went to his bed and slid his feet into soft, velvety slippers, then smoothed the wrinkles from the silk sheets because he needed a moment. Jacob was elbow deep in double-talk and Eb was drowning.

He felt for the ring beneath the pillow, twisted it onto his right hand and looked back; Jacob was bouncing his foot, legs crossed like he did in negotiations when he was waiting for the other party to budge, which meant he'd set a trap and was just waiting for them to walk into it.

And they always did.

"This can't be happening," Eb said. "You're dead, Jacob."

"I know."

"Don't screw this up for me!" Eb shook a stiff finger at the apparition. Then he shook it at the droid. "You're in on this."

"I'm here to help you, sir."

Always with the *I'm here to help you, sir.* It made Eb crazy, but it was what he wanted. If the droid would just do it and shut up.

Eb swung his wrath back to Jacob, the sly grin spreading out, his eyes disappearing in the narrowing lids, twinkling light still flashing his amusement.

"What happened to us, Eb?" he said. "Our friendship?"

"Friendships go away when you die."

"You lost your way, my friend."

"I have a mansion, Jacob. I have twenty-five cars in a subterranean garage. I have a shooting range in the attic. I have a helicopter, for crying out loud! I didn't lose my way, I'm killing it out here, Jacob."

"You're a shut-in."

"I *choose* to be alone. Big difference."

"This wasn't our dream." Jacob waved his arms.

"Maybe not *our* dream, Jacob."

Jacob groaned when he threw his weight forward. Eb flinched at the realism, edging a step closer to the droid, but his dead friend's footsteps fell without a sound. He paced to the window and peeked between the heavy curtains without moving them. There was a view of the Rockies from that vantage point.

"Maybe *you* changed, ever thought of that?" Eb said. "We started this company to have fun, to make money."

"Are you having fun?" he asked without turning.

"A blast. You wait and see what I do with the gaming division. It's full speed ahead with virtual gaming and identity reflection. I'm taking us deep into entertainment. No more medical red tape. You can stay and watch if you want with... whatever you are now. Avocado, Inc., is about to hit warp speed."

Jacob latched his hands behind his back. His favorite Indian hippie shirt bunched over his wrists. His persona was accurate in every creepy detail. He was even humming a Christmas tune.

"What do you want?" Eb asked. When Jacob didn't answer, Eb turned to the droid. "What does he want?"

"Don't ask me, sir."

"Jacob? Did you come to haunt me with your awful version of 'Silent Night,' or can I go to sleep now? A lot of headhunting to do tomorrow, employees to sack, housecleaning, that sort of thing. If you don't mind."

Eb waved his hands, the rings powering down the lights, the computers, even the clocks. But Jacob was still there.

"How is he doing this?" Eb said.

The droid shrugged.

"Find out."

This was unacceptable. A virus in the system. Was that what Jacob was, a loose bolt in a finely tuned ship?

"You're right," Jacob said. "I can't change you."

"Thank you."

"You'll have to do it."

"I promise I will. Scout's honor. It's almost one in the morning, Jacob. I'm sure you don't sleep since you're... whatever you are, but... if you're finished—"

"Merry Christmas, Eb."

"Yep."

With that, Jacob turned with hands still clasped behind his back, the trademark smile concealing his true intentions.

"Very well, Jacob. Goodnight."

Eb climbed into bed, ritually taking the ring from his right hand and placing it beneath the pillow before snapping the blindfold over his eyes. His head sinking into the pillow once again, he lay stiffly beneath the down comforter. He waited a minute then lifted the blindfold.

Jacob was still there.

"Oh, for God's sake, man." Eb slammed his fist on the mattress. "Have you no mercy?"

His features had darkened. Perhaps he was powering down.

"A gift, old friend," Jacob said with a slight bow. "I will celebrate Christmas with a gift every Christmas morning."

The silence dragged out. "You mean like coal?"

"I mean a gift in the true spirit of Christmas, from one friend to another."

"I'm not getting you anything. Is that it?"

Jacob slow-blinked. Eb sighed. That was his old friend's signal that the game was over. Although it wasn't quite clear to Eb who won.

And then Jacob was gone.

Eb hadn't even blinked. "Did you see that?"

"Yes, sir."

They stared at each other, the droid's eyes glowing charcoals, waiting for the encore. One never came. The room remained dark.

The doorbell rang.

4

"Would you like me to answer it, sir?"

The doorbell rang a second time. Then a third.

Eb stuttered. With both rings on his fingers, he threw his hands out and stretched open an imaginary scroll. A holo screen hovered between his hands, projecting a view from the front porch.

Not one but two gifts were wrapped in shiny bows and thick coats. Eb pulled the holo closer. He still didn't believe what he was seeing.

The sidewalk was clean, snow piled on both sides. The entry road was carved from the side of the mountain that no one could access without permission. It was dark and icy.

"Stop!" Eb shouted. "Don't move!"

The droid's dull gray hand slid from the doorknob. He cocked his head questioningly. "They're cold, sir."

Eb pulled his robe on and slid into hard-soled slippers. He pulled the Segway from the wall-mounted loading dock and leaned into it. The engine quietly whirred as he sped toward a ramp that circled along the perimeter wall. From the third floor, he could see another droid through the massive chandelier at the front door.

A wide ramp dumped him into the massive foyer. "Turn down… the lights," Eb huffed.

Despite not running more than a few steps across the bedroom, he was gassed. It was the adrenaline or the stress or the recent conversation with his dead friend. Or the gifts waiting on the other side of the door.

The droid dimmed the foyer, but light from the front porch beamed through the narrow side windows, the fractured glass casting rainbows on the shiny floor. Eb wanted the porch lights killed, too. The droid pretended not to understand.

"Need a paper bag to breathe into, sir?" the droid droned dully.

"Shhh."

The droid shook his head, eyebrows drooping in disbelief.

"What is that?" Eb whispered.

"What is what, sir?"

He jabbed at the door. When the droid refused to play along, he pinched his fingers together and pulled them apart like stringing taffy. A tiny holo screen stretched between them, a view of the front porch and the "presents" Jacob promised.

"That," he said. "What is that?"

"Those are young girls, sir. They appear to be twins."

"Really?" Eb moaned. "Those are girls? I know it's girls, you idiot. What are those things doing here?"

"*They*, sir. Not *things*."

"Are you an English teacher now?" Eb stomped a quiet tantrum, fists quivering at his sides. "You know what I mean."

"They are your inheritance, sir."

"My what?"

"Your inheritance, sir. The girls were Jacob's daughters. You are now their legal guardian."

"You're joking."

"I am not, sir."

"I didn't consent to this!" Eb hissed. "You can't just leave children on a doorstep. Ludicrous! Where are the social workers? The nannies? Somebody!"

"It's all been arranged, sir."

The doorbell rang a fourth time. The droid turned to answer, and Eb grabbed his arm, his fingers sinking into the flexy skinwrap.

"It's cold, sir. We need to let them inside."

"You lied to me. You said you didn't know anything about Jacob and the projection, and now you're playing the good butler. You knew they were coming, admit it."

"All of this information was released to me just before their arrival, sir."

"Did you know Jacob had a daughter?"

"Daughters, sir."

"All right, whatever. Did you know?"

"No, sir. Jacob was very private about his personal life. Very few people knew he had family. Look, I insist we let them inside."

"They're wearing coats; they'll be fine another minute."

"It's eleven degrees Fahrenheit, sir."

Eb paced around the Segway, tapping his chin like an overcaffeinated woodpecker. He pushed his round glasses up his nose and stopped in front of the tiny holo.

"Here's what we do. You talk to them, find out what you can. I'll be over there."

"There's nothing to find out, sir. They—"

"Shhh. Just do what I say, will you?"

A dim light rolled around the droid's eyes. He turned for the door. Eb sped off on the Segway, the gears whining as he disappeared into the dark hallway. He went so far that he couldn't see or hear anything. He stretched open a holo, the luminescence turning his porky cheeks bluish gray.

The door opened.

The little girls waited patiently, their hands in their pockets. They had shiny black hair tied back from their ears—one with a red ribbon, the other was green. The opposite was true for their coats. The one with the red ribbon had a green coat, the green ribbon a red coat.

They were each holding something in the crook of their arm.

"Well, hello there." The droid took a knee. "Would you like to come inside?"

Steam billowed from their nostrils.

The droid ushered them over the threshold and wiped their snowy prints.

"Can I take your coats?" he asked.

They only watched him.

"You must be *coooold*," he said loud enough for Eb to hear. "And hungry. Are you hungry?"

They nodded this time.

"Let's go to the kitchen."

They each put a hand out, their little fingers quivering. The droid took one in each of his dull gray hands. His hands would be soft and toasty, warming those delicate little fingers.

"What are you doing?" Eb whispered. "I said find out what they're doing not bake them cookies... *bah!*"

He eased the scooter down the hall, careful not to squeak the tires. The droid left the kitchen door open. Eb parked on the other end of the dining hall and hid behind a table that could entertain twenty guests, avoiding the light knifing through the dark.

The girls were sitting at the marble island, their shiny black shoes swinging midway down the stools. Their coats were open, revealing festive dresses with frilly trim.

What looked like dolls were sitting next to them.

"Would you like the crusts cut away?" The droid's voice carried from deep in the kitchen. A few minutes later, he slid sandwiches in front of them.

"Would you like juice?" he asked. "Apple or orange? We have eggnog. Do you like eggnog?"

He was doing it all wrong. Eb didn't want to know their favorite colors or if they could count to ten. He needed facts, cold hard ones. *And why do we have eggnog?*

"Get over here," he half-whispered.

The droid looked up.

"Not you." Eb waved off the droid. "Keep them busy. Send another one of you up from the basement."

The droid turned his attention back to the little girls, asking them if they were excited about Christmas and what they wanted. Five minutes later, bare feet softly padded into the dining hall. An exact replica of the droid came up behind him.

"What took so long?" Eb said.

"We're docked for the night, sir."

"Shh." Eb smashed his finger across the droid's lips. "Keep it down or they'll hear."

"Is that bad, sir?"

"Do you swear you didn't know anything about this?"

"Does it matter that I swear to you, sir? Really?"

"Well, then don't you find this a little weird?"

"Which part, sir?"

"That part." His arm locked at the kitchen.

"I don't know what you mean, sir."

"Little girls on our doorstep at one in the morning, you don't find that odd? What are they, like two years old?"

"They're five, sir." A dim light rolled in the droid's eyes.

"Whatever. They're little girls that got dropped off like a package. You don't find this just a little out-of-the-world bonkers?"

"They were transported by automated vehicle, sir. The trip was monitored by legal guardians in California and delayed by weather."

"Is that how vehicles work, really? Really?"

"I was alerted when they arrived at the gate, sir, and was about to let them inside the house when you stopped me. In fact, the car was coming back for them if I delayed any longer."

Eb tapped his chin. "You're saying that if we put them on the porch, the car will come back?"

The droid sighed. "You'll be arrested for endangerment, sir."

Eb balled his fists. This was why he hated Christmas, all these stupid gifts that were now his responsibility. He didn't ask for presents. He was an adult. If he wanted presents, he'd buy them.

He stretched out a holo and dimmed the luminescence to avoid revealing his hiding place. The little girls' faces hovered before him. Eb leaned in, studying their olive complexions, the dark eyes.

"Are they even American?"

"Of course, sir. Jacob adopted them from Guatemala."

"That's not American."

"They are American citizens, sir."

"Why would he do that?"

"Do what, sir?"

"Adopt them. Why would he do that?"

"I don't know, sir. Goodwill, a sense of compassion, empathy. Kindheartedness. That sort of thing."

Eb grunted as he watched their tiny chins move in circles, lips tightly closed after each bite. The droid leaned across the counter, chin propped on his hands, talking about how much he liked their dresses.

"You are their legal guardian, sir," the droid next to him said.

"Pass."

"It's already been arranged, sir."

"Not with my consent it hasn't."

The droid in the kitchen looked up as if he heard the conversation. Of course he did. All these dummies were networked together, a personality with multiple bodies.

"Don't do that." Eb waved off the one in the kitchen and turned to the one next to him. "Call the girls' parents, tell them we want a refund."

"Jacob is dead, sir."

"Her *reeaaal* parents, dummy. The ones in Guatemala."

"It doesn't work that way, sir," he replied flatly.

"Try. All they can say is no."

"They need a home, sir. Especially now. They lost their father at Christmas."

"How do you know?"

"Jacob, sir. He was their father."

"Right."

"It will be good for them to be here, sir. It will be good for you."

"I know what's good for me. It's not that."

The droid sighed. "If you fight legal guardianship, it will be a public relations nightmare, sir."

"What are you talking about?"

"A statement was just released to the media." The droid stretched a large holo that contained several newsfeeds. Eb's face—his original face from ten years earlier, not the projected one used for public appearances—was featured in various expressions of bitterness and agitation.

The newsfeeds were absolutely glowing with good cheer about how a cantankerous introvert opened his doors to his best friend's daughters. How magnanimous of him. Perhaps, many speculated, his heart was not quite as hard and tiny as they believed.

"Shall we send them back to poverty, then, sir?"

"I suppose not."

"I'll put them in the guest quarters in the west wing, sir."

"Good idea. Lock them inside just in case they get a little wandery. Don't want them getting sticky fingers."

"Of course, sir."

Eb remained in the dark. The droid in the kitchen cleared the empty plates then bent over. The little girls climbed onto his back, arms wrapped tightly around his neck, cheeks pressed to the dull gray droid's shoulder, eyes closed.

"Addy and Natty, sir," the droid next to him whispered.

"What?"

"Their names are Addy and Natty, sir."

Eb watched his servant droid piggyback the little girls out of the kitchen. Each with a creepy little doll under her chin.

5

Christmas morning.

At 7:00 a.m., a shot of espresso pulled Eb from foggy slumber.

He remained just below the surface of waking, rolling in the turbulent riptide of sleep, reaching for the rich aroma of strictly hard bean coffee from Costa Rica delivered to his bedside.

Eb reached blindly for the espresso. When two sips of caffeine were in his system, he lifted the blinders and slid the round spectacles up his nose, dialing the lens tint to black. His head was still swimming with the residue of sleep aids.

The details of what exactly happened the night before were a bit fuzzy.

At 7:15 a.m., he reached for the second espresso on his way to the window. The heavy curtains automatically parted, the window graying out the stark morning.

A white blanket extended all the way to the distant Rockies, the scene ripped right from a Christmas card wishing peace and good tidings. Eb still received cards during the holidays with photos of employees and their ugly sweaters or business associates keeping their networking opportunities alive with preprinted signatures.

They went straight to the dump. All of them. *I get it, you have a beautiful family.*

Strange tradition, wishing others happiness with a picture of how awesome you are. Like gloating could lift another's spirits.

This very moment there were millions of selfies circling the globe with peace signs and fish lips and inappropriate shots in the bathroom mirror, all declaring in loud lonely voices, *Look at me! Look what I got!*

Disgusting.

Never once had Eb penned a letter about his million-dollar acquisitions or posted about it. Sure, he was recording every second of his life, but he wasn't showing it to the world. He kept it private. It was more of a hobby. If he did put his life out there, he'd make millions. He was sure of it.

One would think Eb was a bigger fan of Christmas. After all, the holiday season drove Avocado's profits through the stratosphere. *That* he was a fan of. It was the excessive celebration that dug under his skin, spiked an icicle through his heart.

Bah!

He was almost through the second cup when he noticed the snow below Castle Scrooge. A track had been carved through the drifts and extended out to the horizon. He threw up a holo and aimed it at the tracks, enhancing the view.

It could be a bear. But don't they hibernate? Maybe a wolf. A lone wolf with big boots and long strides.

The caffeine cleared out the remaining webs of sleep, and the details of the night before emerged.

Jacob.

Eb grabbed the holo and shifted the view into the guest quarters in the west wing. The bed was made, not a wrinkle on the comforter nor a dent in the pillow. The bathroom spotless.

"I was dreaming. That's it."

Eb completed his morning ritual, a fifteen-minute routine that included lotions and oils and a slick parting of his hair. At 7:45 a.m., he put on his tracksuit and cruised the outer ramp.

The Castle could be a few degrees warmer, he thought as he slowly eased into the kitchen, a thought command that would be relayed to the thermostat.

The Segway squeaked to a halt.

"Crap."

The girls were hunched over bowls of Captain Crunch, slurping spoons almost too big for their mouths, splattering milk on the marble countertop. Eb stared for a full minute.

The droid was at the oven, a frilly hemmed apron tied around the small of his back. He was wearing baggy sweatpants and a football jersey, the number zero on the back.

Eb cleared his throat. He wanted to grab a third espresso, but that would mean passing the slurpy kids.

"Good morning, sir."

"Why are you...?" he started.

"Wearing an apron, sir? Addy and Natty's cook always wore one, they told me."

Eb pointed at the girls, his eyes question marks. *Addy and Natty.*

Neither of them acknowledged him. Their thoughts were drowning in sugar milk. Addy had the red ribbon, but she had a green dress. Natty was the opposite. Both dresses, aside from the colors, were exactly the same.

So were the creepy dolls.

They had bright red hair and button eyes with stitching for a smile. They looked to be a hundred years old. Milk puddles spread from the edges of the bowls and soaked the fabric arms and legs.

"We woke shortly before you, sir."

"You slept..."

"With them, sir. They were very distraught, you understand. This is all very new to them. *Change* is never easy."

"Change?" He seemed to emphasize the word. "What's that mean?"

"Their father died, sir."

"You might want to..." Eb pointed at the milk-soaked dolls. The droid cleaned the mess and replaced the weird little things by their sides.

"They are very impressionable at this age, sir. Their lives will be shaped by these events. I believe it will help if we reduce their stress so they can digest all this."

"Are you a psychologist now?" Eb chuckled. "They'll get over it. That's what kids do."

The droid went back to the oven. Eb watched the girls pour more cereal on the floor than into the bowls. The droid urged him to speak.

"Um. Hello."

They continued their cereal assault, but the spoons slowed as he spoke. The droid silently encouraged him to continue.

"Do you enjoy cereal?" Eb said. "You sure look like you do."

Simultaneously, they stared into their bowls.

"You're spilling it all over, you know. You'll have to clean it up before you leave."

The droid shook his head.

Eb squeezed the Segway's handgrips. Was this what talking to a kid was like? He already hated it. His father never talked about stupid things like eating cereal or grubby dolls. His father treated him like a man, taught him responsibility, that nothing was free. When you spilled milk, you cleaned it up.

"Um. What's your favorite color, green or red?"

The droid nodded, gesturing to pull more words out of him.

"You must like those colors because your dresses are green and red and your ribbons are red and green. So those are the colors, right? Okay. Do you have other clothes? Um, it's really cold outside. Do you like weather? And cereal?"

There was a moment they stopped chewing and looked at each other. Then they went back to eating.

"Do they talk?" Eb said.

"Not about the weather, sir," the droid said drily. "Breakfast is ready."

It was 8:20 a.m. "I have work to do."

Eb took his seat facing the window and distant Rockies. This was surreal. His life was already a dream—a billionaire lifestyle envied by everyone with half a brain—but now it felt like it.

Did Jacob really visit? And if he did, why were there tracks in the snow?

The droid carried a plate of eggs, bacon and lightly done toast to a small kitchenette table, where a silent display of newsfeeds was waiting.

"It's all right, sir."

"What?"

"Just be here, sir. Don't worry about last night. It's over."

It was like he knew what Eb was thinking. The droid drew a circle around his face.

"It's written on your expression, sir."

So he does know. Eb shook it off. The weirdness was crawling under his skin. The morning was getting away from him. He needed to get back to normal. He turned up the newsfeeds.

"It's Christmas." The girls were slumped over their bowls, their backs to Eb.

"Which one of you said that?"

"They both did, sir."

Eb froze with a corner of toast in his mouth. "So."

"People don't work on Christmas." The red ribbon jiggled on Addy's head. *Or is that Natty?*

"I do," Eb said.

"You shouldn't." This time the green ribbon said it.

"Well, that's not how the world works, little girls." He smacked the crumbs off his hands. "Not everything is free. Not everyone gets to sing 'Jingle Bells' and hug scary little dolls and chug eggnog until they bloat like pregnant hogs while last year's ornaments go to the landfill—"

"Breakfast, sir. You know you don't like your eggs cold."

There was nothing worse than a cold breakfast. And what did these little brats know about socialism? Addy started on a third bowl (or was it Natty?) while Eb soaked in the newsfeeds until his plate was wiped clean with the last bite of toast.

The droid came over to clear his table.

"That went well." Eb gestured to the girls. "A little interaction there at the end, not too bad, huh?"

"You're a natural, sir."

There was a full day of work ahead of him, lots of paperwork to square up, reports to read. Avocado, Inc., wasn't going to change course without a captain fully fueled.

"I'll be right back, sir. Girls?" He bent close to them. "We'll bathe this morning, all right?"

Their frayed pigtails bounced. The droid left the kitchen. Eb sipped his third espresso as a recap of the year's financial report began. The girls began to mutter. He turned down the volume.

"Did you say something?"

A spoon rattled. They leaned toward each other, heads almost touching, those dirty redheaded dolls clutched in the crooks of their arms. When Eb went to boost the volume up, they did it again.

"What?" Eb said.

They leapt from their stools and ran from the kitchen, shiny black shoes clapping on the hard floor. The droid caught them in the next room and declared it was time to bathe.

"No, not yet!" Eb shouted. "They have a mess to clean!"

The droid's voice faded down the hall.

Eb would leave the bowls and milk slopped all over the counter. He would make sure if the girls were going to stay for any length of time that they would clean up. The droid wasn't their servant.

He was Eb's.

After the newsfeeds wrapped up, he rinsed his cup. It was 8:45 a.m. He'd log into the office at exactly 9:00 a.m. Something nagged him on the way to change clothes. It wasn't so much the girls' weirdness, it was what they said at the end. He swore they were saying the same thing over and over.

He pushed it to the back of his mind. He needed to concentrate. But it would niggle into his thoughts and wait. And when the time was right, he would remember exactly what they said.

6

"Where have you been?"

The droid hustled into the projection room, his sweatpants and number zero jersey wet. "We were bathing, sir."

It was 11:40 a.m. "How long does it take to bathe?"

"You tell me, sir."

Eb's bathroom ritual sometimes lasted two hours. "They're little girls. Throw them in, scrub their backs and dry them off. Ten minutes, tops."

"You've never bathed twins, sir. We have plenty of time."

Eb fidgeted on the lone chair, crossing and uncrossing his legs, folding his hands on his lap then crossing his arms over his chest.

"Relax, sir."

The droid opened a box and began patting Eb's cheeks with concealer. The domed projection room was blank. He flicked his wrist and their reflection hovered over him. He didn't really need makeup, but his complexion was always so blotchy.

He dialed imaginary knobs, muttering commands until the reflection transformed into his animated self: male supermodel, All-pro quarterback. One eye green, the other blue.

That's real.

He tinkered with the details, dialing back the square chin and broad shoulders. The fashionistas' voices were in his head. It was so much more fun when they bagged on someone else.

"Careful, sir. Too many changes to your image will be obvious."

"Shouldn't the girls be down here?"

"No, sir."

"Perhaps they should sit on my knee."

"Like puppets, sir? It's too soon for that. We discussed this. The public wants your reaction to Jacob's passing. Let's not parade the girls out at the same time."

"When do we sync?"

"In three minutes, sir."

It was 11:50 a.m. The droid dabbed his lips with a shade of color, brushed his eyelids and stepped back to examine his work. The avocado logo was projected on the back wall, looming over his head like fat leathery mistletoe.

Eb took short, stabbing breaths, lips tightly circled.

"You're not giving birth, sir."

Eb continued breathing. It was the moments before a live appearance that were the worst. The droid closed the makeup box and stepped aside. Numbers began counting down.

"You'll do just fine, sir. Just be a much, much, much nicer version of yourself and they'll love you."

He barely heard him. When the numbers hit five, he felt around his face. *Glasses!* With a second left, he pulled them onto his nose and dialed the tint all the way black.

The room dimmed. Details flickered.

A man appeared to be leaning into Eb's face. A small microphone was just off his lips. "Mr. Scrooge, can you hear me?"

Eb nodded stiffly.

The man was a producer. His name was Todd. He stood back and tapped an iPad. There appeared to be studio lights overhead and cameras to the left and right. A Christmas tree twinkled behind Eb.

In front of him, a man and woman were sitting on stools with makeup personnel applying finishing touches. Assistants hovered nearby.

"Wow," Todd said. "This is... impressive."

Eb relaxed and smiled. "Thank you."

"First time we're using a three-dimensional projection in studio, thought it would be appropriate we interview you this way since the technology was perfected by... you know."

Todd gestured to the hanging avocado. Eb turned around to make sure it was visible. The Christmas tree was below it. Eb pulled his hands apart. The avocado grew larger.

"Could it be a bit smaller like before?" Todd said. "It's covering the tree."

"I know."

"Ten minutes!" someone shouted.

The hosts made their way to stools across from Eb. Final tweaks were made, their shoulders brushed and hair patted. They introduced themselves. Eb already knew them. Everyone that watched *Entertainment Nightly* did. Michelle offered a short wave. David reached out, chuckling when he drew it back.

"I forgot you're just a projection," David said.

"Thank you," Eb replied.

Everyone laughed.

"It's very nice to meet you," David said. "Should we call you Ebenezer?"

"Mr. Scrooge."

"Thank you for coming here on Christmas." David peered at the giant avocado over Eb's shoulder. "We just want ten minutes of your time. I'm sure you're very busy with the new family, settling down and adjusting."

"Yes, of course."

The droid was in Eb's periphery, giving him the thumbs-up and whispering, "You're doing great, sir."

"Before we start," Michelle said, "I would just like to say how impressed I am with you, Mr. Scrooge. It's such a tragedy to lose a friend and business partner so suddenly."

"He was like family, yes." Eb knew his projected image would appropriately express sorrow.

"Yes. And for you to accept his daughters into your house is just... *magnanimous*."

Eb beamed with pride. For real. "And may I say that I'm a big fan of your work, too," he said. "You will be asking very friendly questions, yes? Something I can jack out of the park. It is Christmas, after all."

He trusted his alligator smile would be smoothed over on his projection. The hosts laughed agreeably. *Bingo*.

"This is *Entertainment Nightly*, not *Investigative Tonight*," David said. "Softball questions are the house specialty."

"And that's why I love your show."

"Where are the girls?" Michelle asked.

"Bathing."

"Well, your whole life is about to *change*," she said.

Eb twitched. It was the way she said it, jabbing him with words. It was hard to tell if she was talking about the girls or everything else. Or maybe nothing at all.

It's been a weird day.

Assistants tended to the hosts' last minute needs. The droid touched up Eb. It was really unnecessary since his projected image smoothed out the wrinkles and blemishes. Behind the cameras, the crew squared up the mics and lights, rolled teleprompters in place. Several members milled around with clipboards and iPads. Off to the left, a young woman watched the chaos with a small fashionable posse.

Eb pushed the droid away.

"Hey there." He waved at the posse. "Did they catch him?"

They stopped chatting and looked around, unsure if the crazy projection was talking to them. The young woman in the middle—the one with the bright pink stripe down her face, the one that spent Christmas Eve bashing Eb with two other fashion snobs—sneered.

"Did they catch him?" Eb repeated.

She shook her head, silently saying, "What?"

"The guy that spilled the paint."

He pointed to his face, pointed at her. It took a moment, then she caught it and answered with a very rude gesture that involved one finger.

"Todd?" Eb said, smiling viciously. "Are all your employees this unprofessional?"

There was a rush to remove Pink Stripe from the set. A formal complaint and a little hustle and she wouldn't see her cohosts ever again.

A confident smile slithered across his face. *Ebenezer is back.*

The countdown to air began. Michelle and David sat back, their smiles reassuring him that the questions would be fat as sugar plums. The world would know he was a good man after tonight. They would know he was... how did she say it?

Magnanimous.

11:42 p.m.

Pack up the lights, throw away the tinsel and burn the tree. It was almost the day after Christmas.

Eb's favorite time of year.

He cruised out of the projection room, having just viewed the *Entertainment Nightly* segment for the twentieth time and giving it two fat thumbs-up. His image was beautifully sculpted, made for television one might say. He emoted the proper amount of regret when asked about his friendship with Jacob (*I only wish I could have done more*) and beamed with hypersonic joy when asked about the new additions to the family (*indeed a gift beyond words*). Instant feedback among the younger demographics was dazzling.

They love me. They really do love me.

They were going to gorge themselves on Avocado, Inc.'s new line of entertainment gadgets. Once Eb had the ship sailing in that direction, he'd be bathing in money, fill the Grand Room pool with gold coins. Maybe add another castle or two, one for each girl.

Let's not get carried away.

Eb hit the ramp at full speed, exited on the second floor to make a pass through the west wing. The girls should be given some credit for the public's adoration. They didn't do anything. They were just there, being needy. But people loved that stuff.

There was no light beneath their door, but he heard voices. He slowed down and circled back. Yes, definitely voices.

He put his ear to the door.

"Change is difficult," someone said. The voice was gruff. Then something about next year and having patience—

Eb turned the knob.

A quick commotion whirled in the room, a dust devil whipping the curtains. The girls weren't in bed. They were sitting on the window ledge, hands properly folded on their laps. The moonlight outlined their silhouettes, their bows properly tied and shiny. They were still wearing their dresses.

Eb pushed his glasses up. "Who are you talking to?"

They didn't answer.

The carpet was damp in several places. The room appeared to be in order. No one was in the closet, which took two attempts to confirm and two shaky knees.

He half-expected Jacob to jump out.

"Why are you awake?" he asked. "Are you not sleepy? You hungry? Do you need pajamas? What's the deal?"

Their eyes followed him around the room.

"Could you nod or something? Blink your eyes once for yes."

He looked out the window. Snowflakes were soft and large. There was no hint of the tracks he'd seen that morning. The girls remained still, staring across the room.

"You're creeping me out, girls. This is no joke."

The droid entered the room, wearing a robe. His dull gray feet sank into the carpet.

"What are they doing up?" Eb asked.

"They're still adjusting, sir."

Addy and Natty put their arms up and climbed into the droid's embrace. He carried them to the bed and tucked them beneath the covers, wedging a wide-eyed doll in each of their arms.

"Why is the carpet wet?" Eb asked.

"They weren't properly dry after their bath, sir."

"Their bath was like twelve hours ago."

"They had another, sir." He turned to the girls. "Would you like another song?"

They shook their heads. He brushed the hair from their foreheads.

"Goodnight, Jenks," they whispered.

"Goodnight, princesses." The droid elbowed Eb on his way to the door and jerked his head toward the bed, eyes growing wide to say something.

"Oh. Goodnight," Eb said. "Don't let the bedbugs bite."

The girls lay on their sides with one arm on the outside and facing each other, their dolls pressed against their cheeks, bright yarn-hair poking out. Weird, that was how Eb slept, on his side, arm out, hand under his cheek.

He followed the droid out of the room.

"Who's Jenks?" Eb asked.

"The name of their previous servant droids, sir. Jacob employed an identical series, although their skinwrap was a shade darker than mine. It comforts them to use that name."

The name was familiar. Eb had heard it before. They had named a product Jenks once before. *What was it?*

"Is that what you want them to call you?" he asked.

"I'm not a fan of Dum-dum, sir." The droid fetched the Segway for Eb. "If there's nothing else tonight, sir, I will return to the basement."

Eb took the handlebars. The droid nodded once and started toward the ramp.

"What's a humbug?" Eb asked.

"Pardon, sir?"

"I think I heard them say that word this morning... *humbug*. Out of the blue, they just said it."

The droid cocked his head. "Sounds like word play to me, sir."

Eb remained outside their door for quite some time. There were no more voices, no whirlwinds. Just the silence of the house. It was past midnight when he reached his room on the third floor.

Christmas was finally over.

PART II

THE GHOST OF CHRISTMAS YET TO COME

7

2:00 p.m.

The offices of Avocado, Inc., were full throttle. If a picture captured the moment, no one would guess it was Christmas Eve.

There was no tinsel on the walls, no garland around the lights. Just the fully lit avocado logo and the smell of productivity. Gone were the compassionate greens and tranquil blues, the quirky loungers and fully stocked coffee stations.

The Ping-Pong table was the first to go.

If his employees looked up from their desks, they would see an image of a handsome middle-aged man looking down from the glass wall of a cantilevered office. If they went into the office and stood in front of the mahogany desk, they could pass their hand right through their debonair leader. But few ever were allowed into the inner sanctum, so they never really knew if that was him or not. And that was the point.

Either way, they were being watched. They knew that.

There was a mahogany monstrosity in the center of the Castle's projection room, an exact replica of the one in his California office. Even a placard that read *Ebenezer Scrooge*. He watched the employees without ever leaving the Castle. Even the smell of the Avocado plant was piped into the projection room, a hint of plastic and cement, the steamy burn of circuits that wafted in from the plant's adjoining fabrication lab.

There was no difference where his body was, whether he was here or there. They both felt just as real.

He took notes of which employees were making their deadlines—deadlines that were nearly impossible to make. Eb liked to think he could warp reality, could push his people to achieve things they never thought possible, accomplish goals too lofty or ambitious. Eb told them they could, that they would.

And they did.

You could accomplish quite a bit with one-hundred-hour workweeks.

At 2:25 p.m., he had completed his naughty and nice lists, which boys and girls would get a bonus and which would get a lump of coal in their bank account. The naughty list was quite lengthy.

The joyful squeals of little girls zoomed outside the projection room, followed by the chase of dull gray feet. They were not to be in this part of the Castle, and the droid knew that. He leaned back to shout exactly that when a door opened.

A gray-blonde woman entered his California office.

Eb checked the time in the corner of his round spectacles. "You're a minute early."

"Your time is fast."

She appeared to sit in front of his desk, her back to the glass wall. A necklace of tiny Christmas lights blinked around her neck. Eb studied his computer. Jerri Mitchell was at the top of the nice list.

He needed to find another word for "nice." *Productive? Essential?*

"Don't make me wait, Eb." *Longtime pain in the butt?* "It's Christmas Eve," she said.

"So?"

"You can get back to counting your money, the rest of us have family."

"I have family."

She would know that. The whole world knew that. Eb had paraded the girls through a dozen interviews, had posed for photo shoots that appeared in magazines and newspapers. There were videos of the girls playing in the snow, riding bikes, having lunch in the park with kites overhead. They were all digital creations, but what was the difference, really? It was a great story and everyone bought it.

"Lucky little girls," Jerri said flatly.

Not everyone.

"Is that why you called this meeting, to insult me?"

"I want to wish you a Merry Christmas, Eb."

"Anything else?"

She played with her Christmas light necklace. "How long have I worked here?"

"I'm sure you're going to tell me."

"Thirty-one years, Eb. You hired me thirty-one years ago."

"Jacob hired you, but let's not quibble. You've worked here since we started the company, is that all?"

"We met in a café, you remember? First employee you hired, and we did it in person, flesh and blood. It wasn't this... *projection stuff*." She waved at the image she was talking to, wrinkling her nose like he farted.

"Don't forget, you helped create this *projection stuff*."

"I can't tell you how silly it feels to talk to a projection, Eb."

He smirked. "You see me, I see you. I'm here, you're there, what's the difference, Jerri?"

"It's better in person, you know it."

"Did you just want to complain about projection technology?"

"*Why* have I been with the company this long?"

Eb sighed. "Mind reading, is that it?"

"Because I have always believed in our mission, Eb. That's what won me over at that café thirty-one years ago, the vision that was laid out over espressos and lattes. I had three offers, you remember? Avocado paid me the least by far, but the vision, Eb... the vision we created made my decision.

"You pitched me on making the world better through understanding, through innovation, to push the boundaries of creativity."

"More money, is that what you want?" Eb said. "There's no room in the budget."

She chuckled. There was plenty of room, they both knew it. "It's not about the money. That's my point."

She twisted the lights around her neck. You didn't work with Ebenezer Scrooge for thirty-one years without knowing how to roll with the punches. She pushed out of her chair and walked to the glass wall, her running shoes squeaking as she looked across the plant. A woman that always wore pants and baggy sweater shirts, she saved the ugly ones for the holidays.

Eb tapped his pen. "Whatever it is you want, Jerri, can you just send it to me in an email that I can delete?"

"What happened to you, Eb?"

Jacob had asked him something like that a year ago. Or his digital ghost did, an experience he was still trying to forget. Now he was reliving it from his vice president.

"You were so different." She turned around and leaned against the glass wall. "Now I'm looking at this abomination behind a desk."

"Excuse me?"

"Your projection is ridiculous, Eb." She laughed. "I can't figure out if you think you're training for the Olympics or varsity football."

He pulled at his shirt, the hem creeping up his belly, and stopped from checking his hair in one of the dark monitors. Of course, his projection sent none of that reality to the plant. She saw an impeccable version. The only similarity was the round spectacles that sometimes hid his green and blue eyes.

His trademark.

"Jacob had the vision," she said. "He never lost it. You had the vision, too."

"Check the financials. Profits have rocketed since his death. That vision you're touting was killing us. Had Jacob not passed, I'm sorry to say, we'd be bankrupt. So if this is about the future—"

"It's about the present, Eb."

He hesitated. For a moment, he thought she meant Christmas present.

"You have all these new projects—"

"That are making money," he said.

"I don't know where you're going with the company, Eb. These... gaming projects and movie makers and these... *secret projects* no one can see."

"Money, money and—wait, what?"

"You cut the medical division."

"Back up. What secret projects?"

She crossed her arms. "You cut medical, Eb. It's what made Avocado different than all the other tech companies."

"Medical was where our money died."

"It's what made a difference. No one was doing what we were doing."

"Yeah. Killing money."

"We were almost there," she said. "The last strain of stem cells was stable. Market introduction was twenty or thirty years away. No disease would be incurable, no handicap unfixable. Our profits, whatever they are now, would easily increase tenfold."

"*Synthetic* stem cells, Jerri. Synthetic, don't forget that. You're underestimating the ethical and moral blowback from the general public. You, Jacob and all the others just can't accept that it was never going to work."

"In your lifetime, that's what you're worried about. Those profits weren't going to show up until after you passed."

"This is about your granddaughter, isn't it? Let's be honest, you don't need the product to save the world, just to cure your granddaughter."

She tapped her forearm, lips grim. *Bull's-eye.*

"It's selfish, you're right," she said. "I'm watching my granddaughter decline and Avocado might have something that could help her. And if not her, then those like her. My heart's not big enough to hurt for everyone suffering in the world, but it hurts to see those closest to me; it hurts to just watch it happen and do nothing."

She approached the empty desk in front of her, the one where Eb would sit should he ever actually go to California, a desk so orderly it could be a display at OfficeMax.

"You ever care about someone like that, Eb? Because if you do, you can't just shove aside your feelings." She moved a *World's Greatest Boss* mug from one corner of the desk to another. "It's not as easy as that."

Eb paused. His projected image would appear thoughtful, compassionate. Not impatient. And certainly not the eye rolls. "I'm really sorry, Jerri—"

"Don't modulate the emotions. Doesn't matter what all that looks like"—she circled her hand at his projection—"I know you don't mean it. Where are you, Eb? What do you feel, really? Because I don't believe you don't care. I know the Ebenezer Scrooge I met in the café. He cared. And I know he's still there, wherever you are."

Right on cue, the girls went squealing past the room.

"If you can't do it for others," Jerri said, "then do it for the company you love, the vision that started it all. Not the money. You're crushing the heart of Avocado."

He folded his arms. Hope cast its shadow on her face for a moment, that maybe her plea was actually finding fertile ground, that she'd dug through the hardpacked shell and found the real Ebenezer Scrooge deep in the gooey center.

Then he said, "Is that all?"

She hovered over the desk until all traces of hope vanished, then reached into her pocket for a folded piece of paper.

"What's that?" he said.

"A letter to Santa Claus."

Eb pointed at it. The projection room saw what she was holding and put it on his monitor. It was a wish list.

"Dear Santa," she said. "Please reinstate all funding back to our medical lab. If you don't, we'll have to close it by June."

"Santa doesn't work here, Jerri."

"Next," she continued, "please do not discontinue Avocado's annual donations to MPS research."

"Your granddaughter."

"Jacob would want the company to continue supporting the cause, you know he would."

"He—"

"And third, Santa, if you can't bring me those gifts, then I'd like for you to make my third wish happen."

He looked at the third line. *Have a Merry Christmas, Ebenezer Scrooge.*

She placed a small box on his desk before leaving, a tiny bow on top.

The office was quiet again.

The girls' contagious laughter carried through the door. Eb shouted for the droid to control them.

He stayed in his office until, one by one, the employees clocked out to go home to their families, to have dinner, to sit around a fire, to put out milk and cookies and open the fireplace for Santa and his bag of goodies.

At 5:00 p.m., the lights went out.

The avocado logo was dimly lit. No stockings to fill, no gifts to wrap.

Eb reached out for the little gift, but his projection wouldn't allow him to grasp it. No amount of modeling would tell him what was inside. He'd have to go there and open it. And that wasn't going to happen.

As far as Ebenezer Scrooge was concerned, Christmas was just another day on the calendar.

8

Mashed potatoes and gravy, cranberry sauce and the smell of roasted turkey infected the house. *A special meal,* the droid had said. *For the girls.*

Eb twitched. *For the girls.* Everything for the girls. How quickly he had been forgotten. An afterthought! The house was named Castle Scrooge, not Playhouse Addy and Natty. The droids hadn't even asked if he wanted something for Christmas dinner. It should've been obvious why, but still… it would've been nice.

He sped away from the projection room. "Call Rick."

A holo unfolded over the handlebars. The picture was a steel gray blank. He tapped a nervous rhythm with his rings.

"Rick, pick up."

He passed through the foyer and began to make circles beneath the chandelier and was about to make the call urgent—a command that would force his production manager's rings to squeal—when color flickered across the holo. A lamp brightened the corner of a room, garland draped over the shade.

"Mr. Scrooge?" The forty-something production manager stepped into view, unshaven and slightly bleary-eyed.

Eb averted his gaze from the God-awful sweater—tiny bells sewn onto antlers and a blinking red nose.

"I need you to look something up."

"Sir, it's Christmas Eve," Rick said.

"It's Thursday, Rick."

Someone said something. Rick cleared his throat and looked off to the side. "We're opening presents," he said.

"Your presents aren't going to run away, Rick. Unless you got them a puppy. You didn't get them a puppy, did you?"

Rick shook his head.

"Is there a secret project?" Eb cut the chitchat.

"What?"

"Is there an encrypted secret project that I'm not aware of? It's pretty simple, Rick. Look up our projects and find the one that doesn't belong."

Jerri was specific about that. Eb meant to corner her, but then she had gotten off track, and then he was distracted with her gift and all that stuff about medicine and sick kids. There was nothing secret at Avocado that didn't directly involve Eb.

He was the secret-maker.

"Rick?"

"Mr. Scrooge, really... I'm going to be divorced if I work now."

"Goodie." Eb felt personally responsible for many of Avocado's broken marriages. Once an employee was divorced, he or she had nothing else to do but work. *Who said divorce was failure?*

"I'll have to open the database," Rick said, "but it'll take a little while to run a search. I'll do it as soon as the kids are asleep." He impatiently twisted the metal band on his finger. "I'll call later tonight."

"Rick?"

"Yes, Mr. Scrooge?"

"Is your wife looking at you right now?"

He shook his head.

"Are you lying, Rick?"

He hesitated, looking off to the side again. "It's Christmas Eve, Mr. Scrooge."

The Segway eased to a stop. He would've kept going, but the droid was blocking his path.

"Dinner is ready, sir."

"I'm busy." Eb looked at the holo and Rick's uncomfortably pale face then back to the dull gray droid. "What are you wearing?"

"A tuxedo, sir."

"Why?"

"The girls' request, sir."

"You can say no to them, you know that?"

"Yes, sir. Dinner is waiting."

"Well, I'm working."

"It's 6:00 p.m., sir." The droid had him there. It was dinner time. Get too far off schedule and the sky would fall.

"Be there in a minute."

The droid held his position. The Segway refused to run him over even when Eb leaned into it. Stupid safety features.

"Mr. Scrooge?" Rick said.

"All right, all right. Go eat your figgy pudding. And call back when your ball and chain isn't busting your—"

"It's Christmas Eve, sir."

Eb killed the connection. Rick's pallid expression vanished. "It's Thursday. Satisfied?"

"Thrilled, sir. After you."

Eb's eye twitched. He thought it was the girls giving him nervous tics, but now he wondered if it wasn't that droid dressing up in gym clothes and wedding gowns and cowboy costumes and now a tuxedo.

He was making Eb mental.

A FIRE CRACKLED in the dining room.

A massive candelabrum flickered in the center of a long table.

The roasted turkey sat on one side, side dishes on the other. Saliva pooled beneath Eb's tongue.

A table setting was at one end. He dismounted the Segway and stood behind his high-backed chair. At the other end, framed by two tuxedo-clad droids, Addy and Natty waited with ribbons in their hair.

Addy is for apple, red as can be, the droid taught him. *And Natty is neither, but green as a tree.*

But Addy had a green dress to go with her red ribbon and Natty's dress was red. How was he supposed to remember that? Their dangling feet drummed on the chair, hard-soled shoes tapping in rhythm.

"Stop the noise," Eb said.

They giggled behind their hands.

"What?" He didn't mean to shout. The table was ridiculously long, but sound carried like a bullet on the hard floors. His emotions had a hair-trigger, and everything seemed to pull it. Especially two little girls laughing at him. And the droids, too. They looked at him and laughed out loud.

He checked his zipper.

"Why are you laughing?" Eb half-whispered.

"They said you'd say that, sir," the two droids said in tandem. "That you'd tell them to stop the noise."

"They did? Well, if they knew, why were they doing it?"

"Because their feet don't touch the floor, sir."

"Just... serve the food."

These dull gray dingbats were spoiling them. He needed to look at their programming and tighten it up a bit. Maybe insert the word *no* into their vocabulary, require it at least twenty times a day. Not to Eb, of course. He was spoiled, too. But he was an adult.

Big difference.

A third droid entered the dining room and filled Eb's glass with water. Food was dished out by the other droids. The clatter of silverware bounced around the high ceilings. Eb took three bites before chewing.

"Why are you two off your docks?" He pointed his fork at the droids. "We only need one."

"The girls require us, sir," the one next to him said.

"No, they don't."

"They're six years old, sir."

"So?" A red globe caught a flicker of candlelight. "What's that?"

"A candelabrum, sir. The girls thought we should light it for this special occasion."

"You know, can we all just agree that it's Thursday?"

"It's Christmas, sir."

"First of all, I don't care. The girls don't run this place."

"Of course not, sir. You do."

"Don't patronize. Secondly, I know what a candelabrum is. I was talking about that." He shook his finger at the red globes hanging from the candelabrum.

"Ornaments, sir."

"Ornaments?"

"Decorations, sir."

"I know what an ornament is!" His round spectacles slid down. "How'd they get there?"

"The girls thought they looked pretty, sir."

Eb dropped his knife and fork, mopped his greasy fingers with the linen napkin and leaned his elbow on the table. His finger danced left and right, bouncing between the two tuxedoed droids.

"You and you, get out." The droids continued helping the girls cut their turkey. "And take the ornaments with you. How'd those even get in the Castle?"

"The girls ordered them, sir."

"Ordered them?"

"They—"

"Yes, yes, I know what ordered means. They can't just order whatever they want, you understand? They don't make the money around here. In fact, they make none. I make money." He walloped his chest, a wave roiling his belly. That spot would be sore in the morning. "I didn't say they could order anything, now did I? I want to see everything they request, you understand? Nothing gets ordered unless I approve it."

"You did approve, sir." The droid stretched a holo on the table. Eb's signature was on the daily expenditures list.

"When did I—you know what, forget it. From now on, nobody gets anything. How's that?"

It was a forgery, it had to be. But why argue. It was stupid little ornaments today, but then it would be boxes of them tomorrow and a tree the next year. They would have boxes of all new stuff that would be thrown away and then more boxes and more stuff and more garbage.

He had to put a stop to it before it got rolling on ice.

He would have to pay closer attention to what he was rubber-stamping. This never happened at Avocado; he had to watch those people. Every penny wasted was a penny out of his pocket.

He immersed himself in newsfeeds as he shoveled down the meal and basked in the glory of warm emotions. If ever the Christmas spirit were to infect his cold and shriveled heart, it would be hearing the rave reviews of Avocado products.

That was Eb's explanation for the spirit of Christmas or romantic love or whatever gooey emotion made people act a fool. Glue whatever label you want to the feeling, oxytocin was behind it. These good feelings were the result of hormones, a brainwashing that expanded the consciousness, opened the mind, brought a smile to grim lips. *Oxytocin, people.* Whatever triggered that waterfall of hormones invited the Christmas spirit into his house. And right now it was rave reviews.

Eb was bathing in it.

Tom-tom-tom. The thudding of black, shiny shoes was followed by giggling. Eb looked up from his second glass of red wine, the room warmly glowing in the halo of the love hormone.

The droids leaned over to receive a secret. The girls gated their lips with tiny hands, but it did nothing to hide the volume.

"*Ree-ree moi tu,*" they said.

"What was that?" Eb said. "What did they say?"

"They want to give it to you now, sir." The tuxedoed droids stood tall.

"That's not what they said... reeree tuba something."

"*Ree-ree moi tu*, sir."

"Is that French? Are you teaching them French? I didn't say you could teach them French; we speak English in this house."

"It's their own language, sir. They make it up and teach it to me."

"Tell them to stop. I can't understand it."

"Certainly, sir. Anything else you'd like me to stop? Laughing, perhaps? Little puppies and dreams? Hope?"

"I'd like you to stop talking." Eb drained his wine.

None of the conversation slowed the girls' laughter. They hid behind both hands, their nails painted green and red and sparkly, joy spilling between their fingers, their shoes thumping the drums.

The droids whispered in their ears, truly whispered. Eb couldn't hear what they said, but the girls nodded. The droids held out their hands, dull gray platforms where the girls each placed an object. The droids swiftly brought them the length of the table, one on each side, both carrying them like they were delivering the Hope Diamond. They stopped at Eb's end of the table.

They were tiny boxes.

One was green and the other red. The green gift had a red ribbon and the red one had green ribbon. *Addy is for apple, red as can be. Natty is neither, but green as a tree.*

"What's that?"

"Gifts, sir."

"We don't do gifts."

"*You* don't, sir."

Eb stared like screwworms would spill out.

"It's not radioactive, sir."

"I don't want it."

"You just have to open them, sir. You don't have to play with them."

"I didn't get them anything."

"You can talk to them, sir. They're right down there."

Eb hesitated. The girls were peeking between their fingers, stifling giggles. "How about I get you some new clothes?" he accidentally shouted. "Something not green or red."

Laughter spilled out.

"You have everything already," Eb said. "What more could you possibly want? You want your own castle? How selfish!"

"You can just open the gifts now, sir."

"This is just one of the reasons why I hate Christmas. It's the want, want, want and the gimme, gimme, gimme. These insatiable holes that never fill up. It's throwing away perfectly good stuff to replace it with something new and shiny, that's all it is. It's sickening."

"Of course, sir. Why would you want people buying all those Avocado products? It's heinous."

"And don't even get me started on birthdays!" His laughter was slightly maniacal.

"Sir?" The droid nudged the gifts.

"All right, all right. But under protest, you understand. I'm only opening these because you want me to."

Eb pushed the plate aside to make room for the gifts. They were about the size of the box Jerri had put on his office desk, a present he couldn't open. Eb tugged the ribbon. It unraveled. He rubbed his hands, resisted a tiny glow of warmth in his belly as he wondered what was in it, the moment of anticipation setting off fireworks as he pinched the lid between finger and thumb.

Inside, something was wrapped in tissue paper.

Eb picked up the weighty object—smooth and round and black.

"What is it?"

"You have another one to open, sir."

"Is it the same thing?"

"Just open, sir."

He did. It was.

"What are they for?"

"They're down there, sir," the droid whispered.

The girls sank in their chairs. The hard soles of their shoes tapped the floor. Eyes were just above the table.

"What do I do with these?" Eb shouted like they didn't speak the language.

"*Gubmuh*," Addy said.

"*Gubmuh*," Natty answered.

"English, please!" Eb turned to the droid. "Tell them English. I don't speak weirdo. Look, I don't speak—"

"Paperweights, sir. They found the stones on one of our walks and thought you could use it for work."

Eb rubbed his thumb over the rounded edges, the cold smooth surface. There were probably a billion of them just like that in the valley. A billion, at least. And they put one in a box and called it a present.

"Brush your teeth and all that," Eb said. "Get ready for bed."

"Would you care to say thank you, sir?"

"Where are my manners? I've always wanted a rock." Eb shoved his chair back and stood. "Get some sleep now, girls. We're going on television in the morning, and I don't want you speaking ding-dong language, you understand?" Eb turned to the droid. "Got that? I'm not joking."

"Of course not, sir."

"And put a different dress on them. People are going to think I don't pay them any attention, for crying out loud."

Eb stormed out of the dining room.

"We wouldn't want them thinking that, sir."

"I heard that!"

9

The bathroom was painted with fragrance. Eb put the finishing touches on his hair and opened his robe to inspect the bod, swearing he'd lost a pound or two, before cinching up. His mood seethed beneath a stench of face lotions and body creams. No matter how good he smelled, an emotional infection continued to fester. It wasn't the fashionistas that made him feel so foul. They hadn't commented on him whatsoever. Pink Stripe wasn't on the show anymore, but that pleasure was short-lived.

He didn't know what it was.

The snow-laden valley was sharply lit with a quarter moon, the white carpet pure and untouched. Eb teetered on the hoverboard, the bitter cold seeping through the glass.

Someone cleared their throat.

"Did you find it?" Eb said without turning.

"No, Mr. Scrooge," Rick said from the holo. "There's nothing on the project list."

Silence stretched across the room. Rick cleared his throat again before saying, "What... makes you think there's a secret project?"

Eb repeated his conversation with Jerri.

"Why don't you ask her?" Rick said.

The hoverboard wheels whirred in a circle. Rick's tired face was stretched across a holo floating in the bedroom. He rubbed his cheek, the whiskers grinding in his palm.

"Tired, Rick?"

"Exhausted, Mr. Scrooge. It's..." He stopped. *It's Christmas Eve.* "Is there anything else?"

"Did you run through the new launch lines?"

"Yes."

"Conceptual?"

"Yes."

"Read them to me."

Rick looked down at a monitor and yawned. "Uh, alternate reality immersive is on schedule, artificially intelligent infusive game world is going through beta, the cinemaker is finishing self-directed analysis..."

Rick's tone of boredom ran through the remaining projects. It was musical to Eb, poetry in his ears. Avocado was going to flip the entertainment industry on its head. Medical innovation always slogged through red tape quicksand. They would never get anywhere with that; Jerri couldn't get that through her skull. It didn't matter how well-intentioned the project was. If nothing got done, then it wouldn't matter.

Avocado was making a difference under Eb's leadership.

The cinema-maker environment alone would revolutionize entertainment. Actors would become obsolete when every director wannabe stepped inside a cinemaker room and digitally created his scenes and the actors in them—a realism that was impossible to differentiate from fantasy. Want an Oscar-award-winning performance? Can't afford top-shelf talent? Make it up yourself.

First own the world. Then solve its problems. He needed to lay that line on Jerri.

"That's weird," Rick mumbled.

"What?"

"There's an imbedded kernel in the immersive…" Rick tapped a key sequence, the dregs of sleep falling from his eyes.

"What is it?"

"It's using a lot of data."

"What is?"

More keystrokes. "That would explain the occasional data lag…"

Eb dialed his round spectacles until they were clear and sharp. He wheeled right up to the holo, nose to nose with Rick's image. He held his breath while the production manager frowned.

"What is it?" Eb said.

"It's encrypted, Mr. Scrooge. I think you're right. There's no name or tag attached to it. There is a date, but it doesn't make sense." He leaned closer to his computer. "Twenty-five years ago? That can't be right. The system isn't even that old. Something's corrupt. I need to run analysis, Mr. Scrooge. It'll probably run through the night."

"Are you lying, Rick? You just want to go to bed?"

Eb couldn't wait till morning. He'd stare at the ceiling until it was finished.

"It's something that's hidden pretty deep. How did Jerri know about this?"

"How should I know?"

A baby was crying. Rick looked to his left, muttering something. His wife brought the baby into the room and put her over his shoulder. *How is he supposed to type?*

"I'll start the analysis. You'll get the results in the morning."

"Rick?"

"Goodnight, Mr. Scrooge."

"Rick!"

"And Merry Christmas." He killed the connection.

Eb stood in a darkened room with a mystery that weighed as much as a herd of reindeer. He wasn't going to sleep with that kind of pressure. He cruised around the room, tapping his chin, mumbling through thoughts that filled his head until they tumbled like rocks.

"Jerri," he said. "Call Jerri. Now."

The holo hung dead gray.

She knew something. How could his production manager not know about this and she just threw it out like gossip? She had something to do with this, that was what it was. She was in on it. And she wanted him to know.

After a minute of silence, he attached a critical flag to his call. Her rings would sing until she picked up. He coasted back, expecting her tired and angry face to pop into the holo.

Instead, it went black.

"Oh no she didn't."

She killed it. She knew he was calling and killed it without answering.

How could she do this? After everything he'd done for her, now this? He gave her a career and she was going to do this to him now because... *because it was Christmas?*

"Bah!" Eb shook his fists.

He searched for a word that would capture his feelings, a word that summed up all his thoughts and emotions. A word that would squash all those well-wishing, present-giving, joy-singing, cheery-faced joyheads.

And then he had it.

It was a word the girls muttered last year. They gave it to him like a gift to wield when he felt this trapped, this powerless. This frustrated.

"Bah!" He shook his fists over his head and drew a deep breath. "HUMBUG!"

A great tremor ripped through the house.

The hoverboard struggled to keep him from falling. Arms stretched out, thoughts of an earthquake spitting the Castle from the side of the mountain filled his head. Colorado didn't get earthquakes. And the architects assured him that should there be one that *nothing would happen*.

As quickly as it started, it settled.

The house gasped one last time.

The hoverboard had moved across the room in the throes of

balance. He was now facing the window. The snow was still bright beneath the quarter moon. But no longer perfect.

A path had been etched from the horizon.

Then a voice crawled from a dry throat and walked up his spine.

"Ebenezer."

10

Eb's tongue clung to the roof of his frosted mouth, his throat a cold steel pipe. His legs were columns of ice, head carved from a block of granite. He could not turn, could not utter a single word.

There was a rustling sound behind him, perhaps a paper bag dumping a pile of twigs, the clickety-scratch of insects crawling for cover. The musty odor of wet leaves.

"Turn, Ebenezer," the hoarse voice said.

The vise of fear released him, sensation trickling into his thighs. Doubt crept around him. He no longer wanted to turn around. The voice, however, compelled him to step off the hoverboard.

It was standing in his bedroom, the head scratching the ceiling, gangly fingers twitching at its sides. Eb's breath came in short chops. A lack of oxygen caused his brain to float. His eyelids fluttered, eyes half-rolled.

"Ebenezer," the thing said.

Eb found his balance. Sensation had returned to his arms and chest. He still couldn't accept the dark stooping form that filled his bedroom. A word bubbled out of Eb's lungs. It was so large that it nearly lodged in his throat before exploding from his mouth.

"Dum-dum!"

The door immediately opened. The dull gray droid stepped casually around the thing.

"Would you like cocoa, sir?"

Eb lifted his arm. It was locked at the elbow, finger quivering.

"Trouble sleeping, sir? Perhaps you should not have had the second glass of wine. I can fetch aspirin, if you wish."

"N-n-n-n-n..."

"A bad dream, sir?"

"Th-th-th-that."

"That, sir?" The droid looked at the bed and pulled the covers back and fluffed the pillows. "Perhaps a soothing cup of chamomile, sir? Christmas will soon be over and you can get about the business of business."

Eb slobbered through another string of syllables. All he could do was point, yet the droid acted like this was part of a bedtime ritual and not a seizure.

"He cannot see me, Ebenezer," the thing said. A dark chuckle finished the sentence. And then, "That will be all."

"Very well, sir."

"N-n-no-no. Don't—"

The droid left the room. Dark laughter rattled the walls, quaking in Eb's thighs. Rotten, musty air puffed from the thing's lips.

It moved as a tree might swing heavy branches. It took one step toward the bed. Moonlight cast upon the length of its body, illuminating the lanky limbs and narrow head.

The skin was beyond pale. It was porcelain.

The hair was thick and solid. It stuck out from its scalp like twigs. And it moved. The thing slowly sat on the bed. A long sigh escaped like a punctured tire.

The bones of the thing creaked.

"Could I have some water, Ebenezer? It has been a long trip."

"W-what's happening?"

"Water first."

Eb was compelled to walk. His wooden feet thudded the carpet on the way to the bathroom. He brought back a cup of water.

"Jacob," Eb said.

The thing took the cup with long ghostly fingers that appeared to have one too many joints. Ice crackled around the rim in jagged lines. The thing took a long drink.

Black shiny objects dripped from its tattered sleeve. They began to crawl—beetles and cockroaches and centipedes. They fell from the thing's ragged shirt and crawled beneath the covers.

Eb fell back a step, but only a step. He was trapped by the thing's eyes, the pupils black and engulfing, eyes adapted to moonlight.

"What are you?" Eb muttered.

"What am I?" The thing took a thoughtful draught. "A guide. A mirror. A blessing, a curse—I've been called many things, Ebenezer."

"How'd you get in here?"

"Down the chimney, of course."

Eb never believed in Santa Claus. If he had, it wouldn't have been a thirsty, bug-infested nightmare.

"Who are you, then?" Eb said.

"I will tell you who I am," It said, hauling in a deep breath before saying, "if you can tell me who you are."

"I am Ebenezer Scrooge."

"Is that what you are, a name?"

The laughter erupted in mangled coughs, specks of debris showering a moonbeam. The earthy smell cloyed at the back of Eb's throat. He eased around the room as the thing coughed into its clammy fist, a fit of laughter still escaping its haunted chest. Eb made it to the door.

He pulled it open, but there was no hallway for him to escape into, no ramp for him to run down or stairway to leap. Eb had somehow stepped right back into the bedroom as if it were on the other side of the door.

The laughter was hysterical.

He tried again, opening the door first and looking into the hall.

He could see the chandelier, could see the ramp. But when he stepped out, it was the bedroom.

"No matter where you go," the thing said, "there you are."

The air was thick and hard to breathe again. Eb leaned against the wall, clutching his chest. The floor slowly churned.

"Relax, Ebenezer. We have a lot to discuss. Come, have a seat."

It patted the bed. A brief waterfall of black bugs crashed onto the mattress and escaped beneath the sheets.

"I want you out."

"It doesn't work that way, Ebenezer."

"Out of my house!"

"No matter what power to which man lays claim, he can no more affect me than he can grasp the wind or own the sky."

Its laughter flattened out.

This made no sense. Eb was not asleep. This was not a dream. Yet the thing was there as Jacob had been a year before, when his childhood friend claimed to give him a gift. And now he was staring at a nightmare. Unlike Jacob, this nightmare sank into the bed as if it were weighty. This nightmare filled the room with its stench.

This nightmare is very much here.

"I don't understand," Eb said.

"Of course you don't. It is why I'm here."

"I don't want you here."

"No one does. But you'll see, Ebenezer, you don't realize you've been calling for me all your life."

"What are you, some sort of... dream? A monster?"

"I am neither."

It stood with the same crackling creaks as It did when It sat. The insects that had escaped its sleeves crawled back beneath the hem of its shirt. The thing handed the cup back to Eb and thanked him.

Eb dropped it on the carpet, the handle so cold it burned his fingers.

"We're going on a trip, Ebenezer," It said. "One of many."

"I don't want to."

"You're already there."

Eb worked his way to the window, away from the suffocating darkness. The illusion of space brought a small sample of relief.

"Where are you taking me?"

"Where you need to be, Ebenezer."

Its arms spread across the room, long and lanky and nearly touching the opposite walls. The sleeves hung like those of a scarecrow. As It stretched out, gossamer threads clung between its chalky fingertips. They began to vibrate, sweet chords of music shimmering through Eb's feet, filling his head with light, fluffy daydreams.

"You see, Ebenezer," It said, "the fabric of time contains all the possible futures. It is the present moment that does not move, but only seems to."

It let go of the singing threads. They were suspended above the floor, the vibrations making them appear as more than one string. They split into two, then four. Eight. Sixteen. They continued to multiply until countless threads twisted and weaved, knitted and knotted, kinked and crossed from wall to wall, a tapestry of moonlit webbing.

"Life lines," the thing said. "All the possible futures of your life, Ebenezer."

There was nothing he could see with his eyes, they were just glowing lines tracing empty space. But somehow their sound, the music, carried images and feelings, emotions and events. Eb could taste sadness when one particular string sang above the rest. Anger, bitterness and resentment.

"Yes," the thing said. "It is all there, Ebenezer. The path you have chosen. I am here to show you where you are going."

Eb shook his head. "I know where I am."

"Shhhhh." It placed a long finger up to Its bluish lips. "Every journey is different, Ebenezer. For you, we will start with things to come. Tonight, on this Christmas Eve, I take you down the path you have chosen. We will follow it to the end."

The thing reached inside the infinite web without touching a single strand. Its thick fingernails settled on one particular string, as if it were searching for that one and that one only.

It plucked it as a musician would pluck a harp.

It sang inside Eb, his brain a tuning fork struck with the edge of an axe. His limbs stiffened, body rigid. A light sparkled behind his eyes. The strings took on a golden hue, the luminescence blinding. Engulfing.

Until there was only music.

No more web, no more room.

No more anything.

Eb fell into the light, swimming effortlessly in an ethereal ocean of weightless particles, an endless fountain of sunshine.

One moment there was only light, the next he saw his bare feet on a golden floor. He wiggled his toes, the surface hard and polished. Birds fluttered overhead. He lifted his arm and shielded his eyes. Sunlight passed through a transparent dome where colorful birds were trapped. The walls were gold.

Pure gold.

Heaven, he thought. *I'm in heaven.*

Laughter rumbled like thunder. "No, no. Not heaven," the thing said, "Not even close."

Its eyes were lumps of coal stuck in a face of chiseled ivory. It pulled back a smile that exposed crooked teeth. A spider escaped his lips.

Eb's feet were anchors.

As the golden walls dimmed, shapes appeared. Several people stood in two lines, all facing a table. The dull gray texture of skinwrap soon became apparent. The droids were all accounted for, all seven of them—three on one side, four on the other. They wore black and white suits, the formal attire of servants.

It was not a table they faced but an elevated bed. The blankets were folded over a man's chest, his arthritic fingers clutching the fabric. His lips were caving into the mouth, the eyes hidden beneath thin eyelids.

A luscious mop of inky black hair was parted to the side.

"You made it to a ripe age," the thing said. "Bravo."

"That's…"

"That's you, Ebenezer. Definitely ripe."

Eb couldn't turn away, couldn't step back or forward. All he could do was watch the living corpse rattle air through its suckhole, each breath coming slower and farther apart than the one before it.

"What's wrong with me?" he said.

"You're dying, Ebenezer. This is it, the final hurrah. You managed to delay your date with Death for one hundred and thirty-two years, but it couldn't last forever."

"One hundred and thirty-two?"

"Oldest man in the world."

"I outlived them all. Is that why no one's here?"

"Not exactly."

A door opened on the far side of the golden atrium. A woman walked alone, the click of her heels coming in short, even strides. The birds stirred above.

"Where are we?" she said.

"He's fading, ma'am," said the droid to the left of Eb's shoulder. "Perhaps two more minutes."

She hummed grimly then watched and waited.

"Is that... my granddaughter?" Eb said.

"Uh, no."

"Great-granddaughter?"

"You're hilarious. That's the executor of your will." The thing leaned over, half-whispering, "She took control of your estate when you went cuckoo-cuckoo."

"I went *what*?"

"You lost it, Ebenezer. You always were a strange bird, but when you hit about one hundred and twenty years, you started talking about ghosts that visited you every Christmas Eve at midnight."

The thing offered a pleasantly creepy grin.

"Even for you, it was out there, Ebenezer. You began using Avocado's money like your own piggy bank. Well, you always have, but then you went over the top. Exhibit A." The thing gestured to the golden atrium. "Despite the protests of your legal team, a judge ruled in favor of Avocado's board of directors. They took control of everything."

"You..." Eb pointed.

"Don't blame me, Ebenezer. This is *your* path."

The ancient body of Ebenezer Scrooge stopped short, his breath catching in his throat. His chest arched a few inches. The young woman leaned over, turning her head to listen. A long, gurgling breath broke the blockage in his lungs and the painful journey continued.

"The end is nigh, chiller," she said.

"What's that?" Eb said. "Why did she call me chiller?"

"A nickname. You've had many over the years, Ebenezer, but this is the one you will die with, one you earned."

The young woman crossed her arms.

"How do you think you made it to one hundred and thirty-two, Ebenezer? Bitterness and loneliness is not a youth serum for the body."

"Good living?"

"You reinstated the medical research division when you turned ninety."

A surge of goodwill passed through him. He'd done something good. He knew he would.

"Yes," the thing continued, "you fast-tracked the development of artificial stem cells that could rebuild organs and replenish tired blood cells. That body there is almost completely rebuilt. Some thought you were going to live forever."

Eb would've been responsible for revolutionizing the health industry. Why was the young woman so angry?

"Because you kept it for yourself, Ebenezer," the thing said. "For almost forty years, you refused to allow your discoveries into the public, afraid everyone would become immortal. There was only room for one immortal, you believed."

The thing twirled a finger around its infested hair.

"The media dubbed you *the chiller* because only a man with ice blood could withhold such a gift. Even when you relented, you charged exorbitant prices. Just business, you told the public. If they wanted to develop a cure, then they could start their own research and development division."

One of the droids checked the body's pulse. The young woman checked her watch. Eb tried to move and nearly fell over. The thing caught his elbow. An avalanche of roaches hit the floor like a box of cereal.

Eb would rather eat those insects than watch another moment.

"You sued them over the name, of course," the thing announced. "You sued everyone, especially when you ran for president."

Its hearty laughter echoed in the atrium.

"One hundred and twenty years old and you decided to run for president. It was a charade, of course. You were bored. You insulted everyone, made ridiculous propositions. It was as if you wanted to see just what would sink your campaign. You ranted these crazy ideas from your projection room, sent out surrogate droids to kiss babies and shake hands. And then you did that with your face."

The thing pushed up the corners of his mouth.

"You called it a smile."

"I would never."

"Oh, you would, Ebenezer. You did. It was your way of showing the world you had so much money that you could do whatever you wanted."

The thing sighed laughter.

"And you did, Ebenezer. You succeeded at exactly what you set out to do. The fruits of your labor are all around."

All the droids shuffled.

The young woman put her ear to the old man's lips. The droids checked for a pulse. She stood up and nodded. Before making the long walk, she pulled a plastic item from her pocket. She pulled the string dangling from the handle.

A spray of confetti exploded from the top.

"What's she doing? On my deathbed... she can't. This... this is..."

"Unconscionable?"

The door slammed behind her. The birds stirred one last time. The droids pulled the sheet over the old man's head.

"That was how you celebrated the death of your enemies," the thing said. "You even televised it."

Eb turned cold.

The droids marched out of the atrium. The bed was left alone, the sheet still. A sudden urge to vomit filled him. Cold fingers were on his shoulder, a creepy-crawly sensation flooding down his back. A horde of beetles raced from the sleeves and marched up his neck, through his hair. Eb bolted upright, raising his head before they crawled into his mouth—

Gone were the gold walls.

Gone the ceiling and floor, the old man beneath the sheet.

Eb was looking at a gray sky. The wind watered his eyes.

"O Lord," a man intoned, "You who are the Father of mercies and the God of all comfort, look with compassion."

The man was not in robes or any special garb. Just a man dressed in black, holding an open book with two hands. He stood at the head of a gold coffin, the lid buffed and polished, the handles inset with jewels.

The droids were there again. Heads bowed.

"Million-dollar view." The thing loomed over Eb's shoulder. "You can see in every direction."

The site was on a mountain. To the left was a valley; beyond were the white-capped mountains. There were no funeral markers, just rolling hills and swaying grass.

The preacher's words rang in Eb's chest, carving out his heart. The bitter breeze sifted through him. He swayed like a sea of wheat awaiting harvest.

"No family," the thing mused. "No friends."

The droids, Eb thought. *They were my friends.*

"You only wanted the droids to do what you told them," the thing said. "That's not a friend, Ebenezer."

The preacher finished the sermon, carefully placed a marker in the good book and bowed his head. Birds of prey circled overhead, their shadows gliding over a pile of dirt, shovels stabbed in a row. In unison, the droids latched onto the diamond-studded rails. A slight sense of vertigo buckled Eb's knees.

"This is what you built, Ebenezer," the thing said. "Your investment."

They carried the coffin to a rectangular hole. Eb felt it jostle. He swayed as they tipped the coffin. The slight thrill of descent lifted his stomach.

The sky dimmed.

"This," the thing said, "is your legacy."

The golden coffin was gently lowered into the earth. The dark walls surrounded it on all sides. Eb could taste the musty organic matter, could feel the damp soil envelop him.

Felt the hard tamp of the earthen floor.

He was no longer standing.

No longer outside.

Darkness wrapped around him with cushioned arms and a suffocating embrace. Dirt trickled near his face. He attempted to shield his face, but his arm hit something hard and unrelenting.

And then a load of soil hit the lid just above him.

"It's beautiful in here." The thing's voice was next to his ear. "Silky linens, brand-new pillow."

Stricken catatonic, Eb listened to It sigh. With each wallop of soil, the weight pressed down. Something crawled up his pant leg.

"It won't be like this, Ebenezer. You won't feel the emptiness or panic when they lay you to rest."

Dirt thudded more distantly.

"You won't hear the hole filled above you. You won't hear the silence. No one will mourn. The droids will fill the earth, their last duty to perform. Your gold will remain locked away, your castle empty and cold."

The air became thin and frigid.

"This is the end of your path."

Eb's breath came in tiny gulps. Little by little, they became shorter. Less frequent. It was pitch black when they ended.

Death stood on his chest with both feet.

Cold.

And alone.

And then air whooshed into his lungs.

The first breath was long and desperate. He fought against a tangle of fabric, punched a wall of pillows and rolled across a mattress. He did not hit the coffin or a wall of earth. Instead, he fell off the edge. His head slammed hard on the carpet.

Bright lights lit up the bedroom.

On hands and knees, he scampered into the corner. He hid behind crumpled handfuls of linen, filling his greedy lungs. Wide-eyed, he stayed there until the sun cut across the window. And in that time, not a creature was stirring.

Not even an insect.

11

"Perhaps you should speak to a psychologist, sir."

"Shhhhh!" Eb planted his hands on the droid's mouth. "This can't get out."

"Why are you whispering, sir?"

"Where are the girls?"

"Bedroom, sir. On the other side of the Castle."

"You're sure?"

"Positive, sir. They asked to have breakfast brought up."

Eb twisted his rings then pulled open a holo. They were sitting in their bedroom, playing with those dreadful dolls. Green dress and red bow. Red dress and green bow. Even the black shoes.

"Perhaps you were having a bad dream, sir."

"Shhhhh!"

The droid shook his head, heavy eyes looking off. Eb looked out the kitchen doorway. The dining room was empty, the Castle silent, but his heart was attempting to escape through his throat.

"It wasn't a dream. I told you."

"Really, sir?"

"Yeah. Really."

"You spent the night with a tall man with sticks for hair, sir?"

Eb shivered. "And bugs."

"Bugs, sir. How could I forget?" The droid tied an apron around his back. "You just described the boogeyman."

"He was there. Trust me."

"And then you died, sir?"

"No." Eb paced beneath the rack of pots and pans. "I saw it."

He described the strings the thing had plucked, how It took him to the future to see his lonely old body in the atrium. The gold walls and rows of droids, the popper the young woman set off.

He didn't talk about the burial.

"It doesn't take a detective to know your future, sir."

"What does that mean?"

The droid sighed. "You're alone, sir. You know it, I know it. Everyone at Avocado knows it. Your subconscious knows it, too. Perhaps you have guilt for ignoring the girls. They have lived here a year and you have spent a total of ten hours with them."

"So you're saying it's their fault?"

"Many psychologists believe dreams are the window to the soul, sir."

"I told you it wasn't a dream."

"Regardless, sir. What did you learn from this experience?"

"That I don't want to die."

"There's that, sir. Anything else?"

The droid wasn't getting it. Something came into Eb's castle, into his bedroom and... what, drugged him? Performed dark magic? Eb tapped his chin, the ring chafing his finger. He wasn't wearing his glasses. That was a first. Even if he were, he wouldn't check the time. His schedule was toast.

There had to be an explanation. The boogeyman was there. He touched him!

He pulled open a holo. The girls were still playing with dolls. They were muttering nonsense, made-up words that only the droid would know. Their room was in order, the bed made. No sign of foul play.

"Where were they?"

"The girls, sir?"

"Yeah, the girls."

"Sleeping, sir."

"All night?"

"All night, sir. Believe it or not, that's what six-year-olds do at night."

Eb started to reach for his glasses. "Do you have security footage from their room?"

"You can't be serious, sir."

"I don't know what to think!"

The droid went to the stove. An egg sizzled in an iron pan. He began shredding cheese into a bowl. Eb started another round of pacing beneath the pots and pans, a tender spot developing on his chin. His head was a snow globe of shaken thoughts. Why did this happen? How did it happen?

I'm losing my mind.

He had a company to run. He couldn't be appearing on television looking like a lunatic that just spent the night with a ghoul. This wasn't Halloween. This was a full-scale catastrophe. He'd lose everything he worked for.

But then the future wouldn't happen.

"Breathe into this, sir." The droid held up a brown paper bag.

The room was turning and Eb wasn't breathing. The droid fit the bag over his mouth and told him to breathe easy. Eb drew slow, deep breaths. The snowstorm in his head eased, the flecks of thoughts settling in place.

"This is stressful, sir. Perhaps if you retrace your steps of what you did last night?"

Eb crumpled the bag and nodded. The droid watched him pace. The thoughts began churning again, this time slowly and methodically, something he could follow. What had he done different that night?

"Rick." He snapped his fingers. "He found that program."

Eb pulled open a holo, but the droid took his arm. "It's Christmas morning, sir. Perhaps call him later. What else did you do last night?"

A spark of irritation lit up his stomach, but the droid was probably right. If Rick didn't answer—and he wouldn't—then Eb would go nuclear. He needed to not do that.

Not right now.

"What else, sir?"

He tapped the tender spot and recounted the night. He'd taken a shower, watched the newsfeeds. It was all good news, nothing out of the ordinary. He'd spoken to Rick. He'd found that secret program but couldn't tell him anything about it.

Eb's finger locked. "*Humbug.*"

"Humbug, sir?" The droid cocked his head.

"Something changed when I said that."

"Said what, sir?"

"I said that last night and... and the house shook. And then there were tracks... in the snow. Remember? You came to my room. Yeah, you were there!"

It was all coming back now, how the thing laughed as the droid wandered around the room and offered him chamomile.

"Sir?" His eyebrows pinched, mouth turned down. "I did not go to your room last night."

"Yes, you did. I showed you the tracks outside, and the, the thing was in the middle of the room, and you... you couldn't see it." His breath was beginning to shorten again. "Remember?"

The droid dragged a stool from the bar and eased Eb onto it. Hands gently on his shoulders, he said, "I believe you had a dream, sir."

"But it..."

"Seemed so real, sir. Yes."

He had touched the thing. Its skin was ice cold. Its laughter dark. And the insects and coffin and the earth... all a dream. In a way, that was good. Dreams weren't real.

"But it wasn't a dream," Eb stated.

The droid sighed. He went to the breakfast nook and looked out the wide window that faced the valley. Shading his eyes, he peered left. Then right.

"It did not snow last night, sir."

"So?"

The droid stood back and gestured to the window. Eb shuffled across the kitchen. His knees ached. That, he thought, was proof enough that he'd walked where the thing had taken him. He hadn't been on his feet that long in forever.

But when he looked into the valley, the snow as white and clean as a child's comforter, his conviction was shaken.

There were no tracks.

He saw them. It was how the thing got to the Castle, It had cut across the snow like a knife through a watermelon, ascended the mountain until It entered his room to work its future magic. And now there were no tracks.

Tracks don't disappear. Unless they were never there.

"You'll be there?" Eb muttered.

"Where, sir?"

"My funeral."

"It was a dream, sir."

"But you'll be there?"

"If you make me, sir."

"Make you? You don't want to be there?"

"I'm a droid, sir. I have no preference. I'm here to *help* you."

"Right."

The droid offered a smile then went back to the stove, where the egg sizzled fiercely. Smoke billowed up as he scraped it onto a plate. He broke another egg to start again.

"It's true, then," Eb said.

"What's that, sir?"

"I'll die alone."

A dream, sure. But it would come true. Dream or not, they both knew it wasn't a future that was hard to predict. It was the path Eb had chosen. The thing dredged it up from his subconscious and simply showed him what he already knew.

The thing appeared at the stroke of midnight. Perhaps that was Jacob's gift.

A horrible, terrible, awful gift.

"There are worse ways to die, sir." The droid flipped the egg and sprinkled cheese. "Your death will not bring sorrow to the world, so that is good."

"What?"

"No one will be sad when you die, sir. You will not cause sorrow."

"You're really digging for a bright side here."

"Of course, your life will not bring happiness to the world, either, sir."

The droid slid breakfast in front of Eb, licking cheese from his thumb. And a half-empty glass of orange juice.

12

"I'm not feeling well."

"You haven't eaten all day, sir." The droid brushed dandruff from Eb's shoulder and straightened his collar. "Perhaps your sugar is low."

"Perhaps I shouldn't do this."

"Shall I remind you of the social wealth you'll collect from this viewing, sir? Your fans want to see you, want to know where their gifts came from. It's your duty."

"Fans." He scoffed.

People didn't care who invented their stuff, they just wanted it. Eb was the one that shoved it at them faster and faster. They wanted stuff; he wanted money. Seemed like everyone should be happy.

"Stop it." He slapped the droid's hand. "They'll be seeing my projection, not me, you idiot."

"How you feel about yourself affects the projection, sir."

"And I feel like a garbage can. A spritz of cologne won't change that."

"You're overweight, sir." The droid stood back. "Is that my fault?"

"Now? You're going to start that now?"

"Your weight is not a secret, sir."

"Get out of here." Eb pointed at the open door.

"I'm not finished, sir."

The droid held a white shirt up to Eb's shoulders. He hadn't showered yet and was still wearing a two-day-old tracksuit. Begrudgingly, he stripped off the top and draped his arms across his jelly belly as the droid pulled the shirt over his head. It was fresh from the drier.

The droid was right. But he still hated interviews.

The technicians estimated a surrogate autoresponder was still a few years out. Once his sensibilities were adequately copied and uploaded into the database, he could send his projected self out to these stupid things and no one would know the difference. He could be relaxing in a bubble bath while the projection joked and laughed and turned his social presence viral before he was done drying his toes.

That was why he kept the company's projects secret. Some secrets meant more to Eb than money, hard as that was to believe. The world could enjoy the fruits of his labors when he was dead and dusty, but not before he thoroughly test-drove them into a mountain of wealth.

"What would you rather be doing, sir?"

"Anything but this."

"Keep your eye on the money, sir."

"I always do."

"That you do, sir."

The droid gently lifted Eb's chin, careful not to gouge his second chin. He had enough jiggling.

"Where are the girls?" Eb said.

"We are cleaning them up, sir." The droid brushed his hair. "They'll be down momentarily."

"They're wearing new dresses?"

"Of course, sir."

Eb didn't need the world to think his girls couldn't afford new clothes. He slumped when the droid was satisfied with his look—there was only so much he could do with the doughy splotchiness.

What did it matter anyway? He had on a fresh shirt, the warmth fading, but it smelled clean.

He was supposed to feel better when he woke up from a bad dream. It took a little lying to himself over the course of the day, but he finally accepted the fact that the thing he saw was a dream. But if it was just a dream, why did he still feel like he'd swallowed a carton of expired milk?

The sound of dirt hitting the coffin.

The line of droids.

The loneliness.

"Checking your projected image, sir."

Eb looked up. A younger man appeared to be seated in front of him on a chair just like his, shoulders slumped. His hair was cut close to the scalp, his chin square and cleft.

"More cheer, sir?"

The image began to smile; eyes twinkled behind the darkened round lenses.

"Down a bit," Eb called. "Don't make me psychotic."

"Wouldn't dream of it, sir." The droid muttered something that Eb couldn't hear. The handsome projection of Eb appeared to smile like a male model in his prime.

Eb ran his hand over his head, his thick hair sliding between his fingers. His projection mimicked his move, but only the short stumble of his severe haircut ran beneath his palm. The style was the droid's idea, said it would look a tad less narcissistic. More masculine. Eb couldn't get used to it.

It was lacking class.

"A hat, maybe?" he said.

"A hat, sir?"

"Something for the projection. You know, unique and deserving. Memorable."

"Memorable, sir. Of course."

A series of hats appeared—a baseball cap, a bowler, cowboy, panama, boater, beret, beanie, flat cap, fedora, trilby. The projection appeared to be sadder beneath the spinning parade of lids that popped on and off his stubbled scalp.

"There."

The droid paused. "A top hat, sir?"

"That's the one."

"You're positive, sir?"

Eb stood up. The projection imitated him. "Match the clothing."

The projection's denim was faded at the knees. It transformed into a loose-fitting tuxedo, reminiscent of what the droids were wearing the night before.

Eb walked forward and the projection did the same. His forehead nearly hit the curved wall. The tips of their noses were almost touching, their round spectacles mirroring each other. He could see himself looking at himself looking at himself.

A stir in his belly dispelled the rotten grossness of the thing in his nightmare. A rugged gentleman looked him right in the eye—a steely blue iris and a green iris behind the rose-tinted lenses, a rigid brow, and a smile denting one cheek that suggested arrogance that came only from a long line of success. But classy.

This was how the world needed to see him.

Why did he have to change when the world would see what he wanted the world to see? Standing toe to toe with his projected self-image, he bathed in the luxury of swarthy good looks and intoxicating confidence. He could almost smell the leather of a horse saddle, the iron taste of blood from scuffed knuckles after a bar fight. The feel of money was on the sharp edge of the top hat—not too tall, not too short.

Just right.

A smile bent his lips. As it did, the image shattered on the wall. For a second, his bloated reflection looked back with rheumy eyes and saggy cheeks.

"What was that?" he shouted.

"Connecting, sir."

"No, wait—"

The room flickered; shards of dark and light reorganized to

project camera booms and tripods of bright lights. Eb stood nose to nose with Todd the producer.

"Whoa!" Todd jumped back. "You scared me, Mr. Scrooge. Thought you'd be seated."

Eb blinked. Was Todd seeing the top hat projection or a sloppy mess?

"Merry Christmas, Mr. Scrooge."

Eb said nothing. If there was some miscalculation, if Todd was seeing the real deal, then Eb could bluff his way through it. He stood perfectly still, scheming a way to explain how a bloviated geezer arrived instead of a top-hatted stud.

"Do we have a connection? Mr. Scrooge? Can you hear me?" Todd waved. "Hello?"

"Sir?" the droid whispered. "Are you all right?"

The sound of grinding marbles minced inside Eb's cheeks. He was going to grind his molars into dust.

"We're all right on this end, sir," the droid said to Todd. "Do you like the new hat?"

"The hat?" Todd stepped back and nodded slowly. "Yeah, yeah. Top hat, yeah. Haven't seen one of those in forever, but it's looking dapper on you, Mr. Scrooge."

He can see the hat. Eb stood upright. An image of a tuxedoed young man stood on the monitor behind Todd. There he was, in full attire. And he looked good.

Top hats are back, baby.

"Is that one of your personal droids, Mr. Scrooge?"

"Get out of here." Eb bug-eyed the droid toward the open door.

"Impressive," Todd said. "Never interacted with one so advanced before. He sounds so real. I mean, the speech pattern is almost human. When are you going public with that version?"

"I don't know what you're talking about." Eb sauntered back to his chair.

"Is he not ready for release?"

Eb turned a key on his lips. "Don't you have presents to unwrap or something?"

"Be quiet, okay. I get it."

The hosts were behind him. He recognized David but not the other one.

"Why are they turned around?" Eb said.

"We want to keep fresh, avoid chitchat before cameras are on," Todd said. "It works better to be spontaneous. Can you hear me all right, Mr. Scrooge?"

"Yes, it's a beautiful day, the birds are singing, children are dancing. Now who's that?" He pointed at the woman next to David. Her hair was too long to be Michelle's. It was the wrong color, a natural red. And she was shorter.

"Marie," Todd said. "She took Michelle's seat a month ago."

A month? "Where's Michelle?"

"She moved on to her own show. We'll be lighting up in five minutes, Mr. Scrooge."

Eb understood quite clearly—Michelle had been sent out to pasture. The old lady was in her fifties by now, far too old to keep it fresh. This new one was younger and prettier. That was how it worked. People like Michelle could have used a projection like Eb, but eventually she'd have to go out in public, greet fans, do events. None of those pesky requirements shackled Eb; he stayed safe from the world.

No one was replacing him.

Once Avocado's CineMaker™ technology hit the scene, projected images would take on a life of their own. These digital characters would read us the news, play sports and make us laugh. Michelle would be a relic by then.

Real looks are for suckers.

"Hey!" Eb shouted. "David! Marie, hey!"

The hosts looked over their shoulders, their makeup artists holding brushes. Wide smiles broke on their faces. Their eyes moved to the top hat.

"Merry Christmas!" Marie said.

"Okay," Eb said.

"It's so nice to meet you." She held out her hand and then

chuckled when she realized she was attempting to shake hands with a projection. "Oh my goodness, I'm such a goof. Your projection is so real, Mr. Scrooge."

Beauty. Manners. Eb had already forgotten about Michelle.

"I love your hat." Her grin faltered. "You look so fashionable."

"I keep up."

"Where are the girls?"

Eb drank in her beauty, bathed in her sincere flattery then turned to the door. "Dum-dum! Bring the girls!"

Marie and David flinched. So did the assistants behind them. The volume must've been up.

"Is that... someone's name?" Marie asked.

The door opened. The twins were herded inside the room. The droid stopped outside the range of their view. Eb stared wide-eyed at the girls wearing the same dresses with the same ribbons.

"You said the dresses were new," Eb growled.

"They are, sir. Addy is wearing a green dress now. And Natty is—"

"Are you out of your mind?" Eb just got accustomed to the poem. "By new," Eb said, smiling back at his hosts, "I meant different."

"You didn't say different, sir. You said new."

Eb's top-hatted projection on the studio's monitor smiled without a hint of fuming rage. The hosts waved at the girls as they stepped into view. Addy had her redheaded doll locked in a two-armed vise grip. Natty dragged hers by one arm. They started to climb onto Eb's knees.

"Oh, oh." Todd ran back into the studio. "Nice, nice, I love it, but can we save it for the cameras? We'll have them walk into the shot once we're on the air. Do you mind, Mr. Scrooge?"

"Whatever gets this train rolling."

"Super."

David turned around. Marie wiggled her bright red fingernails at the twins before Todd turned her back to makeup. The droid ushered the girls back to the doorway. Natty tugged on the doll's leg that escaped Addy's death hug.

"*Moe bee!*" Addy jerked away. Natty hissed.

"Hey!" Eb spun on his seat. "Put a cap on the nonsense, you hear? I want English for the next ten minutes, you got that, Dum-dum?"

"I haven't said anything, sir."

"You tell them."

The droid sighed. He took a knee and corralled the girls, speaking in hushed tones.

"That better be English!" Eb turned back to the studio. "Can we get started already? I'm not feeling hot. Too much nog."

He rubbed his face, cheeks clammy. His projection tipped his top hat instead of mopping his face in frustration. Even Eb was surprised by the intuitive reactions of his projection. Very uplifting.

"Everything all right?" Todd asked.

"You my therapist? Let's go before the figgy pudding gets cold."

A murmur rolled behind the scenes. Even Eb's projection couldn't stanch the sarcasm on that last outburst.

The intro music blared as assistants ran for cover. This was the last time he was doing this show. Despite what the droid said about social clout, Eb had become barely more than a parade balloon hovering above the road for entertainment and a fine target for pellet guns. He could hear the fashionistas cackling at his top hat and tuxedo.

Why did I wear this?

Pink Stripe wouldn't be laughing, at least. If she was, it was in a dark room by herself. Eb made sure she wouldn't find work on that side of the camera again. It was safer running the Pamplona streets with a bright red target painted on your butt than messing with Ebenezer Scrooge.

As the hosts turned around with big fake smiles, a stir of joy melted the butterflies in his stomach. It wasn't the lights and camera or the sound of money filling his accounts that did it.

It was the thought of Pink Stripe all alone.

"Merry Christmas!" David and Marie shouted in unison.

"Yep."

"Thank you so much for being here." Marie clapped.

"Sort of like tradition," David said. "We had you last year."

"Sure did."

"Did you get everything from Santa?" Marie asked.

"Totally."

"It's been quite a year for you," David said. "The release of not one but two of the most popular video games, an upgraded gaming console, and the introduction of immersion wetware. I mean, wow. Avocado is on fire, Mr. Scrooge. You've got to be happy."

"Like a schoolgirl, David."

"You must feel a little like Santa."

Eb covered his belly. "You saying I'm fat?"

"No, no, no." David and Marie competed for the most nervous laughter. "I'm talking about the number of presents that were under Christmas trees this year, most of which came from Avocado. A banner year for the company, indeed. You must love this holiday."

"Everybody loves money, David."

Thankfully, the projection beamed a million-dollar smile and tipped his hat. There was a short discussion about his new look, how they loved it and, if he wasn't mistaken, they meant it. He looked great, a fact that couldn't be argued by the sane. Marie stayed on script and asked about what the public could expect from Avocado in the coming year, and Eb discussed groundbreaking technology that would blow their minds.

"How are you doing this?" Marie asked.

"Doing what?"

"Coming out with so many great products. Before the untimely death of your partner, you weren't half this productive."

"I'm a motivator, Marie." Eb winked. His projection did, too.

"We understand you cut all of your medical funding," Marie deadpanned off-script.

"What?"

"Since Jacob's death, you've stopped development of important synthetic stem cell research that, according to your late partner, could heal millions."

"Nonsense." Eb waved at the droid. "Don't believe everything you hear, young lady."

The twins trotted into view. Marie began clapping, her expression rosy red and Christmassy again. David waved with both hands. The girls waved back just like they were taught to do, before climbing onto Eb's knees, their bony butts grinding into his thighs.

"Hi, girls," Marie said. "How was your Christmas?"

"Good," they said.

"It must be nice having Ebenezer Scrooge as your father."

They nodded.

Father? He wasn't their father. He wasn't even a guardian, really. More like their banker.

Marie asked about their dresses, said she loved the ribbons, asked what their dolls' names were and if they got them for Christmas even though a troll could tell you those germ bags appeared to emerge from a dumpster dive at the turn of the century.

"What a great, beautiful family, Mr. Scrooge," Marie said. "Thank you again for taking the time to visit with us and wishing everyone a Merry Christmas."

"I didn't say that but okay."

"You know you made Christmas happen all over the world today."

"If Christmas is about money, then all right."

David giggled about getting his kids not one but both games from Avocado this year. Marie said she didn't buy anything from Avocado, but Santa must've and, oh boy, did they laugh about that. Meanwhile, the twins whispered back and forth. Eb lightly pinched their arms.

"Just two more minutes, girls," he said without moving his lips.

"Can I see your dolls?" Marie asked. "They look very special."

Natty held her filthy little puppet by the arms and made it dance on her knee while singing something in the twin language that the hosts would think was singsong. Addy squeezed her doll tighter, but once Marie started clapping and laughing, she loosened her grip.

Now there were two dolls dancing.

Marie and David hooted like proud parents. "I love your doll, Addy," she said. In an attempt to learn her doll's name, she ignored Natty's dancing fool.

"*Moe bee!*" Natty snatched Addy's doll by one of the floppy legs. It snapped from her fingers. Eb felt Addy's buttocks clench as Natty leaped to the floor and twirled the doll like a raggedy lasso.

"*Moe bee! Moe bee!*" Addy cried. "*Moe bee!*"

The hosts didn't have time to ask what in the world they were shouting. Natty stiff-armed her sister in the face and hit her on the crown with the doll before hurling it across the room. Before storming out of the room, she held her doll over her head, victorious.

Eb stood in horror.

He could've grabbed Natty for an apology, could've picked his crying daughter off the floor and hugged her as the show signed off. Instead, he stared at the monitor behind the hosts. His projection in the top hat stared back.

"Thank you from everyone," David said.

"Yeah. Uh-huh."

"Merry Christmas," Marie chimed.

The room went blank. Eb was alone. He slumped in the chair so deeply that he almost slid onto the floor. The segment was a disaster, sure. But that wasn't what paralyzed him with horror.

It was what he saw when Natty held up her doll in victory.

The droid snuck into the room.

Eb shook his head, eyes seeing something that wasn't there. His mind was playing tricks again. And the world saw him when it happened. The world watched his spoiled brats make him a fool. He was awake this time.

"I anticipate sympathy from the audience, sir. Parents will know how hard it is to raise children. They will have pity for you."

"Pity?" The word echoed.

"Pity, sir. Yes. They'll feel sorrow for you in your castle."

"Where are they?"

"Sir?"

"The girls, idiot. Where'd they go after they *ruined my life*?"

"They're in their room, sir."

Eb wasted very little time. He tipped the Segway as far forward as it would allow. The droid's elastic footsteps drummed in long gummy strides. As he approached the bedroom door, Eb stepped off the

Segway too soon and ate the floor. The droid helped him up, but Eb shrugged him off, wiping blood from his lip.

He kicked the door open.

The girls were in the middle of the room, back to back, playing with their dirty redheads. They backed away from the raging fat man wheezing in the doorway.

"You." He pointed at Natty. "Give me that."

She crabwalked behind the bed with the doll clamped under her chin. Eb caught her before she crawled under the bed and yanked the wretched doll from her grip.

"You think this is funny? That this is a joke?"

He tore it limb from limb, stuffing falling like snow. The fabric ripped down the back; the head dangled from the frayed seam. Natty clung to his arm, screaming. Addy tugged on his other arm, crying for her sister, who had only a short time ago shoved her to the floor.

"What is this?" Eb shook a handful of white fluff. "Where did you get this?"

Natty was crying as loud as Addy. The droid put his arms around the girls, shielding them from the towering menace. Eb's cheeks were flush and jiggling. His knees quaked.

"Shhh-shhh-shhh." The droid stroked their hair and wiped their cheeks. "Now, now," he said.

"Things are changing around here, right now!" Eb shouted. "I want my way, you hear? I pay the bills; this is my house, my rules, you understand? This isn't a joke!" He took a deep fiery breath. "I want answers!"

"Stand back, sir."

"Stop coddling them." Eb grabbed the droid's arm, but he was immoveable. The droid sensed danger. Six other droids arrived from the basement. They crowded behind Eb and waited impatiently.

"This is the problem, you see." Eb's breath rattled, spots dancing in his vision. "You spare the rod, you spoil the child."

Had Eb a belt, he would've pulled it from the loops and doubled it over. The snap of leather would've sent a message that could not be denied. But had he a belt, he never would've gotten it unbuckled.

The droids were there to stop him.

"You." He shook his finger at Natty. "You know."

"What, sir?" the droid said. "She knows what?"

"Humbug. She knows."

The droid put them on the bed and pulled up the covers but remained between Eb and the bed. "Humbug, sir?"

"They speak their language. They... they know something about... about *you know what!*"

Eb's knees were about to unhinge. One of the droids brought him a chair and he collapsed. He needed another paper bag to breathe into. The shaking wouldn't stop. Three of the droids put their hands on his shoulders. One of them kneaded his neck.

"May I suggest a softer approach, sir?" The droid guarding the bed approached. "Perhaps speak with love."

Eb rested his elbows on his knees. When the shaking settled to a slight quiver, he stood and swayed. The droids steadied him as he raised his finger. Addy held her doll to her cheek. Natty clutched a wad of white stuffing.

Their heads touched.

"You call me father from now on," he said. "And there will be no doll for you, you hear? Dolls are for good girls."

"What are you saying, sir?"

He stormed out of the room. His legs were too weak to go any further. He leaned against the wall and slid to the floor. One by one, the droids left the bedroom to return to their docks. The last one closed the bedroom door quietly.

"I want her gone," Eb said.

"Who, sir?"

"The bad one. Natty. She makes me hate her. Call the lawyers; there's got to be a way to find her another home. She has to have an aunt or uncle, a long-lost cousin or something. I'll make them rich just as long as she's out of here."

"And Addy, sir?"

"She can stay."

"I see, sir." The droid sat on the floor next to him. "Would you care to talk about it?"

"No. Just get rid of her."

Eb crawled to the parked Segway and climbed onto the platform. He wasn't sure he could stay on it long enough to make it to his bedroom. It wasn't exhaustion that nibbled at his strength or low blood sugar.

It was fear.

What he saw in the studio when Natty lifted the doll in the studio, when she held it above her head in victory, Eb saw it on the monitor behind the hosts, saw the doll swing between her clenched fists. It wasn't raggedy and soiled, worn out with love. It didn't have faded red hair and button eyes. It was long and bleached, the arms and legs stretched thin. The eyes black as coal. The head covered with a mop of sticks.

A thing covered with bugs.

13

"You can't get rid of her, sir."

Eb paced the bedroom. It was 11:45 p.m. He'd tried to nap that afternoon, but he was still wide awake, his legs rubbery from incessant walking in an attempt to outrun the thoughts pecking at his head.

The doll. It was the thing.

That was not something to be forgotten in a day or a week. Or ever.

"Have the lawyers look at it tomorrow," he said. "Don't stop until they figure it out."

"I can do that, sir. But I feel you should know that you will risk the company if you do so."

"What?"

The droid had analyzed the legal contracts Eb and Jacob had signed throughout the years. Somehow his partner had made iron-clad arrangements that should something happen to him, Eb would become their legal guardian. Both of them.

And if not, there would be repercussions.

"You will risk your stake in the company, sir. I think you know what I mean."

The illegal acquisition of Jacob's share... if that snake pit were opened up, then everything would die. So if he had to keep the girl, then he would. But only until she was eighteen; then it was out the door. No one could fault him for that.

There was always the chance he could do a reality show. If the world saw how awful she was, they wouldn't blame him for cutting the cord. Problem was they'd see him too. That would need some work.

"There's got to be a way." He tapped his chin. "Keep looking."

"Honestly, there's some blame to take here, sir."

"Me? You saw the way she was acting. How is that my fault?"

"You pay the girls no attention, sir. You rarely talk to them aside from telling them to pick up their messes and chew with their mouths closed."

"And they still do. Whose fault is that?"

"And now you want them to call you father, sir? Really?"

"I pay for everything." He thumbed his chest and stalked away from the window. "The bills, the castle, food, heat, entertainment... *everything*."

A draft snuck beneath his robe. He changed into silk pajamas before continuing his nervous parade, swinging his finger to point out all the things he paid for in the castle, and what did he get in return? A thanks? Respect?

Tantrums.

"I make sure they don't starve or freeze. What else do you want?"

"You treat them like props, sir."

"Hey!" Eb aimed a knobby finger. "You work for me. I can turn you off. Remember that."

"Then who will listen to your complaints, sir?"

"Maybe I'll just turn off your vocalization, ever thought of that?"

"Working for you doesn't mean I have to agree with you, sir. Nor should I. You're very wrong here and you should know it." He cocked his head. "I'm here to help you."

Eb opened his mouth only to find no words. With finger cocked and loaded, he broke the stalemate to have another pass around the room, ending up at the window again. The snow was sparkling beneath a bright moon.

He felt the need to walk again. But he couldn't do this all night. Exhaustion would break him down before morning. And if all these thoughts still haunted him when sleep came, there was fear the dream would return.

And he couldn't do that again. Not now. Not ever.

"The doll." He half-looked back over his shoulder. "Natty's doll… it changed when she held it up."

"Changed, sir?"

Eb filled his lungs with nervous air and purged the rattling fear before describing what he'd seen on the monitor. That was not the redheaded raggedy doll she dragged around day and night that looked back at him. It had turned into the stick-headed thing grinning back.

"And that is why you destroyed her doll, sir?"

"I know what I saw."

"You should be aware that what you saw was a projection, sir. As real as it feels to be in the projection room, you only viewed a representation of what she held. You did not look directly at it."

"You're saying it didn't happen?"

"The senses are easily fooled, especially when you only witness reflections of reality, sir. You have not left the Castle in years. I suggest you go out into the world, to be in it, to experience it directly. The projection room is a delusion, sir. In essence, you believe you are making reality what you want it to be when, in fact, you are only deluding yourself."

Eb tapped his chin then shed his glasses to rub his face. An urge to cry lodged in his throat. The dream was unraveling his sanity. He couldn't come undone, not now.

"May I suggest you speak with a therapist, sir?"

"No."

"There is much to benefit from a skilled counselor, sir."

"What you just said was good, I like that. I think, yeah, I'll do something like that."

"Like what, sir?"

"Not the therapist part. The other thing." He fluttered his hand at him, already forgetting.

If he was honest, he had no intention of leaving the Castle. His life's work was aimed at never having to expose himself to risk and danger ever again. The world was a dangerous place. Just ask the animals still stuck in the food chain. Eb hovered far above the food chain; he didn't intend to go back.

Too vulnerable.

"Do you think I'm crazy?"

"You're asking a machine, sir."

"You're a good one, though."

"Was that a compliment, sir?" The droid covered his chest.

"No. I'm just saying that you can analyze past cases of insanity and match them to me, maybe evaluate brain activity. You're objective." Eb cleared his throat. "What's your analysis?"

"Stress, sir," the droid said after a long pause. Eb suspected the silence was for his benefit, that the droid had the answer all along. "There has been a lot of change over the last year, and you live alone."

"What does that have to do with it?"

"Loneliness can empower self-centered thoughts, sir. Wishful thinking, deluded behavior, that sort of thing. There are other contributing factors involved with your state of mind."

After another long pause, Eb said, "Like?"

"Your past, sir. I don't know your childhood, but I would guess you don't either."

"I know perfectly well how I grew up."

"Most people see their past through distorted lenses, sir."

"What does that mean?"

"It means memories are not often reliable, sir. Yet they determine much of your present behavior, in particular the memories you don't recall. Speaking about your past with a qualified therapist can clarify much of your life, sir."

"You want me to talk about my feelings?"

"Studies suggest talking can relieve stress and balance the emotional life, sir."

He was already a quaking bowl of jam, emotions jiggling just under the skin. One touch and he would explode into a thousand pieces that no one could put back together no matter how qualified or how many king's men they had.

No. Touching the emotions was a horrible idea. They needed to get back in the dark where they belonged. *How did they get up here anyway?*

"Call the doctor tomorrow." Eb turned his back to stare out the window. "Get me a prescription."

"What shall I say, sir?"

"Say severe anxiety. Not depression or panic attack, nothing like that. In fact, don't say severe. Just nervousness or something. But get the strongest pill out there, whatever's working these days. And turn down your sarcasm."

"You prefer not to be challenged, sir?"

"I'd rather be married than listen to you."

"And there's ample opportunity for that, sir," the droid sneered.

The small hairs sprang up on the back of his head. A clip of angry words was loaded and ready to fire when all the fear, all the delicate emotions putrefying beneath his skin simply drained away, as if a plug had been pulled on a vat of bitter sadness.

He stood a hollow vessel of a man. The switch on his emotional activity had been turned off, a faint sense of relief filling the void. The answer was in the corner of his glasses.

12:00 a.m.

The house was silent. No wind against the windows, not a snowflake scratching the chimney. No tracks in the snow.

Christmas is over.

Eb pressed his hands together and held them between his closed eyes and sighed. His rings began to hum. An incoming call rattled his fingers.

He waved the droid away.

"Sorry so late, Mr. Scrooge." Rick's face filled the hovering holo, the snow-covered hills sparkling through the translucent display.

"If it's bad news," Eb said, "you're fired."

"It's good news... I mean, it's great news. Sales are beyond what we projected. There's already an increase in orders since this morning. We're a hit... you're a hit. You owned Christmas, Mr. Scrooge."

Eb suppressed a toxic smile. "Make sure everyone is aware, Rick. I want the plant at full tilt in the morning. Christmas is over."

"Yes, Mr. Scrooge. Also, I just wanted to say that your television appearance was fantastic."

"I've had enough sarcasm for the day, Rick."

"No, I'm not joking, sir." Rick looked over both his shoulders before leaning closer and whispering, "Our social media director says you're trending, sir."

"Trending?"

"Yeah. In a good way. There's a ton of sympathy for the way you handled your children. You appeared to be patient and accommodating despite the meltdown."

"I did?" His projection must've defaulted to acceptable reactions. Eb hadn't seen the replay. Until the arrival of midnight, he probably would've cried had he done so.

"There's speculation that your appearance is contributing to the increased sales and orders. I mean, not just the way your girls behaved but your whole look."

Rick sat back and tipped an imaginary hat. A goofy grin spread across his face. It took a moment before Eb caught on.

The top hat. They're digging the top hat.

He couldn't stop the smug grin blooming deep within him, imagining what the fashionistas were saying now. They couldn't deny Eb was becoming a fashion icon. The public had spoken. And the public was never wrong.

I'm trending.

"A bit of bad news, though."

"What is it?"

"The unknown program, the one you called about earlier."

"Yes, I remember." Now Eb leaned in but didn't whisper. "What about it? What'd you find?"

"Well... *nothing*."

"Don't tell me that, Rick."

"No, I mean it's gone, Mr. Scrooge. It just disappeared. We were running an analysis, but it was encrypted. We don't know what it was doing or how it got there. IT doesn't think security was compromised. They believe it was put there by someone on the inside."

Of course they didn't think it came from the outside. If it did, they were all fired. Those idiots would deny a hacking attack as long as they were on the payroll. This meant he'd have to bring in outside intel.

Talons of impatience clawed at Eb's underbelly.

"We still don't know what it was for," Rick continued. "It wasn't a virus, as far as we can tell. And then it just... *vanished*."

"Keep searching."

"Of course, Mr. Scrooge."

"I want a full report in the morning."

"Okay." Rick hesitated.

"Is there a problem?"

"It's after midnight. I'll be in first thing in the morning."

"Rick?"

"Yes, Mr. Scrooge?"

"You just had a vacation. You should be rested. Sleep is overrated."

Rick looked over his shoulder and swallowed. Eb hoped his wife was close enough to hear that. He killed the connection before Rick could respond. If he looked well rested in the morning, Eb would begin searching for a new Rick. Someone hungrier.

More willing.

He bathed in the moonlight's view and let the good news fill all those empty spaces vacated by the emotional turmoil. The juice of winning lifted him up, charging him with life. Made it all worth living.

How could he sleep now?

It was 12:55 a.m. when he activated a holo. The girls were sound asleep, their foreheads touching. Arms on top of the blanket, thumbs in their mouths, Addy with her doll pressed to her cheek. Natty with a clump of white fluff.

Before closing the screen, he sent an order to the printer.

He wrapped a robe over his pajamas, stepped onto the hoverboard with fat, cushioned slippers, and cruised to the first floor. The printer hummed and vibrated.

Printing heads zipped around the inside of a three-dimensional printer, making their last pass as he closed the door. The foggy scent of warm fabric hung near the ceiling.

Eb reached inside to retrieve the item, still pliable. He pushed it over the crown of his head, followed the rim with his finger and thumb, then pointed at an imaginary crowd and smiled.

He was an entrepreneur. A pioneer.

He would lead the world into a new era of technology and fulfill dreams and wishes. And while he hated the name, they could call him Santa Claus if they wanted. Because that was what he was, except with loads of money and no little people.

Except the two living in the west wing.

Eb went to sleep with the top hat on the pillow. He forgot all about the future his dream monster had showed him. True or not, the future was tomorrow.

He was only interested in today.

PART III

THE GHOST OF CHRISTMAS PRESENT

14

Black smoke spewed from the trucks.
The drivers waited for the droids—barefoot in their insulated coveralls, spits of snow sticking to their dull gray scalps. With an aggressive shove, the droids pushed the black gates open. The contractors made their exit down a narrow road carved from the mountain.

It was 11:40 a.m. *They better be finished.*

The project was behind schedule. They were supposed to be done on Labor Day, then Thanksgiving. Now it was Christmas.

Eb had paid absurd amounts of money for this project. There was no way for him to expand the Castle. The engineers were too short-sighted to think he'd want to add a room or two.

Idiots. All of them. That was what he posted on Yelp.

A fire blazed on the far side of the room, the flames' reflection dancing on a black grand piano. Eb went to warm himself before returning to the window.

The last truck departed.

A shiver rippled down his back, as cold as it was nervous. This must be what it was like for children on Christmas Eve, fluttering excitement fanned by anticipation. He didn't need Santa Claus to rubber-stamp his wishes, didn't need to be good to get what he wanted. He took it.

A droid stepped into the room.

"Well?" Eb said.

"It's finished, sir."

"They're finished, with everything? It's not even lunch. They said it would be tomorrow."

"It's done, sir."

"You've inspected it?"

"Top to bottom, sir. Side to side. They were motivated by Christmas."

Why couldn't everybody work like a vacation was waiting? Every other day of the year they grazed like lazy cows.

"Don't release the final payment," Eb said. "You know contractors once they're paid. I want a second inspection."

"An outside firm already provided one, sir."

"Then I want a third. You can't be too careful."

The droid cocked his head with an incredulous smile. "This project didn't even scratch your fortune, sir."

"And don't give them Christmas bonuses, either. They already dragged this out."

"I wouldn't dream of it, sir. They did exactly as you asked, why reward them?"

"Reward them for doing their job?" Eb laughed hysterically. If they didn't do exactly what he wanted, exactly what he paid for, they'd get nothing. And he'd sue for pain and suffering. It hurt not getting what he wanted.

"Would you like to go up, sir?"

Eb paced to the piano. He adjusted his glasses and tapped his chin along the way. The anticipation roared inside him, a sweetness that trembled in all his chins. He started to answer, almost said yes, then made another pass around the room.

"You've waited all this time, sir. You rushed the contractors, and now you want to wait?"

The droid couldn't understand. It had to be perfect. When you wanted something, it had to be absolutely perfect or it was no good at all. If there was a single fracture, a tiny scuff, Eb's head would explode in a red mist.

"Perhaps we could launch the drones, sir, and see it from the outside first."

Eb snapped his fingers. "Perfect. Yes. You're not so stupid."

"Of course not, sir."

The droid forwarded a request to the basement, where an army of quadcopter drones were docked. They patrolled thousands of acres to report trespassers who, on occasion, snuck out to camp or hunt or whatever on Eb's property. They were then persecuted to the full extent of the law.

The rings were icy bands around his sausage fingers. He clapped his hands—the heavy rings clinked—and stretched open a holo until it curved around his periphery and immersed his senses.

"Ready, sir?"

"Go."

Snowflakes slashed across the slate gray holo. The view swayed as a gust of wind buffeted the drone. The view surged toward the ground. Eb clawed at the armrests, his stomach dropping. He tipped his head back and the drone ascended toward the sky. The flight settled, swinging left and right as he tipped his head, steering it into the open field before banking steeply to the left.

So immersed in the view and the response to his movements, he'd forgotten his body and become the drone. He soared unfettered by his flabby body and knotted emotions. The tangle of thoughts that weighed him down vanished.

The Castle came into view.

The architectural marvel was padded with snow. The broad windows reflected the mountain range. Atop the grandeur sat half a glassy dome—a black-mirrored snow globe perched on an extension like the tongue of a cuckoo clock.

Skeye™ dome.

It converted sunlight into energy, but it was so much more than that. The design was his idea, not Avocado's. The name, too.

Pure Ebenezer Scrooge was on display.

"Satisfied, sir?"

Eb sat back and closed his eyes. His chin sank into his neck. A dopey grin dimpled his cheeks. The wait was over. Anticipation congealed into a drop of molasses—sweet and thick on his tongue.

From somewhere outside the room, a pair of screams pierced the silence. It was followed by the thump of something on the floor. The patter of footsteps faded.

"That better not have been expensive," Eb said.

"It's Christmas Eve, sir. The girls are excited."

"That's not an excuse."

"You have a television appearance in two hours, sir. Would you like to experience the Skeye™ dome beforehand?"

"Is it ready?"

"It's everything you dreamed of, sir."

The droid helped pull him from the chair. Before he could mount the Segway, his rings began to vibrate. A quick swipe revealed who was calling.

Rick.

He thought about this for several seconds. He needed to take the call but didn't want it to contaminate his Skeye™ dome experience. First impressions only came once. And the anticipation was already so yummy.

"Run my shower," he said. "It can wait."

"Are you positive, sir? Skeye™ dome is quite spectacular and—"

"Yes, I'm sure," he whined. The mood was starting to spoil. This was exactly what he wanted to avoid. Why couldn't everyone just leave him alone?

The droid exited.

Eb pulled open a holo. "What?"

"Mr. Scrooge, sorry to bother you on Christmas... um, I'm mean today."

"Is it important?"

"I think it is."

Eb's projected image—the handsome, chiseled face that Rick was talking to—wouldn't reveal the flush of frustration currently coloring his cheeks.

"What is it?" he said.

"We're wrapping up end-of-year projects because, you know, the office will be closed tomorrow. Everything has gone smoothly, Mr. Scrooge, but we noticed this morning that the systems had bogged down, so we checked into it."

Rick held out his hands like a rhino was charging. Eb's frustration must have leaked through the projection.

"Everything is all right, though," he said. "I promise."

"Get to the point, Rick."

He sighed. "The program is back."

"What are you talking about?"

"The program from last year."

Eb shook his head. A sinking feeling punched him in the groin; a distorted moment threatened to erase him. He hadn't forgotten about the nightmare—the stretchy-armed, bug-infested *thing* that dragged him through his so-called future—but he had forgotten about the secret program that disappeared. IT promised it had been taken care of. And it had been.

"Is this a joke?" Eb said.

"No, Mr. Scrooge. But it doesn't appear to be doing anything. All the data is backed up, the system files are okay, security is green."

"The program has to be doing something, Rick."

"We... we're looking into it. There's nothing to worry about as far as we can tell."

"So you called to tell me what, Rick? You're incompetent?"

"I don't want you to worry, Mr. Scrooge. Last year it was a little unnerving, but we caught it early this time. We'll figure out who put it there and what it's doing."

"I wouldn't worry if you hadn't called."

Truth was, he would've been furious if he didn't call. Rick couldn't win. But that was sort of his job, the not-winning part.

A stampede of clapping shoes passed outside the doors again. This time the girls were babbling instead of screaming shrilly.

"Rick." Eb held up a finger. "Will you excuse me a second?"

He split the sliding doors open and poked his head out. The girls had turned the corner, their shoes tapping into the distance, their psychobabble echoing *gubbagubbagubbah*. If he prattled on like that, they'd say he was losing his marbles. Seven-year-olds did it and they were bubbling bags of joy.

Or are they eight years old? Either way.

This recklessness would get handled now. Eb locked the holo onto the Segway, Rick watching him mount up.

"I know you're busy—"

"I want you to stay at the plant until this is resolved," Eb declared.

Rick looked up from the Segway's handlebars, his expression dimming.

"I know, I know," Eb said, "It's Christmas Eve and blah, blah, blah, excuses, excuses. This is your job, Rick. This is what you do. You put out the fires; you make sure there's water in the troughs. We are Avocado, Rick. We are the biggest nut on the tree, and you are one of the branches holding it up. You bend but don't break, you understand?"

Eb leaned into a turn.

"When the storm hits, you don't run, you don't take vacation. You weather it, son. You protect the nut. People are jealous. They want to be us. They want to dominate the holiday season; they want our sales, our innovations, our domination. I don't care what kind of pruning you have to do, you make sure that nut is safe. Am I making myself clear?"

By pruning, Eb meant trimming back family time. By family time, he meant Rick's family.

By nut, Eb meant fortune. His fortune.

Whether he understood what Eb was saying didn't matter, really. The tone was making the point. Based on Rick's nodding and pasty complexion, Eb was certain the message was received.

"Yes, Mr. Scrooge."

Eb killed the connection as he cruised by the girls' bedroom. The door was open. They scurried behind the bed. He could hear them whispering. Eb leaned back and reversed the Segway.

The ruckus went silent.

"Girls, come out."

The bedroom was spotless. The floor picked up, the bed made, the corners crisply tucked. It had been some time since he'd been up to their room. He'd peeked on it through a holo screen every once in a while, but actually walking into the room? *Probably last Christmas.*

"I know you're hiding, girls. You're not in trouble."

Yet.

When they didn't come out, Eb stepped into the room. He was stopped by a peculiar smell. An earthy scent. Fresh compost. But not a speck of dirt anywhere. He went to the bed.

"All right, that's enough—"

They weren't there.

He was certain he saw them, knew he heard them. He dropped a knee on the carpet and felt it squish. The floor was damp and cold. Similar spots darkened the carpet across the room. Eb dipped his head below the bed.

It was empty.

There were two lumps beneath the bedspread. Eb peeled it back to reveal two redheaded dolls, still worn and dirty. He had wrecked one of them last year after he saw it change into something quite terrifying. Maybe she had another one all this time, and he just didn't notice. *But where did it come from?*

Something shuffled behind him.

"Girls?"

A light flashed inside the closet. They must've crawled under the bed and snuck to the closet when he bent down. Panic transformed into frustration, replacing the weakness in his legs with steely strength. He plodded to the closet and yanked it open.

Strands of Christmas lights hung over a dozen dresses, the flashing lights turning them different shades of green and red. An equal number of black shiny shoes were lined against the wall. In front of them was a small plate of cookies and a glass of milk. One of the cookies already had a bite out of it.

Eb grunted.

He bent over with much effort and took a bite from the uneaten cookie. Chocolate chip. It was still warm, too. This would be discussed at a state of the union later that night. Rules would have to be reinstated. He dropped the cookie then decided to eat the rest of it. The plate shifted as he grabbed it.

The torn corner of a piece of paper stuck out.

Eb, breathing heavily from the effort, unfolded it. *Dear Santa,* it read in big, loopy letters. There was a list beneath it, each line numbered. He couldn't read the items but not because they were poorly written.

It was jibberish.

The same nonsense the girls whispered to each other, what the droid called their secret language.

Another scuffle by the bed.

Eb's heart jumped. Blood pulsed through the racetrack of arteries in his forehead. The dolls were propped up on the pillows, relaxed and watching. His mouth was cotton. Like the stuffing that filled them.

"Silly," he said to no one and walked stiff-legged to the bed.

He grabbed the dolls, one in each hand, and squeezed. They felt familiar. Something tugged at the back of his mind, attempting to pull memories out of the basement and dust them off.

They were old-fashioned rag dolls with round eyes and no hint of a nose. Their hands were mittens, dirty from the girls chewing on them and harboring a billion germs. His throat was beginning to itch. A strange tickle ran up his nose, an army of bacteria invading his sinuses and attacking his brain—

"Are you all right, sir?"

"Ahhh!"

The dolls hit the ceiling. Eb leaned against the wall, clutching his chest to keep his heart from blowing an escape route through his sternum.

"Don't... ever... do that again," Eb said.

"I sensed your vitals were unusual, sir. I came to see if you were feeling unwell."

"I've been calling you for the past half hour."

"I'm sorry, sir. I did not receive a call." The droid returned with a warm damp cloth, patting Eb's clammy chins and the back of his neck. "Did something startle you, sir?"

He wasn't about to admit the dolls just totally freaked him out. "That," he said instead, pointing at the closet. "What's going on in there?"

"It appears the girls are celebrating, sir."

"And you didn't know anything about it?"

"Obviously they were hiding it, sir."

"Obviously." Eb got his wind back. "You're supposed to be watching them."

"I'm not a spy, sir."

"Just clear out the closet and don't let it happen again."

"Of course, sir. I'm all about helping you. Would you care for another warm washcloth?"

"Would you care to explain this?" Eb shook the dolls.

"The girls' dolls, sir." He cocked his head. "How are you not aware of their dolls?"

"Don't give me that. Where did this one come from?" It was impossible to tell which one was which—they both looked a hundred years old—so he shook them both. "One of these had a little accident last year."

"They have more than one doll, sir."

"No, they don't."

"Of course they do, sir. How would she have another one?"

"That's what I'm asking you!"

They had showed up at his front door with a doll in each hand and no luggage. Now they had a closet full of identical clothing and dolls that multiplied like rabbits.

"Where are they?" Eb said. "Where are all these dolls? Show me."

"They're not here, sir."

"They're gone?"

"Just not in this room, sir."

"Then. Where?"

"I will find them, sir. If that'll make you happy."

Eb squeezed the little pillows. A pile of these raggedy dust mite motels made him itch. They would probably burn without an ounce of lighter fluid—just a match and *whoosh*.

Then, for some odd reason, he had the urge to push them against his face and breathe the musty fabric.

"I must be losing my mind," he muttered.

"That's quite possible, sir."

"Is it?" Eb sneered. "Get the girls up here to... to clean up or something."

The room was already spotless. The closet would take exactly five seconds to reorganize. Maybe they could scrub the bathroom or shovel the sidewalk. Something besides giving him a migraine.

And where are they?

15

The bow tie was giving him fits.

Eb blamed his fingers. They were still soft and pickled. He'd taken a marathon steam shower and actually nodded off for a spell. The fog had a clearing effect on his thoughts, like a section break in a long narrative of nightmares, a swish of water to cleanse the mental palate.

He propped his top hat forward and stepped back from the mirror, turning left then right. An over-the-shoulder look back. From an inside pocket, he withdrew a silk handkerchief and tucked it into the front pocket of his jacket. He dialed the tint on his round spectacles to match the kerchief.

Rosy.

"Bah." He blew his nose in the kerchief and threw it in the garbage. Every little detail seemed to bother him because more money, more problems. Poor people complained about what they didn't have. Try a mile in Eb's slippers and they'd see it ain't all rosy on this side of the spectacles.

The interviews. The haters. The endless details.

And creepy dolls.

He had managed to squeegee the memories of the dolls from his mind. And that earthy smell. Where had he noticed that before? A little voice told him he didn't want to remember.

It was 1:50 p.m.

Get the interview done and get to the Skeye™ dome. That was all that was on his calendar. After that, his problems would vanish like a magician's assistant.

"Ten minutes, sir."

"This." Eb held up the bow tie.

The droid flipped the white collar and worked the bow tie into place. It was quite snug beneath chin number two. *Or is that number three?*

"We may need to print another tuxedo, sir."

Eb just had the three-dimensional fabricator print the tuxedo six months ago. "It must've shrunk in the wash."

"Of course, sir." The droid stuck out his tongue as he began squaring the knot.

Eb's projected image would be stellar as usual. He didn't have to dress the part, but he found it lifted his spirits and made him feel closer to the handsome fellow the public was watching. If he held very still and closed his eyes, he could feel the square chin and high-rise cheekbones. As if that were really him, that he could wish himself into the projection.

One day, maybe.

The droid brushed the jacket and straightened the collar. Eb did a slow circle, examining his backside in case he should ever walk a red carpet.

He looked over the glasses. "Do you think a pipe would be over the top?"

"Why stop now, sir?"

Of course it would be over the top. What were they calling him on social media? *Eccentrically charming.*

"Five minutes, sir."

"Are the girls ready?"

"They weren't invited, sir."

"Good." That meant less baby talk from the hosts. "Where are they?"

"Their bedroom, sir. No cookies or milk."

"We're going to talk about this after dinner. I want to meet in the Grand Room."

"A state of the union, sir?"

"A state of the union."

"Perhaps it could wait until after Christmas, sir. Why smash their spirits now?"

Eb took three steps back and took in the whole Ebenezer Scrooge show from the top of the tilted hat to the bottom of his bare feet. With two minutes to showtime, he hopped on the Segway.

"Now is now, Dum-dum!"

He rolled into the projection room at exactly 2:00 p.m. The *Investigative Tonight* studio was already on the air when he arrived. A wide, shiny desk with curved edges protruded from the domed wall. Michelle Barrows, the blonde attorney-turned-entertainment-host sat on the other side, her cerulean blue blouse snug around the neck. She smiled as he approached, her peach lips glossy and full.

"Mr. Scrooge," she said, "pleasure to have you."

"Wouldn't miss it for the world, Michelle." His projection pretended to kiss her hand. "Congratulations on your new show."

"We've been airing since last year, but thank you."

The set was less Christmassy than her last gig on *Entertainment Nightly*. No tree or ornaments or distracting lights. Just a strand of twining garland over the backdrop.

I can dig this.

"It's nice to have a very dapper gentleman on my last show of the year," she said. "Merry Christmas to you, sir."

"Okay."

"Why do you always say that?"

"I'm sorry?"

"I notice when someone wishes you a Merry Christmas, you say okay. It's sort of like grunting when someone says good morning."

"I don't know what you mean."

"Why do you hate Christmas, Mr. Scrooge? It made you a very wealthy man; I would think you would love it."

"Are we on the air?"

She chuckled. "Yes, we are."

"I, uh, never said I hated it."

Michelle let a pause drag out. Eb glanced at the monitor off set and saw his projected image smiling with the entire set of pearly whites.

"Jacob Marley died two years ago," she said. "You two were good friends."

"Yes, uh-huh. We were."

"It must've been hard after all that time."

"It was."

She let another pause hang. Eb's image didn't falter despite the fact he had already sweat through his shirt.

"You took custody of his girls, too," she said. "Very selfless."

"Yes, thank you."

"Well, legally you had no choice but to take them in, but you haven't sued them for it."

"You're not being very nice, Michelle. What's that mean?"

"Your legal team is trigger-happy, Mr. Scrooge. What are the girls' names?"

Eb crossed his legs twice. The tuxedo was becoming a straitjacket. "Um, Addy. Natty."

"Addy and Natty. Sweet names. What did you get them for Christmas?"

"What they wanted, of course."

"Whatever they wanted, that's nice."

He didn't say *whatever*, but he couldn't quite figure out her angle. Did she want to fight?

"Where are they from?" she asked.

"Guatemala."

"Have you ever contacted their birth parents?"

"Of course not."

"I'm assuming their parents made an adoption plan because they were very poor, not because they didn't want them."

"I never said that."

"What's their favorite food?"

"I don't know."

"Their favorite color?"

"Look—"

"We know their favorite clothes."

Those dreaded dresses. Social media was beginning to catch on, scolding Eb for never buying them anything else when, in fact, there was a whole room of little girl clothes. Somehow they always ended up in those dresses.

"We can't find their birth parents." Michelle flipped a page over. "We did a search of Jacob's custody and can't find a single picture of the children or where they came from."

Her long stare drilled for oil between his eyes.

There were rumors that the girls were made up, some sort of publicity stunt to appeal to the public. If only he would've thought of that before, then he wouldn't be stepping in milk puddles when he walked through the kitchen.

"You're not being kind to me," Eb said. "I was very nice to you on the other show, so it's very unfair of you to treat me this way."

"Jacob had a vision."

Michelle had not flinched, her shoulders square and taut. Her image was replaced by a video of Jacob visiting a children's hospital, sitting at bedsides with gifts for juvenile patients, their eyes dark, scalps bare. He would smile that wide Jacob smile—the smile that all the newsfeeds ran, the smile that captured Philanthropist of the Year —as he went bed to bed in his Santa coat and pulled stuffed animals from his Santa bag. One year it was lions, the next tigers, then rhinos, then bears. Always something new. Something special.

Every year.

Eb went once but couldn't take the smell. It was the antiseptic and old skin, the smell of an open wound.

"Since his death," Michelle said, "you've cut all medical spending. How has the mission statement changed at Avocado?"

Eb grimaced, but his projection appeared serious and empathetic.

"We entertain the world, Michelle. It's what people want. The proof is sitting right in front of you. Every dollar spent is their vote cast. They've spoken very loudly. Who am I not to give them what they want?"

"How about giving them what they need?"

"People are responsible for their own decisions, Michelle. Quite frankly I'm surprised you feel like we should decide for them."

"You don't give booze to a child."

"Nor have I. And the public are not children. They're adults, Michelle."

Score.

"Jacob envisioned technology that could rebuild organs, could eliminate cancer. The test trials were all very promising and you cut the investments entirely for what, entertainment? I find that irresponsible, Mr. Scrooge."

"I didn't cut the spending, not entirely."

"Really?" She raised an eyebrow. "Do tell."

"It's confidential, Michelle."

He was telling the truth. He had reinstated a portion of medical research, pretending to give way to Jerri's request when, in fact, he was hoping to find something that would eat fat from his belly and chins.

"We're not expecting immortality," Michelle said. "We're talking improvements in the quality of life, enhanced recovery from accidents, stable mental health. You, Mr. Scrooge, could deliver the greatest Christmas gift to the world instead of entertaining us into a coma."

"You can't change the world overnight, Michelle."

"Change happens one person at a time."

"Is that what you're trying to do, change me?"

"Only you can do that." She blinked slowly.

Eb flinched. His projection also flinched, less so. Eb had nearly fallen out of his seat. *Where have I heard that?*

"You have money, Mr. Scrooge. You have power. You have opportunity. Don't squander it. Make Jacob happy."

His projection maintained a pleasant smile while tracks of sweat pooled on Eb's eyebrows and dripped down his cheeks. His teeth hurt. She asked another question. Eb couldn't hear it over the sound of grinding molars.

"Have a pleasant day," Eb's projection replied, an automated response to whatever hateful question she spewed. Then the projection smiled brightly, waving like a beauty queen in the back of a convertible.

The walls turned blank.

Eb clutched the edge of the desk, holding his breath until his inky periphery began to close on him. He sucked in a long breath and choked on saliva as he looked around the vanilla room, the walls the silvery shade of a dead theater.

"Noooooo!" The scream vibrated through his foaming lips. "No! No! No!"

He flipped the desk on its back, kicked it with his bare feet, and picked up one of the splintered legs. It spun like a throwing knife, the sharp edge sticking into the far wall.

The screams continued. His protests mingled with the sounds of a dying animal, the wet slap of sweaty palms against the floor, the crumpling of compressed wood as the desk was tortured into unrecognizable pieces. His reflection had appeared on the wall and watched him flail on the floor.

A sloppy beast in a top hat and crooked bow tie looked back.

Eb tore the shirt open, buttons popping like plastic bullets. He ripped at the bow tie, but it refused to budge beneath his pudgy grip. His hat took the worst of it.

The top hat.

He put his foot through it, ground it beneath his heel, pulled it apart, beat it with a table leg until black shreds covered the floor like black snow. He only stopped to breathe.

On his hands and knees, a single strand of drool hung from his lip like a sagging instrument. He dropped on his back, sobs clogging his windpipe. He rolled once, twice until he came to the edge of the room and sat up, the curvature of the wall pushing his head forward.

His enormous belly was tacky with sweat.

Sooner or later, the haters attack.

Only the sound of raspy breath, a plump uvula rattling in his throat, filled the room. When the door opened, he was half naked, hunched over with a knotted bow tie squeezed between chin number two and chin number three.

The droid stood with a stack of neatly folded clothes on his forklift arms. Eb continued massaging his stomach, curly hair swirling around the vortex of his belly button.

"I need a vacation" he said.

"How about Florida, sir?"

He shook his head; the round spectacles were shattered. All his anger and agitation had been incinerated by the nuclear tantrum. Only a hollow of exhaustion remained.

His heart was granite.

The droid cut away the bow tie with a pair of scissors. "I took the liberty of printing a larger shirt, sir."

"I'm going to put more money into medical research."

"Wonderful, sir."

"I'm so fat." He slapped his belly, wet and sticky.

"Would you care to lose weight, sir? I have an exercise program and diet menu that will guarantee results."

"No, dummy. We'll use Jacob's research to develop fat-eater cells."

"Fat-eater, sir?"

"Instant results. We'll start with that and see where it goes."

The droid helped him to his feet, dried him with a towel and dressed him. The freshly printed shirt was toasty. Eb left the projection room with a table leg stuck in the wall.

"Cancel all my interviews," he said. "All of them."

He would never do another one.

16

Eb faced golden doors.

Dry and naked beneath a fresh robe, he smelled like baby powder. Nothing was tied around his neck, no belt cinching his waist or collar choking his windpipe. He was free.

It was 11:00 p.m. He was ahead of schedule.

Eb watched the girls on a holo. They were curled up in bed—lying on their sides, arms on top of the bedspread, foreheads touching. Dreaded rag dolls crushed against their chins. The closet doors were closed, the room clean. No jibberish to be heard.

He didn't go to dinner. Skipped it altogether. It was time to shed some weight. After the interview disaster, he went for a steam shower. Then another after that.

He cancelled the state of the union address. No need to bring the girls to tears about the cookies and milk in the closet and the dirty little doll that looked too much like the one he'd shredded. Those were answers he would get, just not now. He needed the night to end on a high note. If not a high one, then at least a quiet one.

The droid kneaded his shoulders, whispering affirmations past the cloth hood draped over his head.

"You're good, sir."

Eb's fingers were wrinkled worse than wet cotton. The lotions were nice; the baby powder soothed his chafed belly folds. The droid was only expressing what Eb wanted to hear. He didn't really mean it, didn't really believe that nonsense.

"You're a very good boy, sir."

Wait. Did he say 'boy'?

"I will send up food, sir."

"Do not disturb me."

"Of course not, sir. You deserve this. You earned this."

He had earned it. Who were these self-righteous reporters that could tell him what to do with his money? They were jealous, plain and simple. He started Avocado; he dominated the gift-giving season. She needed to accept that.

Quite simply, he won.

The golden doors slid open. An evergreen breeze fell over him, the minty exhalation of an ancient conifer breathing on him. A vague mist wafted beneath his hood. Eb vacuumed it up with his nostrils. He nearly wept.

The spoils of war.

Funny how he thought of it as war. But business was a battle. Take it lightly and you'd be filling potholes. Life was a business. And no one *wanted* to fill potholes.

The droid guided him inside the elevator, a golden tube with polished walls. Eb fell onto the bench seat along the back.

"I will see you soon, sir."

If everything went right—and it better—he wouldn't see that dull gray face until morning.

Eb avoided his reflection on the inside of the elevator doors. The tube began a slow rise. He braced his hands on the bench and felt something papery next to him.

Two gifts. One green, the other red.

He shook the weighty boxes. There was no need to open them; he recognized the heavy rattle, the same gifts they had given him the year before, the smooth-edged rocks that he could use to weigh down paper. Or skip across a pond.

The elevator stopped so smoothly that he didn't notice his arrival. The evergreen scent captured his attention. He closed his eyes once again and inhaled.

On his feet, he could no longer avoid his gold-tinted reflection. The concave surface slimmed him down a shade. The image was distorted but better. He was wheezing just from the two attempts it took to stand.

He thumbed the only button on the wall, a button that would only respond to his fingerprint.

The ceiling slid open; the floor began to rise.

A warm breeze fluttered his hood. The night sounds of crickets and cicadas called forth. A nervous buzz sang in his stomach. He tipped his head back as the floor lifted him out of the Castle and into the Skeye™ dome.

Dizzy with anticipation, saturated with insect song and fresh-scented boughs, he opened his eyes.

Pines and hemlocks, spruce and cedar. Rhododendrons in bloom.

A veritable forest.

Between sagging branches, the sky was littered with celestial diamonds. There was no hint of a dome, nothing that seemed to separate him from the outside world. As if he were in it. Of course, he wasn't, but what was the difference?

A temperate breeze ruffled the hem of his robe. Eb walked the paved paths that journeyed through the miniature forest, a conservatory of hidden ponds and small alcoves for meditation. Chairs and loungers could be found in larger niches, a place to rest and relax. Even sleep.

The face of the mountain soared over him.

He cautiously approached the stone wall. Snow crusted near the bottom of the invisible dome, the first hint of a barrier. As he neared the perimeter, the surface of the dome turned milky white. And when he backed up, it turned transparent.

A proximity warning. Genius. And beautiful.

He wiped away tears.

It had been seven years since he'd left the Castle, not since the day he moved in. Now he had the experience of being in touch with nature again, with real trees and seventy-two-degree breezes and the stars and the mountains. The insect sounds were simulated—miniature speakers strategically installed in the trees and little burrows. He wasn't going to do real bugs; he could only take so much nature.

A gentle mist fell over him, warm, comforting.

Life is beautiful.

Eb began to weep. He stifled the sobs, the tiny blinking light inside his round spectacles reminding him that he was recording this life moment. He didn't want to sound like a baby. Instead, his shoulders quaked quietly, his eyes glistened. He made another pass through the forest, the serpentine routes never seeming the same.

He collapsed on a lounger, the cushion swelling around him, and looked into the star-spattered sky.

Nothing could spoil this moment. Not the haters. Not the jealousy. Not the fact that Rick hadn't called back.

Nothing.

This was ecstasy. Heaven. Nirvana. The end of the road.

He would never want more than this. That was until he walked the paths so much that he memorized them and the trees all started to look the same and the sky was just another sky instead of a magical canvas, at which time he would build something even bigger and even better. And then he would be happy again.

Until then, he never wanted anything else in his life.

For now, the sleep of angels descended upon him. He rolled on his side, and something stuck his hip. Attempting to avoid the fallen branch or stray zipper, he flipped to his other side. The pain wasn't going away. If it was a pair of pruners, someone was getting sued. He pulled a pokey mess of wire from a crease in the cushion and considered throwing it into a nearby pine.

It had been twisted into tight curls.

He held it by one of four spindly limbs that could've been arms and legs. A loop for a head. The proportions were stretched out. He turned the figure by the foot, spinning it like an aberrant ballerina.

A bored electrician, perhaps?

Sleep dusted his eyes. At 11:59 p.m., he pulled off his glasses. The dreaded day was almost over. A word limped from his lips, one that aptly captured his disdain for the frivolous holiday.

He didn't hear the distant thunder.

"Hello, Ebenezer."

17

A man stood at the foot of the lounger. Eb was heavy with exhaustion, cast in concrete repose, helpless in the presence of a stranger. His lips popped, strands of saliva stretching in gasping attempts.

Ropey hair hung over obsidian eyes, a mop of black dreadlocks dancing on the man's head. His complexion was the color of mulch. His teeth tapped like pearls.

Eb struggled to move.

"Relax," the dreadlock man said. His voice was deep and scratchy, resonating deeply.

This did not put Eb at ease. Fear tugged at his intestines and stomped the air from his lungs. The dreadlock man's fingers were long and boney, spidery as they unfurled.

The hands.

The black eyes.

"You," Eb croaked.

The dreadlock man's smile grew warmer, spread wider. Somehow, it eased Eb's strangling panic. The invisible grip loosened. Eb struggled to sit up. Gravity had tripled.

He rubbed his tired face, lips and cheeks dull and slightly

rubbery. This couldn't be happening. It was midnight. Had he learned nothing from the past two Christmases?

"I'm dreaming again," Eb said.

"Does it matter?"

"You're not real."

"And you? Are you real?"

Eb had no answer. If this was a dream, why couldn't he wake? Why did it feel so real?

Does it matter?

The green scent of the forest was around him. The night sky above, the paved path below. The wire man that was hidden in the cushion was now biting the palm of his hand. Dream or not... *this feels real.*

The dreadlock man nodded.

The eyes were the same as *the thing* that had visited him a year ago—the blackness, the bottomless depths—yet his skin was darker.

The dreadlock man moved forward, a graceful step that glided toward Eb, his loose clothing fluttering around a bare foot, the tendons taut and flexing. His hand emerged from a wide sleeve, the fingers once again unfolding. Eb flinched but couldn't avoid his touch, a cold shiver brushing his cheek.

"No," Eb chanted. "No, no, no... this is not happening again. You are not real. This is not... *not my future.*"

His words, however, would not take root. Eb trembled all the same. And laughter bubbled out of the dreadlock man. It started low and built to a roaring cascade that echoed around the invisible dome. His entire body quaked, head thrown back, chin dancing. Eb felt it pulse through him, as if his cold bones were struck with a mallet.

The dreadlock man snapped his teeth.

"You have seen your future," he said, his voice now as silky as his movement, "yet you have changed nothing."

"No. No, that was a dream, nothing more. That was not my future."

"This dome you have built. What is below it?"

It took a moment for Eb to visualize the Great Room over which the Skeye™ dome was built, the wide-open pillared space with golden trim. In the dream, where the deathbed held his body and birds fluttered in a domed ceiling. The great room had a flat ceiling—ornate crown molding and a dual step trey ceiling. It was nothing like the dream.

Unless...

And the dreadlock man laughed again, the moment of realization seizing Eb's brittle sanity, shaking it into a million tiny pieces. Because if the Great Room ceiling was removed, the Skeye™ dome would be revealed.

That will be where I die.

Did he build Skeye™ dome because of the dream, a self-fulfilling prophecy?

"The future rarely changes behavior," the dreadlock man said. "No matter the certainty. You know your future, Ebenezer; you know how it will end, you know the dread and discomfort and, more importantly, the regret that will follow, yet you have done nothing to alter your life. You are like so many, Ebenezer. People know the consequences of their habits yet continue to embrace them."

He pointed a long, accusing finger. "You are no different, Ebenezer Scrooge."

"I... I don't smoke."

"But you only care about now. You don't care about tomorrow, Ebenezer. You only want what pleases you, regardless of how it affects the world around you, regardless of the tomorrow it creates."

"This isn't happening."

"Therein lies your problem, Ebenezer."

The dreadlock man began walking through the trees, his voice carrying through the limbs. He would appear in small openings, suddenly upon the path and then gone again. Eb tried to run for it. He would dive into the elevator and scream for the droid. They would lock the doors and never let this dreadlocked horror out.

"Tomorrow is now, Ebenezer."

Suddenly, he stood in front of Eb, his toes appearing very human from beneath pant legs.

"I demand to know who is doing this to me."

"Tell me who you are, Ebenezer, and I'll tell you who I am."

He tapped his teeth like bouncing pearls.

Last year, the thing had appeared at the stroke of midnight. The ground shook and there were tracks in the snow. Eb had muttered a word. As he had this year.

"Humbug," he said.

The dreadlock man took a step back, ropes of hair hiding his black eyes. He smiled before turning away, the elongated fingers weaving behind his back. His footsteps fell upon the path silently, veering into the mulched ground, disappearing into the forest.

Cicadas filled the empty space.

"A beautiful creation, Ebenezer," the deep voice called from the trees. "Quite a vision."

"Don't patronize me."

"You believe I have come to hurt you?"

"You aren't here to help."

"On the contrary, Ebenezer. You have worked very hard for all of this. I commend you on a job well done. A visionary, you are. Let's not sidestep the fact that you have achieved amazing feats." Sticks snapped behind Eb. "And wealth in the process."

"Is that what this is, a shakedown? You want money?"

Laughter shook the trees.

"What, then? What do you want from me?"

The dreadlock man appeared in a narrow gap. He was at the edge of the Skeye™ dome, the transparent surface turning milky white. He was too close to it.

"You don't know who you are, Ebenezer." His voice reverberated in Eb's chest as if he pressed those long fingers against his sternum. "And you don't have a clue as to what you've done. Tell me what's out there, can you? Are you aware of the world, what is happening presently? Or are you caught in a tangle of self-centered thoughts, an increasingly sad man creating the reality he wishes to see." The dreadlock man smiled a knowing smile. "An image he wishes others to see."

For a moment, a top hat appeared on the dreadlock man.

"Whatever you are, leave me." Eb pushed off the lounger, strength returning to his body of sand. He took two lumbering steps and pointed, fixed a stony eye—an expression that brought employees into submission, convinced his enemies he was not one to bend to intimidation, a look that produced results.

"Leave me now!"

The dreadlock man folded his hands behind his back. Eb continued the mad charge of a bull protecting his turf. He neared with a roar, fists clenched, a fierce cry that was no bluff.

The dreadlock man began to laugh.

Eb froze on the inside, a cold presence that brought him to one knee. Then he was in the dirt, hands clutching the earth, bones rattling. On the verge of losing consciousness, a blessing he would welcome, to wake up or sleep.

Anything but now.

The laughter had stopped. Eb's body continued to vibrate. Dreadlock curtains framed the man's brown face, black eyes like holes.

Teeth tapping like stones.

"You live in a glass house, Ebenezer. Your power is an illusion, these walls nothing more than your projections, no different than dreams. Your reality, self-delusion. You are a child hiding from the world." He held out a long-fingered hand. "Why am I here, you wonder?"

Eb was pulled quickly to his feet as if he weighed no more than a sparrow. The man's touch was unpleasant, not cold nor hurtful. Just deeply unwanted.

Quietly, the man walked to the edge of the Skeye™ dome. He dragged his manicured fingernails along the foggy surface, the disturbing sound of a violated chalkboard.

Four deeply etched lines appeared.

"You have confused wealth with value, Ebenezer."

He passed his left hand over the Skeye™ dome, the cringeworthy fingernails biting into the glass, a crisscross of tracks. The dreadlock man approached Eb, reaching out, fingers curling over Eb's shoulders.

Fractures sprang from the crisscrossed Xs, crackling ice echoing in the miniature forest. Jagged lines raced to the top of the Skeye™ dome. An icy draft slipped beneath Eb's robe.

The insect sound effects died.

"I come to show you, Ebenezer."

A hole blew out the X, an invisible fist punching into a black, snowy world. A vortex inhaled the contents of the Skeye™ dome. Branches twisted, needles and pinecones soared. Eb's robe fluttered and snapped. The dreadlock man held him steady, frigid hands on his shoulders, black eyes relaxed.

The dreadlocks pulled off his face.

Laughter roared.

They were sucked into the night, tumbling over the edge of the Castle. The ground raced toward them, a painless plunge that would end this dream.

Instead, they were thrown over the horizon, a blur of details below, stars streaking above. Blistering wind scoured his face, squeezed tears from his eyes, pierced his eardrums. Eb could still feel the man's hands on his shoulders.

And laughter in his bones.

18

Stars twinkled green and blue.

They twined around the branches of a tree and drooped along the eves of a three-story house. An inflated snowman was looking at Eb, the carrot nose pointing to the right while the body listed to the left. Its color alternated beneath the tree—green, blue, green, blue.

"What is this?" The words scratched Eb's throat.

"The world, Ebenezer."

"How did you—"

"Watch out." The dreadlock man pulled him aside.

A pair of headlights came around the curve, splashing festively decorated houses with light. Loose gravel crunched beneath the tires. A minivan eased up the driveway and parked beneath a basketball hoop.

The dashboard lights softly lit the driver's face.

"Jerri?" Eb said.

She turned toward the back of the van. There was laughter and scrambling. The door almost hit Eb when she opened it. She smelled like the sun and green grass. He'd noticed that about her the day they met at the café, the day they hired her. Here it was in the middle of Christmas and summer was climbing out of the van.

Eb held still, afraid she would freak out when she saw him. But she didn't notice, didn't even turn his way.

"When's the last time you saw her?" the dreadlock man asked.

"Just the other day."

"That was a projection. I mean really saw her, in the flesh, with your eyes, Ebenezer? When's the last time you shared a space with her?"

They'd had a meeting two days ago; Eb was talking to her in his projection room. But when had he seen her in the flesh, actually stood in front of her?

Years.

She popped the sliding door open. A young girl waited with arms out, leaping into Jerri's grasp. They started for the house. The little girl held her tightly, wiggling like an overwound toy.

"Her granddaughter," the dreadlock man said.

Yes, her granddaughter. Something's wrong with her.

"MPS," the dreadlock man said. "Mucopolysaccharidosis if you want the long version. It's a genetic disorder. She can't produce certain enzymes and that causes a progressive degeneration of her body. You remember, Ebenezer?"

He didn't know the details. People were sick all over the world; he couldn't be expected to remember the particulars. Just that she was sick.

Jerri climbed onto the porch, where a fat Christmas tree sat outside a big window. It was outside the house, not inside. The branches glittered with silvery tinsel and tiny lights, homemade ornaments dangling from the tips—painted tongue depressors, paper-cut snowflakes.

She rang the doorbell.

"This isn't her house," the dreadlock man said. "She comes here quite a bit, though, especially this time of year. Every Christmas, in fact."

The door opened. Shrill sounds of excitement shotgunned out of the house. Christmas music blared. The child climbed out of Jerri's arms and charged inside. A brigade of children leaped around the house like a spilled barrel of monkeys. Jerri hugged the woman that answered the door.

"Come on." The dreadlock man tugged Eb's elbow. "Let's have a look."

"What is this?"

"This is now, Ebenezer. This is the world you do not know."

"How... how can this be? How can we be here? This isn't possible."

The dreadlock man crossed the driveway. The Christmas lights turned his cream-colored clothing various colors. Eb was chattering, the soles of his feet cold against the concrete. A draft chilled his thighs.

The dreadlock man went to the window. "There's a fire inside, Ebenezer."

Eb slipped on the driveway as he made his escape and crashed. The road bit into his hip, tore his robe open and exposed his lower half. He found his footing and started down the middle of the road, his feet slapping the wet asphalt. Slabs of flesh bounced along his belly and swung from his arms.

He made it exactly one house before his lungs caught fire.

The houses all looked the same—multistoried and bleeding Christmas cheer. Not until Jerri's van was well out of sight did he stop. He wheezed at the end of a three-car driveway, hands on knees, vomit climbing his esophagus. Icicle lights glittered off the gutters.

A man sat beneath a lamp, his bald head in the window.

Eb limped to the front porch and dry-heaved into the bushes before pulling himself to the door. This wasn't a dream. Somehow this... this dreadlock man... this thing that haunted him on Christmas Day was transporting him all the way to California.

As crazy as that sounded, it was true. Eb believed it with all his heart. He would hide until morning. Then call the police.

He banged the front door, his fist sounding like the fat end of a baseball bat. The impact rattled his arm. He hit it again. The bald man beneath the lamp turned. Eb fell on his knees.

There was a leaning snowman in the front yard, colored lights blinking across its back. The door opened. Pearly teeth tapped together.

"You're cold, Ebenezer," the dreadlock man said.

How is he making this all so vivid? So real? How could I run down the street and end up exactly where I started?

I'm going nowhere.

"Why are you doing this?"

"You need to know the world, Ebenezer."

Long fingers wrapped around Eb's arms, numbing his flesh.

A stone hearth was blazing. Eb stood near it, his robe soon toasty. His toes still numb. No one seemed to notice the front door had opened or that two strangers had entered. They were sitting around the storm-wrecked room with mugs of hot chocolate and eggnog among mutilated boxes and shredded wrapping and an avalanche of toys.

Picture books open.

Blankets tossed.

Coats and colorful socks abandoned.

Three girls were destroying the room, one of them Jerri's granddaughter. Currently, they were consumed with colorful shapes that had been mined from one of the discarded gifts. They breathed through their mouths, eyes focused on leaning stacks and interlocking pieces. They finished building something, squealed and bounced and chucked the pieces against the wall, chased them down and started all over.

The adults were oblivious.

They leaned closely to talk over the rumpus. One of the women was on the phone, a finger in her ear. Occasionally one of the adults would run down a wild throw or corral a wild animal.

There was a fourth child. He watched from a wheelchair, his head quivering.

"This is Christmas, Ebenezer."

He barely heard the dreadlock man. The chaos rattled his head. But it wasn't unpleasant. An undercurrent of joy buoyed it. The room was warm and alive, the children squeezing joy out of every second. This was the last place Eb would want to be.

Yet he didn't run.

A stuffed lion hit him in the stomach. He held his robe closed with one hand and picked it up. Its nose was wet. A voice box roared when he squeezed it. *One of Jacob's animals.*

One of the girls crawled over and sat on her haunches, panting. Eb dangled it by the tail and she took it with her mouth like the old man in the dirty robe belonged there. She scrambled past a bookshelf bolted to the wall.

"It's a strange disease," the dreadlock man said, his breath tickling Eb's ear, teeth clacking. "They become more energized as it progresses. Hyperactivity can go on for days with no sleep. Televisions get pulled down, tables turned over. Their curiosity becomes a raging current, like half-pint tornados ripping through the house."

He pointed at the Christmas tree on the porch. It wouldn't survive indoors.

"But you know all about that," he said. "Jerri being an advocate for the disease, I'm sure she told you hundreds of times."

The woman on the phone was frowning. She was the one that answered the door. Her dark hair pulled back, she pressed her hand against her ear and left the room, eyebrows rigid. A few minutes later, Jerri followed her.

"Who is that?" Eb asked.

"Carol. You met her last summer."

Names didn't stick with Eb. They were just labels. Faces he recalled, not names. Carol, though, wasn't registering. She obviously didn't work for Avocado, he'd remember that. And she wasn't a contractor or a contact or someone important, at least no one he'd met, despite what the dreadlock man said.

They had gone into the adjoining kitchen. Carol leaned against the sink, arms folded.

"He's still there. On Christmas Eve," she said. "I can't take this anymore, Jerri. He's got to find someplace else to work."

"I know," Jerri said.

"We didn't sign up for this."

"Of course not."

Carol sniffed. "It's just hard sometimes. You know?"

Jerri put her arm around her then poured two glasses of wine. The tornados stormed in and out of the kitchen but didn't disrupt the moment. Jerri and Carol watched them strip magnets off the refrigerator. Coloring book papers and letters to Santa scattered in their wake.

The refrigerator door was plastered with magnetized letters and words, pictures, and a dry-erase board, where five stick figures were outlined in black marker. Family photos were mounted in clear plastic frames. One was from the beach, before their third child was born. Carol and her husband held one of the children. Their other child was in the wheelchair.

Eb pulled the plastic frame off the freezer. "Rick."

"That's him," the dreadlock man said.

This was Rick's house. Carol was his wife. Of course, it made sense now. He'd met her on Rick's first day at the plant. They came to the office and spoke to his projected image. Her expression wavered between laughing and getting sick.

Now she just looked sick.

"He never said his children had this... this condition."

"Yes, he did," the dreadlock man said.

Eb couldn't argue. He probably did and Eb didn't care. That was their problem. Eb had his own issues to deal with. He didn't have space to even remember their problems, too.

Let alone care.

Rick and Carol were smiling in the photo. They looked like they hadn't slept in days, eyes weary, cheeks sagging. But they were smiling.

"Jerri recruited him," Eb said. "She brought him to Avocado five years ago. But I never knew about their kid being sick and..." He stopped. It was a lie.

He knew.

"Jerri and Rick met at an MPS conference," the dreadlock man said. "They got to talking about Jacob's medical program. Rick wanted to be part of it, so one thing led to another."

Jerri swirled her glass and took a sip. She looked into the red wine, the answer floating somewhere below the surface.

"Why are you still there, Jerri?" Carol asked. "Why do you still work for that man?"

"I believe in him," she said. "He'll do the right thing."

"The crazy old curmudgeon? I'm sorry, Jerri, but you have to let go of hope. Unless he can make money from it, he's not doing anything different. He's not changing."

"I don't know."

"I've been watching him for five years. He's always been an awful small man, even when Jacob was around. And when he died, it only got worse. He deserves to be loathed and pitied. He only thinks of himself, you know that. He's insulated from the world, there's no saving him from himself. And now with the stupid hat, he's just mocking us, Jerri. It's like a child playing dress-up and I can't take it anymore. I don't know how you do it."

Jerri continued swirling the red wine. She was nodding to herself, the sort of nod that you knew better than to keep doing what you were doing, the sort of nod that was betting the long odds that kept getting longer. She put her arm around Carol, their heads touching at the crowns—two warriors that had seen worse.

The tornado train chugged into the room for another round. The women caught the children as they raced around the island counter, tickled their ribs past the refrigerator, past the crazy old curmudgeon in the dirty robe and his dreadlocked companion.

"I see Santa!" someone shouted.

The front door opened, followed by a *ho-ho-ho* and a collective squeal that could slice an eardrum. Eb wanted to join them, wanted to watch the children sit on Santa's lap, watch them spill eggnog on his shaggy red pants and bomb the house with half-eaten cookies.

The dreadlock man had his hand on the refrigerator.

When he pulled it open, a frigid wind inhaled the room. Pots and pans clattered, wineglasses tipped, and letters to Santa were vacuumed inside. Eb held his robe with both hands. The dreadlock man threw the door wide open.

And inside they went.

Eb was lost again, tumbling through darkness. This time he landed without confusion. There was a ceiling high above and an enormous avocado backlit on the wall. The lights were off. Three men, their backs to Eb, were huddled in the glow of a computer.

"That's the one." Rick's tie hung around his neck. "Can you let that run?"

"Yeah," Kyle said.

Kyle was the head of IT. Eb didn't know the other one's name. They were like ants that fixed stuff and went back into hiding. Now they were in Rick's office. Across the open floor and cantilevered over the plant's office space, a glass office was lighted. The image of a slender man stood with arms folded. Top hat tipped forward.

Eb's projected image was watching.

Oily fumes seeped into the room, the fabricated smell of new parts fresh from the plant. Somewhere, incense was burning.

"That's it." Kyle tapped the space bar. "That's all for now."

"But it's isolated?" Rick asked.

"Far as I can tell. Never seen anything like it. Seems to be connected through the Avocado network. How we never seen it before, I can't figure out."

"Think it's a virus?"

"If it is, the company's doomed. It's dug into the backups, too. If this thing has a fuse, everything blows." An explosion sound effect filled his cheeks.

Eb cringed.

"We'll have some answers in the morning," Kyle said. "That's all for now."

"All right," Rick said. "Listen, thanks for staying. I know it's Christmas; you guys didn't have to do it. This means a lot."

The IT guys mumbled something about family and video games.

"Here." Rick handed them green boxes. "Little something for the girlfriends."

"Unless there's a girlfriend in this," Kyle said, "it's for me."

"I'm not telling you what to do with it."

They locked up and shut down. Rick grabbed his briefcase and a velvety red bag from the desk drawer, the glow of the monitor lighting the way out. Eb and the dreadlock man watched from inside the office.

It was late, but Rick didn't run for the door. He dug into the red bag for gifts identical to the ones he'd given the IT guys—green boxes with red ribbons and a paper tag dangling from each corner. Rick's handwriting glittered in gold ink. He began hiding them in desk drawers at each cubicle.

"He does that every year," the dreadlock man said. "Puts it somewhere—"

"So I don't see it," Eb finished.

When each gift had been delivered, he searched for one last item. As he punched the security code at the front door, he pulled a Santa hat out of the bag.

Avocado was quiet. Dark.

Not a string of garland tainted the room. Not a flash of red or green polluted the walls. The frozen image of a top-hatted figure continued staring down.

"What do you want from me?" Eb said. "You want me to give them presents, sing them Christmas carols and bake cookies? Should they get more vacation? Hard work is what made this place great; honest hard work put us on top. We earned that, and I'll be damned if I give it back so they can—"

"Laugh? Love?"

"Don't put this on me!" He shook his finger in dreadlock man's face, brushing his nose. "I give them work, pay them money. They live in giant houses with stocked pantries and cars—*cars* with an S, mind you, more than one in their garage. So I'm demanding, so I push them. I make them better. I make them more than what they are."

Eb went to the computer where data scrolled and the hard drive was grinding. These were the times he could deliver a deathblow speech about work ethic and dedication. But his gut stirred with a toxic emotion that weakened his knees and clogged his throat.

"What do you want from me?" Eb asked.

"I want you to be present."

Images flickered on the monitor. Faces of children, of beaches and mountains and cities and farms.

"To be in the world, Ebenezer. To know it."

The room grew dark; the computer appeared as a window on a passenger train, a landscape of images racing past. Homeless men and women sleeping beneath streetlight decorations. Men and women fighting, singing, hugging and slapping and kissing and celebrating.

Images of everyone. Everything. Hopeless, righteous and loving.

The world.

Somewhere in the dark, a child began to cry. Eb turned toward the blackness behind him, a room that was endless and mysterious. Out there, the sobs grew louder.

Footsteps.

The monitor brightened, light penetrating the darkness to reveal a long hallway, doors on both sides. An exit sign. A receptionist desk. Folders and the medicinal smell of antiseptic.

A woman with tightly wrapped hair brushed past Eb. Her athletic shoes were silent. She pushed open the door on the right. The cries peaked.

Eb drifted forward.

He stood in the open doorway. The nurse bent over a bed. Tubes hung over silver rails; monitors chattered while she soothed the little girl's tears. The little girl that was crying for her mother.

On the windowsill, there was a vase with wilted flowers and a deflated balloon. Between the flowers and the balloon, a toy leaned against the blinds. It was dusty and old, but watched over her nonetheless.

"Don't forget the world," the dreadlock man said.

Eb walked into the room without notice. He propped up the

balloon, reached for the toy, and wiped the dust from the glass eyes of a stuffed tiger. It roared when he squeezed it.

"And the world won't forget you."

The ceiling cracked.

A concrete block shattered on the floor. The walls fell inward. Eb clutched the guardian tiger as the world collapsed into darkness.

Streaks of ochre and maroon painted the morning sky. The droid found Eb quivering on the lounger, squeezing the collar of his robe to his chin.

19

The theatre room was musty and forgotten.

Eb paced around a fat chair that faced an arcing gray screen. He had not been down to this part of the Castle to watch a film since the immersive experience of the domed projection room had been built.

Had it been any other day, he would chastise the droid for neglecting the film room. Good money had built it, there was no excuse for letting it smell like that. He wouldn't have bothered coming down there if he didn't need the antiquated technology to talk to someone that couldn't connect with his projection room. But there were bigger problems to boil.

Such as walking, talking nightmares.

One of the droids stood behind the comfortable chair. Another one entered with a teacup and saucer. The sudden movement threw off Eb's stride as if someone had jumped from the bushes and shouted *boo*. He clutched his chest.

"Would you care to sit, sir?" The droid placed the teacup on a small table. Peppermint aroma filled the room. "The doctor will be ringing soon."

Eb shook his head and muttered something even he didn't understand.

Both droids remained in the room, a pair of sentinels at the corner posts of a cushioned throne, watching their master circle the room, nightmarish thoughts dragging like tin cans. It was exhausting to keep ahead of them, but what choice did he have? If he stopped, they would find their place in his head, the memories of a dreadlock man and the places he took him.

Places Eb didn't want to go.

"I need help," Eb told the droid that morning.

It was the first time he had ever uttered those words that he could recall. He had always dealt with troubles head-on. Anything that got in his way was either pushed aside or run over. But this... these... the dreadlock man and *the thing*... he had never encountered anything like this. They could not be ignored. And Eb couldn't handle another midnight visit, not another nightmare trip to the future or anywhere else without going clear off the rails.

Perhaps he already had.

"Dr. Chase is connecting, sir."

The gray screen turned silver. A thread of static crackled across it. Eb stood in front of the cushy chair, his lotioned hands crawling over each other. Colors spilled from the static. An abstract painting appeared above a bookshelf. Someone off-camera cleared their throat.

Eb's heart rate climbed. What if no one was there? What if he couldn't get help? It was Christmas morning, after all. Worse than that, what if the dreadlock man sat down?

What if I'm still dreaming?

His noodly legs spilled him into the chair, the robe falling open. He pulled it closed just as a dark form filled the screen. He pulled the robe's collar closed. The droids each massaged a shoulder.

"Good morning, Ebenezer," Dr. Chase said.

She sat at what he presumed was her office desk. A small image of Eb's projection popped up in the corner. It wasn't the square-chinned handsome projection made for public consumption. It was the ruddy-face fatso filling the La-Z-Boy like a jar of quivering jelly.

"Hello?" she said. "Can you hear me, Ebenezer?"

He tried to nod. Dr. Chase was a black woman, her flesh darker than the dreadlock man and her hair cut very close to the scalp. Her eyes were dark. Not black holes, but the resemblance temporarily paralyzed him.

"We can hear you, Dr. Chase," one of the droids said.

"Stop it." Eb smacked their hands. "Go. Get out."

Suddenly they were a nuisance. One second he couldn't be alone, now he didn't want to be treated like a child. He pointed at the door and shook his finger. Dr. Chase sipped from an oversized mug. Her face filled the twenty-foot-tall screen, an African-American goddess staring over a cup of coffee at her helpless minion.

"What can I do for you?" she asked.

"I'm in need of a prescription, something to control dreams and bad thoughts."

He could've just acquired something and taken it. He didn't need a prescription, that was for the general population. The droid had done the research and suggested several psychotropic drugs, but it was all too confusing. Popping random pills seemed like a bad idea. But he needed something that would work definitely.

Immediately.

"Tell me what's going on?" she said.

"Nothing, really. Just need to feel better."

"I see. And why is that?"

"Because I want to. Doesn't everyone?"

She sat back, nodding. "It's Christmas morning, Ebenezer. I have family waiting for me, but I took your call out of respect for Jacob—"

"Are they in the next room?"

"What?"

"Your family, can they hear us?" Eb sat forward, his hands strangling each other.

"No, Ebenezer. This is a private conversation. Nothing you say will leave this room. You have my word."

"I just want some drugs, that's all. I know you helped Jacob with that sort of thing, that's why I called."

"My work with Jacob is none of your business. The application of medicine is not something I use lightly, you understand?"

"You're a psychiatrist. Psychiatrists give drugs. It's sort of why I called you."

"My family's waiting, Ebenezer."

"You already said that."

She pursed her lips, raising an eyebrow.

Normally, he would unload on her before dramatically storming out. She was making the rules, not something he allowed. But this was not a negotiation. And she was the only person outside his ring of trust he could talk to about this.

And that was debatable.

Actually, there was no one in his ring, but she was someone that Jacob always recommended, insisting she was the best therapist, or life coach or whatever she called herself, he had ever witnessed. She wasn't all touchy-feely, so there was that.

He flopped back into the fat chair, exhaling like a popped balloon. "It's this holiday stuff. I don't like it, brings me down. That's all. Nothing to talk about, really."

She stared, unblinking. It was the sort of X-ray look that exposed the bones and guts of a person, turned them inside out, shredding the phoniness. Nowhere to hide.

"Here's what I suggest, Ebenezer. Be honest with me. I want to help you, but I can't do that if you don't tell me where you are. I'm not interested in wasting time. There are plenty of doctors that will get what you want. I'm not one of them. If my coffee gets cold and you're not on with it, we're done."

She lifted her cup.

Eb cleared his throat, shifting in the chair. He had rehearsed a story just in case this happened. Now he felt cornered. Anger extinguished the nervousness twirling his stomach. It refueled his legs and reinforced his armor. She was challenging him and he liked that. But she was challenging him to drop the armor.

He didn't take armor off.

"Okay, all right," he said. "I'm just worried about the girls. You know, they've been through a lot since Jacob died, I'm sure you're aware of that. I'll never replace him, you know that. I just want to be the best father I can be and I… you know, I just don't think I can handle this without some help. There's the company and the stress and I don't want to ignore them."

Eb sniffed.

"I'm doing this for them," he said. "I just want them to be happy."

He suppressed a grin. He would bury this hard-driving psychiatrist beneath a mountain of snow and get what he wanted. He'd even rehearsed a victory dance for the moment she relented, something he'd do in private, not in front of her. Yet.

Dr. Chase nodded before leaning forward. Her chair groaned as she reached for the monitor and began to stand.

"Wait!" Eb shouted. "What are you doing?"

"My coffee's cold."

"But… it's only been a minute."

"Goodbye, Ebenezer."

"I'm having bad dreams!"

Her thick turtleneck appeared frozen on the screen. If she had killed the connection, it would've gone blank. Then she moved. She backed up until she was in full view again.

"Go on."

"You… you wouldn't believe me if I told you. I was just trying to save you some time."

"Try me."

"Okay. Well, I don't know where to start."

"Start with the dream."

"I don't usually dream, that's the thing."

"Then it must be very strange for you, a person with all this vision that doesn't dream."

"What's that mean?"

"You have a company that builds dreams for other people, yet you say you don't usually dream. Tell me about your dream, Ebenezer."

He chuckled. He was a grown man having nightmares. It sounded so stupid now that he thought about it. "I... I don't know how to start."

"Start with the first one."

"How'd you know there were two dreams?"

"I didn't. You said you had bad dreams. I said start with the first one."

He weaved his fingers over his chest and sank back, staring at the vaulted ceiling. Why did it feel like she knew there were two dreams?

"Last Christmas," he started, "was the first one. It happened at midnight, almost exactly."

He recalled the tremor that shook the house, the tracks leading up to the house and the ivory-white thing with stretched limbs and sticks for hair, the bugs that crawled throughout them, the way his tongue snapped them up.

A thing that was feeding itself with the things that were feeding on it.

"He said he was there to show me the future. And then we were there, standing in my house, in a room with an elegant dome and golden pillars and what looked like a solid gold floor and... and *me*. I was dying. And I was alone."

A lump swelled in his throat.

"This woman, she was an assistant or something, celebrated when I took my last breath."

He left out the funeral part and the coffin. He was uncertain he could talk about being buried alive without having to pace the room, and that would give away more emotion than he wanted.

The doctor was sitting down. *She's buying it.*

"Do you believe it?" she asked.

"We all die."

"Not alone."

He shrugged. "I like my own company."

"So it didn't bother you?"

"Maybe a little."

He threw her a bone with a little emotion on it to keep her seated.

It *did* bother him. And he wasn't going to forget that assistant, either. As soon as he saw her, she was fired.

"Did the dream change you in any way?" Dr. Chase said.

"I started drinking smoothies."

Her eyelids grew heavy. She leaned back with mug in hand.

"Yes, of course I changed. I'm trying to be, you know, nicer and happier and blah, blah, blah. It was a dream, though." He chuckled a bit maniacally. "It's not like I believed it, come on."

"Dreams are the voice of our subconscious, Ebenezer. This one is speaking loud and clear. Maybe that's why it came back."

"How'd you know it came back?"

"I'm assuming that's why you called this morning."

His knuckles ached. Two seconds ago, he was talking about stupid dreams and thoughts. They suddenly felt real again.

"Are you afraid to die?" she asked.

"Yes."

That came out without premeditation. It was honest and direct. He was afraid to die. More than that, he was lying. *I'm afraid to die alone.* All this stuff he'd collected—this castle and wealth, these self-serving droids—would mean nothing when he was on his deathbed. His life would have no meaning in their wake.

His breathing had become choppy. His eyes, glassy. He kept them open until they itched and watered. When he lifted his head, tears fell down his cheeks. It looked like he was crying. She put down her coffee when she saw this.

We have a winner.

"So what did you do?" she asked.

"About what?"

"After the dream, what did you change?"

"I walked it off, forgot about it. It wasn't doing me any good thinking about it. I can't do anything about the future."

"Interesting. You did nothing."

"I didn't say *nothing*. I said I walked it off, got back to living."

"Despite knowing your future."

"It was a dream."

"A very real dream."

"Yeah." He wiped his cheek to remind her he was crying.

"Why do you think you had a dream that believable?"

"Stress? Something I ate?"

"Could it be true?"

"A stretched-out monster that broke into my house and took me to the future?" He jolted upright "Are you insane? What kind of doctor... did you get your degree online? This is absurd—"

"Things yet to come, Ebenezer. Could it be true?"

"That I'll die? Of course!"

"In that manner. Will you die all alone, with nobody at your side, with people celebrating? Will your life have meaning?"

"Do your patients commit suicide often?"

"You sounded remorseful, Ebenezer. It was more than death that bothered you."

"What do you want me to say, I'm scared? Okay, I admit it. I'm scared. I don't want to die alone and, and..."

He flopped back to stare at the ceiling. *Unloved.*

That was what he didn't say. He didn't want to leave the world with a bunch of mindless droids staring at him. No one would care he lived. Or died.

At least no one will be sad at your death, the droid said.

"And what, Ebenezer?"

"Nothing."

She paused. "There was a second dream?"

"Yes. Last night, pretty much like the first one."

"Pretty much?"

"You know, a little time and some pharmaceutical assistance would help. I don't want to keep you from your family."

"Details, Ebenezer. Every dirty detail."

He sighed. This was a horrible idea. The woman was squeezing him like a sponge. But he felt better. Well, maybe not better. More... empty. Was that it?

"I was sleeping this time," he said. "When he came."

"He?"

"The monster, the person. The *thing*."

"Where?"

Eb described the Skeye™ dome in great detail. The joy he'd felt at such a creation would forever be tainted with the memory of the dreadlock man. That was the real bummer.

"And then what?" she interrupted.

He lost track of how long he'd been sitting there, the memory of the journey sweeping him back into the experience like metal shavings to a junkyard magnet. He shook his head like a wet dog, shedding the sticky thoughts. This wasn't why he called her. In fact, it was the exact opposite.

"More of the same," he said.

"The stretchy bug man?"

"Mm-mmm. Can we wrap this up? I'm a little tired and your family is waiting. What do you think about the medicine?"

She tipped her head and turned on the X-ray vision. He turned his shoulder, like that would block it. The problem was that his emotions weren't showing on his insides. They were etched on his face.

"Would you like to share any more about the second dream?"

"No."

It was too real, too immediate. What if she told him to call Jerri, see what she was doing last night? What if it all matched up, that she really drove a van over to Rick's house? What if Carol really said that in the kitchen, said he was an "awful small man," that he should be "loathed and pitied"?

Is that what I am, small and awful?

He knew the answer.

"What do you want from me?" The doctor cupped both hands around the mug. The coffee was definitely cold.

"I'm pretty sure I made that clear."

"You want medicine, sure. To do what?"

"To feel good, to forget... look, we've been through this—"

"Why do you want to forget?"

"To feel good. Are you charging by the minute?"

"Your dreams have something to tell you," she said.

"You said that."

"They touched a nerve. Perhaps when Jacob died, it set off something in your subconscious. You never got to say goodbye, perhaps? Were there things left unsaid between the two of you?"

"Nooo," he drawled, "everything definitely got said."

There was the bit about Jacob appearing in his room, the mysterious matter in which the girls appeared. Eb decided to leave that out of the conversation because this session was already too long. And expensive.

"If you think about it," she said, "it was almost a year after Jacob died that you had the first dream, right at midnight when you uttered the word *humbug*."

"I didn't tell you that."

"What does that mean to you? Humbug."

"Seriously, I didn't tell you about that."

"The droid told me when he called." She took a sip. "The one you call Dum-dum. I insisted on knowing the details before accepting your call, Ebenezer. I expected you would be elusive."

"Whoa, whoa, whoa. You're getting the story from that dummy? Listen, this breaks therapist-patient confidentiality rules and you know it. I can have your license."

She chuckled behind her mug, her dark-lined eyes squinting with amusement. "What does *humbug* mean to you, Ebenezer?"

"You think it's a magic word? Is that where you're going with this, that it summons the boogeyman from beneath the bed or in the—"

Closet.

He was going to say closet but remembered the noise under the girls' bed and cookies in the closet, the damp spots on the carpet.

He swallowed a rising knot.

"What does it mean to you?" she asked again.

"What do *you* think it means?" Two could play the question game.

She thought for a moment, cuddling that stupid coffee mug. "Perhaps it means nothing, but I think you've assigned some meaning to it."

"Tip of the iceberg sort of thing. Smart."

"I suggest you investigate what the word means to you, Ebenezer. See how it feels, what's underneath it, at the root. You had dreams about the future and present. I suspect your next dream will take you to the past, and that's where you should dig. The past builds the future, but it's all really happening now. This moment."

"The present." Eb narrowed his eyes, tapping his chin. "I didn't tell you the dream was about the present. What's going on here, Doctor?"

"The droid, Ebenezer. And stop calling him Dum-dum. He serves you."

"We're done. I've given you enough time and money. The prescription, please?"

"To forget?"

"That's the idea."

"I think you want to remember, Ebenezer. That's why you're having these dreams. You want to resolve whatever's lurking in your past, that's manifesting in your future. You must go through it to resolve it, but first you must find it. Your past will help you."

"No medicine? Is that what I'm hearing?"

"You don't strike me as a joyful person, Ebenezer. Medicine isn't going to change that."

"This is a waste of time." He shot onto his feet. "Humbug!"

The room didn't tremor; the light didn't dim. Eb, however, did cringe until he was certain nothing had happened.

"See?" he said. "Nothing. Go drink your eggnog, Doctor. Bye."

"There is one way to change your future, Ebenezer."

"I know, give up dairy. Goodbye. Have a nice life."

"You don't have to die in that golden room." She leaned over the desk, her face swelling to titanic proportions, the goddess lips grinning.

"Just destroy the Skeye™ dome."

20

Second level. East wing.

The sun had breached the distant mountains. Shadows stretched across the valley. Eb coasted into the room that was just above the film room. This one smelled of chlorine.

The corner walls were thick glass from floor to ceiling. The room cantilevered from the castle, enough to bring a toe-curling, gut-clenching sense of vertigo when he stood too close to the glass. For that reason, he rarely came to this room.

That and the exercise equipment.

Rows of ellipticals and rowing machines and stationary bicycles and treadmills faced the glass wall, their seats gleaming with Armor All polish. Television monitors hung obsolete from the ceiling, their black panels collecting dust. Jazz played softly, the kind heard at a café in the French Quarter.

At the far end of the room, the droid was bent over a bubbling Jacuzzi. Eb sped past the section of free weights and nearly hit the kneeling droid.

"How was your appointment, sir?"

"Don't talk to me."

The droid looked up, unsurprised. His gray skinwrap was moist with chlorinated vapor, beads clinging to his face like perspiration.

"I seriously doubt she has a degree," Eb said. "I'm considering having her investigated for malpractice or fraudulent representation. Have the lawyers look into it."

"I don't believe that's something we can—"

"I said don't talk."

He drove around the hot tub. He had left the film room and toured the Castle hallways for nearly an hour. By the time he finished the cruise, he had come to the conclusion that she was an idiot.

Just destroy the Skeye™ dome. His deathbed was in the Great Room below the Skeye™ dome. One day he would knock out the ceiling and connect the two, and that was where he would die alone. And Dr. Chase figured if he destroyed the Skeye™ dome, then it wouldn't happen and he wouldn't die alone.

Brilliant!

She was trying to ruin him. They all were. He didn't exactly know who *they* were, but it was true. No one liked the people at the top.

"Talking makes things worse." Eb climbed off the Segway. "Nothing good came of it. I feel worse than I did this morning and that's impossible."

"I don't think—"

Eb snapped his fingers at him. "How could you do this to me? Don't answer. All I wanted was to feel better and you made it worse. I never should've listened to you, never should've talked about it. All I wanted was medicine. That's it. I'm feeling sick and sick people need medicine. You understand? Don't answer that."

He collapsed on one knee a bit too forcefully, painful shards biting his thigh. He splashed hot water on his cheeks. The droid handed him a towel and helped him to his feet.

"Are you all right, sir?"

"Do I look all right?"

"You appear malnourished, sir. Have you eaten?"

Of course he hadn't eaten. His skin felt three times too small for his fat body. He was a grown man squeezing into a child suit. The world was tight, the air was thick and lacked oxygen, the walls too solid.

"Get medicine," he said. "Nothing that makes me foggy, either. I need to think clearly without fat lips and swollen hands. I want to feel normal again."

"What is normal, sir?"

"Normal is good. Just do it."

"May I remind you that acquiring a controlled substance without a prescription is a felony, sir?"

Eb pulled his face out of the towel. "Now? You want to remind me of that now? Get a prescription!"

"Well, I think it would be prudent—"

"I don't want to hear it! I have a net worth over a billion dollars, you idiot. Do you know what that means? That means I tell you what I want and you get it. That's the end of it. I have a team of lawyers; I have doctors for every ache and pain. Why I listened to you this morning with the quack... I must be losing my mind."

That was indisputable.

He hung the towel over his shoulder. This dreaming business was picking at the loose strands of his sanity. When he woke in the Skeye™ dome, he couldn't think clearly. That was what happened, that was why he took the droid's suggestion to speak with Jacob's life coach.

Life coach.

Eb didn't need a coach. He just needed people to do what he wanted, to do what they were told. And she wondered why he called the droid an idiot?

"This is Rome." Eb threw the towel over the droid's head. "And I have all the gold. Get me some help. The pharmaceutical kind."

"May I remind you that Caesar was assassinated, sir?"

"May I remind you that your job is to shut up?"

"My job is to help you, sir." The droid peeled the towel from his bald gray head. "There is a difference."

"I've had enough help. Get out, now. Go. Make me happy. You

know what, I'll take care of the medicine myself. Don't let me see you until I call."

"The girls are having breakfast, sir. Perhaps you would like to join them?"

"Do I look hungry?"

He hesitated. "The gathering is not about eating, sir."

"Then why is there food?"

See? Dummy.

Eb waved him off, teasing him out of the room like a wheezy matador. He leaned against the wall to catch his breath. The Segway was still by the hot tub. He slid to the floor to rest for just a minute and fell asleep.

10:30 a.m.

The schedule was a total loss.

It was clear that his diet or his health was causing these dreams. It was time to get into shape. He could look like his handsome projection if he wanted. All it would take was a bit of consistent exercise for a few months.

Six, at most.

He passed the machines like a dictator choosing from a fleet of cars—each of them luxurious and perfect. He settled on a treadmill with wide armrests and not too close to the glass. The dashboard welcomed him with lights and music, but no matter what he said or what button he pushed, the belt wouldn't move.

Everything should be intuitive. Everything should know his desire and fulfill it. Was this the Stone Age?

The manufacturer would refund him for this piece of crap; he wasn't paying for a hack design. Instead, he chose a recumbent stationary bicycle. A better choice, really. Exercising while sitting.

Genius.

He called up the music. Head back, legs moving, he soaked in the billion-dollar view. About thirty minutes of this followed by a jacuz and the dead weight of haunting thoughts would shed like dead skin.

He was bored in five minutes.

Sleepy after ten.

At 11:10 a.m., the billion-dollar view was interrupted by one of his drones. It passed within twenty feet of the Castle and doubled back, hovering just outside the window like a bird fascinated by its own reflection. The silver shade window would be like a mirror.

He got up to stretch his legs that were now like rubber. The drone was hovered eye level with Eb while he buried his finger up to the first knuckle into his right nostril. Another drone joined the first one. And then a strange thing happened.

It kamikazeed it.

Just bashed right into the rear propellers. They both tumbled out of sight.

Eb stretched open a holo. The translucent screen flickered with images. The droid appeared with a frilly apron tied around his neck. The girls were giggling at the counter, their plates stacked high with pancakes, rivers of syrup cascading over the edges.

"Having a good sweat, sir?"

"Didn't they already eat?"

"We're having pancakes for lunch, sir. Care to join us?"

"Check the drones. I think they're suicidal."

"I'll have a look, sir."

"Also, I changed my mind. You find the medicine and have it here by this afternoon."

Eb killed the connection before the droid suggested talking through his feelings about lunch. He needed to change his programming. Jacob was the one that created this personality, said it would mimic human interactions and fulfill the need to connect. If anyone was responsible for Eb's isolation, it was his dearly departed friend. Maybe if Eb didn't have the droid, he wouldn't have become a successful shut-in.

You're lonely, Jacob told him. *I'm worried.*

Creating an annoying sidekick more concerned with helping than listening was not the answer. That was obvious.

Eb went back to the exercise bike. At 11:30 a.m., he needed another nap. He also needed help getting up. His legs were elastic, his mind dull. He tipped onto one buttock and grunted. Exercise made him gassy. When he let his weight fall back onto the seat, something bit into his thigh. He shifted back onto one cheek and reached underneath his leg.

"Ow."

He pulled out a loose wire. His first thought was to sue the manufacturer. But then he realized the wire was bare and coiled.

He stopped pedaling.

The ballerina.

He'd found that in the lounger cushion and left it in the Skeye™ dome. What was it doing down here?

Someone giggled.

"Hey!" he shouted.

It was near the hot tub. There was a flash of green. One of the girls had snuck into the room. *Did they hear me fart?*

"Come back here!" He struggled in the bucket seat. It was too deep to climb out. He threw his weight over the side and crashed on the carpet. His legs were nearly useless. By the time he pulled himself up, he was out of breath. The stupid Segway was by the hot tub.

The girls laughed again, this time from the other side of the room. *"Gubbagubbagubbah."*

"Girls!" They were laughing at him. "Come here, please. Now!"

The hallway was empty. He propped against the wall, his sides stitching. Maybe they ran back into the exercise room. He wouldn't hear them over his breathing. A train could sneak past him. It sounded like CPR being delivered to a pet squeeze toy. There was no sign of the pugnacious rug rats.

And the kitchen was on the other side of the Castle.

How'd they get over here so fast? Surely they were done with breakfast. But if he called the droid and they were still sitting at the counter... that would mean...

I'm nuts.

Eb let out a cry that could be mistaken for seven-year-old girl. His rings were humming. He needed to sleep for three days. Without dreaming.

He sniffed back the swelling knot and stretched a holo. It was some man. The avocado logo jolted a memory from last night's dream.

"Hold, please," Eb shouted.

Eb crawled back into the exercise room. He reached the hot tub and splashed his face.

"Get a hold of yourself. You're successful. You're good. You're super rich." Eb pulled himself onto the Segway and steered in front of a projection screen. A slender, fit man cruised up like a reflection—shoulders round, chin square and dimpled.

Top hat squarely on his head.

"No, no." He waved off the hat. He didn't want people to think he slept in the stupid thing.

Ten deep breaths and the floor felt solid again.

"Okay," Eb said. "Okay, all right. Here we go." He cleared his throat and spoke deeply. "Go ahead, Kyle."

The IT guy looked up. "Um, good morning, Mr. Scrooge. I mean, Merry Christmas."

"What do you want?"

"Rick wanted me to call you about the analysis."

He fell on the Segway. A cold chill liquefied his knees. His projection appeared to be leisurely propping his elbows on the handlebars.

Eb wanted to suck his thumb.

"Mr. Scrooge? You all right?"

It could be coincidence. This guy, his name was Kyle just like the Kyle that was helping Rick last night. If Rick was investigating the mystery program, then he would get Kyle to help him, naturally. And it would make sense that Eb dreamed of Kyle helping him. That wasn't impossible. In fact, it was more than likely.

It didn't mean he was actually there.

"Where's Rick?"

"I don't know. He wanted me to update you on the program. You know, the one from last night. Should I… call back?"

Eb mopped his forehead. "No. Continue."

"You sure? You look a little—"

"Yes, I'm sure. It's cold and flu season, so go ahead before I drop dead."

Kyle cleared his throat into his fist. "Okay. I want to assure you that the program has been quarantined and there's nothing to worry about."

"Quarantined?"

"It's under control, Mr. Scrooge."

"Is it quarantined or not?"

"We, um, well, it's gone. We're not sure, but we think the quarantine erased it."

"I know what a quarantine is, Kyle. Programs don't erase themselves in quarantine. What happened?"

The avocado logo was glowing in the distance. A few employees were milling about. Someone leaned into Kyle's office to say something.

"Kyle?" Eb grimaced. "Attention on me. What happened?"

"Our best guess is a self-destruct trigger. More importantly, the program appears harmless. A security sweep showed no tampering; everything's secure. No sign of macros, memory residents, overwrites, direct actions, webscripting, polymorphic—"

"Trojans?"

"We're all good, Mr. Scrooge."

"Run the sweep again."

"It's running now. Third time."

Kyle sniffed in confidence. Perhaps he didn't like being told how to do his job.

"How did it get there?" Eb adjusted his glasses.

"We're not sure."

"Santa Claus, maybe?"

"I'm sorry?"

"How did it get there, Kyle?" Eb leaned in. "Programs don't install themselves. Either Santa Claus pulled it out of his toy sack or someone's up to shenanigans. Now how did the program get on our servers?"

Kyle looked at his shoes. "I can't explain it. There's no evidence of an upload, no one infiltrated the firewall. It's... I don't know."

"It's hiding. Say it, Kyle. The program is hiding and you don't know where it is."

"I assure you, Mr. Scrooge, everything is secure."

"How can you be sure?"

"It wasn't doing anything out of the ordinary."

"What was it doing?"

"Networking."

"What does that mean?"

"As far as we can tell, it was interconnecting all our resources, sort of drawing on all the company's projects, running them in the background. Nothing's been manipulated, though. It just seems to be observing, sort of screening them."

Eb squeezed the Segway handlebars. "Company secrets?"

"No data was outbound, Mr. Scrooge." Kyle threw up his hands. "Not even an email. Everything is secure, the firewalls intact, I assure you. All dataflow appears to fall within ordinary limits. Just, except for one thing."

Kyle coughed into his fist.

"What is it?" Eb said.

"Your, uh, portal, sir. There was a bit more outboard dataflow entering your house. We analyzed your activity, but nothing was out of the ordinary."

Eb blanched. He had the sudden urge to put his head in the hot tub. "You're monitoring me?"

"No! Of course not. It was just—"

"This is a secure outpost, Kyle. What I do here is none of your business, you understand?"

What I do here? Could he have said anything more suspicious? It sounded like he was hiding aliens from the government. Or worse.

He began driving the Segway and completed a lap around the

room, cruising along the glass wall. When he returned to the holo, Kyle was turned toward someone at his door.

"This from you?" someone asked him.

"No," Kyle said quietly, shrugging. "It's from Rick."

"Kyle." Eb made sure his projected image appeared calm. "Listen carefully. Tell me exactly what you monitored at the Castle and who knows about it."

"Castle?"

"My home, Kyle. Tell the truth, what did you see?"

"We didn't see anything, Mr. Scrooge. Just looked at dataflow metrics. That's all."

"You're sure? You're positive?"

"Absolutely."

Eb relaxed his death grip on the Segway. He believed him. If he was lying, Eb would launch a lawsuit his great-grandchildren would feel.

"There was... one thing," Kyle said.

"What?"

"A spike."

"A spike?"

Kyle shrugged. "The program appeared to respond to some increased demand at your... *castle*."

"Last night?"

"Yes. About midnight."

The Segway rolled backward. Eb felt faint. He righted his balance and leaned forward, exhaling sharply.

"What time exactly, Kyle? Be specific."

He tapped at a keyword. "Midnight exactly. Right on the second."

"Okay. All right." Eb rode around the hot tub. There was something here, a connection. An explanation. Maybe this wasn't a dream. Maybe there was some sort of... rogue program that caused hallucinations or immersive software that went haywire.

Maybe I'm not crazy.

"We checked the records." Kyle cleared his throat. "The same pattern showed up the last two Christmas Eves. Exactly at midnight, there's a spike in outbound dataflow that lasts until morning. We attributed it to your Skeye™ dome, but I'm not sure what would've caused it the last two years."

Eb was shaking his head. Understanding was settling, each conceptual kernel locking in place.

His legs were weak, but his spine was strong.

He stopped at the room's corner, the valley displayed below, his breath fogging the glass wall. The last piece of the puzzle clicked into place to complete the theory.

"Jacob," he whispered. "You dog."

His former partner, his childhood friend, was somehow fooling Eb into believing his thoughts. Somehow he had left an Easter egg in the Avocado system that was piping these nightmares into the Castle; somehow making him see a stretched out *thing* and a dreadlock man. Perhaps he was using some of the immersion software to create the illusion. There was the lucid-dreaming project that never got off the ground.

There were a lot of unexplained details—like how it all felt so real—but the explanations would come in time. Real mysteries weren't solved in a day. But the culprit had been exposed. Why was he doing it?

Eb began laughing.

It was the first time in a long time. The laughter exploded from his belly; it filled the room. Tears wet his cheeks. He blew his nose and laughed some more.

"I'm not mad," Eb muttered. "I'm not mad."

Eb wiped his eyes and sighed. His projected image wore an exaggerated joyous grin as big as the one on Eb's face.

"Is everything all right, Mr. Scrooge?"

"Couldn't be better, my boy. It couldn't be better."

Kyle smiled hesitantly. "Okay. Well, have a merry... um, a good day, then."

"Will do. And you as well. If there's nothing else?"

"No, Mr. Scrooge."

Eb turned his back. He wouldn't be needing the pharmaceutical help after all. It was as if he'd shed a cloak of chains, simply walked out of a suit of fear. Perhaps he would have a soak in the hot tub after all.

It was 12:20 p.m.

"One more thing, Mr. Scrooge?" Kyle was sitting on the edge of his seat.

"Yes?"

"There was a redundant line of code that didn't make sense, but it was the only thing we grabbed. I don't think it matters."

"Okay. What is it?"

Kyle squinted at a side monitor. "Gubba…"

Eb sat down.

"Gubbagubbagubbah."

He'd heard that before. He couldn't remember exactly where and when, but that didn't matter. He recognized the language.

And who spoke it.

21

Snowbanks lined the driveway.

The pavement had been cleared, the distant wrought-iron gates trimmed with snow. A stocking cap rose out of the snowbank like a wary prairie dog, a fluffy ball bouncing on top. Black pigtails shined from beneath it.

The droid lifted Addy from the igloo and placed her next to a stack of perfectly molded snowballs. A red scarf fluttered around his neck. Their backs were to the valley and the precipitous drop at the edge of the driveway.

Eb could hear her giggling.

Another stocking cap was visible on the other side of the pavement, this one green. That was Natty. *Addy is for apple and Natty is a tree.*

"Now!" the droids shouted.

The air was filled with cross fire, powdery tracers streaking across the driveway, exploding on the opposite snowbanks. More droids joined the action, three on one side and three on the other. The ones with Natty wore long green scarves that snapped in the fierce wind. Addy's team of droids wore red.

They sculpted more snowballs and loaded them into Addy's

outstretched mitten. Her shots would shatter on the pavement, barely halfway to the other side. Natty's would do the same.

Their laughter came in rapid-fire giggles, the kind that lit bellies with bliss. It was the sound only a child could make, the joy possessed by the innocent. The kind that made others smile.

Eb, however, did not.

Their joy neither sparked pleasure in his soul nor crinkled his cheeks with delight.

In the decorative windows, the snowballs fractured in flight. The narrow panes beside the front door were beveled and cold. His breath was hazy on the surface. It was the nearest he'd been to opening the front door since the girls arrived.

That was two years ago.

And look at them, a couple of powdered puffballs, snow slipping under their scarves, beneath their gloves, yet they still laughed like nothing mattered. Addy was only twenty steps from the railing and a fatal drop to the valley. The droid would keep her from doing something foolish, but she didn't know that.

The naiveté of youth.

Or stupidity. Whatever you wanted to call it spouted endless joy that pulled at the corners of his mouth. It wasn't clear what was stoking a fire of agitation in the pit of his stomach. Was it their fearlessness? Their bubbling essence? Their interminable dance of joy?

Was it envy?

Of course not. He didn't want to be in the blistering cold with snot running over his lips and snow melting down his back. Who would?

If he was honest, he would. But he was an adult. Had been for a very, very long time.

Eb smudged the glass. His fingertip slowly numbed.

He wanted what they had. Whatever that was.

But they know something.

That redundant line of code was their super-secret language. *What was it doing in the program?*

Perhaps they overheard Jacob, that in the wee hours of the night he would sing them off to sleep with his lines of mystery code instead of lullabies. Did his childhood friend know he was going to die? He had an ironclad agreement in place that Eb would have to take these little orphans into his castle. And now they spoke the language of a program that was somehow visiting him on Christmas Eve.

He needed to get to the bottom of this. The program needed to be unraveled and blotted out of existence. Not another word from stretched-out weirdos and ropey-haired bullies. But who could he trust? Who would investigate without word getting out? If the world discovered these nightmares, he'd be branded a psycho. A mentally unstable sociopath.

They already do.

"Why, old friend?" Eb whispered onto the window. "Why do this to me?"

"I'm here to help you, sir."

Eb thumped the glass with his forehead and rolled his shoulders against the door.

"I'm sorry, sir. I thought you were calling me."

"Don't... ever..." His breathing slowed.

This droid wasn't wearing a scarf. He wore a wry smile, one that seemed to have scraped an ounce of pleasure from the surprise even while retaining the usual repose of servitude. Jacob had given the droid the irritating sense of humor. *You won't be lonely, old friend,* he had said.

"Is everything all right, sir? You seem relieved yet troubled."

"I think, um..." Eb peeked through the window. The girls were back in their snow forts.

"What is it, sir?"

"Shhhh." Eb shoved his finger over the droid's lips, leaned in and whispered, "He's haunting me."

"Who, sir?"

"Jacob."

"I know, sir."

Eb stepped back. For a moment, it seemed the betrayal was finally in plain sight.

"Two years ago, sir. He projected into your room shortly after his untimely death."

"What? No, no, I'm not talking... he's doing it *now*, you ding-dong. The dreams. He's the one—" Eb looked around "—he's making the dreams happen."

In a very rare instance, the droid was speechless.

"The girls." Eb mouthed the words and pointed outside. "I think they know."

"Why are we whispering, sir?"

"Shhhhhh!"

This time he clamped his sweaty palm over the droid's mouth, the skinwrap lips plasticky and slightly sticky. Warm putty.

"Go, get." Eb pointed to the back of the house. "The study, now."

"The study, sir?"

"You know what I'm talking about, go now. Not another word."

Eb mounted his Segway and sped to the back of the house. Just past the second-floor master bathroom was a narrow hallway, the lights dim and yellow. This part of the house was set deep in the metamorphic rock of the mountain. The hallway split in two directions.

Eb turned right.

He was beginning to chatter when the double doors were in sight. Big, loopy gold rings hung from tarnished plates. The furnace couldn't expel the dank, frigid spirit in this part of the Castle.

Inside was an old-fashioned study with velvet loungers and polished furniture. A humidifier hummed in the corner. An ornate rug was centered on hardwood, imported directly from India. The atmosphere smelled of rare books and tobacco smoke, despite the fact he'd read not a single book or lit one of many pipes in the display case.

Eb shrugged a leisure coat over his shoulders, the silky lining cool. The droid's hurried footsteps slapped down the hall. Eb waved for him to slide the study door closed and only then did he reach for the bookshelf. Next to an original Edgar Allen Poe was a frayed and faded copy of *Zen and the Art of Motorcycle Maintenance*. Eb had never read it, but that wasn't the point.

He slid it halfway out, turned it so the spine pointed down then shoved it back in place.

The bookshelf clicked.

Gears turned.

The towering wall of books lifted up then silently swung open. The whole charade was corny and cliché—a secret panel activated by an obscure book (most people would try *The Tell-Tale Heart*, he reasoned)—but so corny and cliché no one would expect it.

Eb slipped into the safe room.

The light was warm; the air incurably cool.

A fireplace roared to life, a dragon exhaling gas flames to expel the dank spirits. A small table was to the left, a pantry with a year's worth of food and water—the inventory checked monthly for expired goods. A couch was to the right, a desk with an assortment of monitors and controls next to that.

The walls were embedded with metal screening, a faraday cage that shielded against electrostatic and electromagnetic eavesdroppers.

The ultimate man cave.

The secret door snapped shut. The lock bolted into place. The droid waited patiently. Eb hogged the fire's warmth.

"Would you care to explain what we're hiding from, sir?"

"From inquiring minds, dummy." Eb pointed at the bookshelf. Out there, someone could hear what he was about to say. From now on, he needed to be careful who heard what.

"Minds, sir?"

He sighed. There was so much to understand. He had just put it all together. Where to start? The rings grew hot on his swollen fingers. He twisted them off—they were useless in the man cave anyway—and turned his backside to the flames.

"Here's the deal," he started.

The droid cocked his head and listened to the conspiracy spew out in no particular order. No interruptions, no attempts at rational explanations or logical thought. He just listened. Eb occasionally paced the room before returning to the fire, adjusting his glasses and tapping his chin to process another batch of thoughts.

The mysterious program used all of Avocado's resources to communicate with the Castle on Christmas Eve. Coincidence?

No way.

The only code to be mined from the cryptic operation was nonsense babble that sounded like who? The girls. Fluke?

Not a chance.

And it all started after a stupid ghost appeared. The whole thing had Jacob's fingerprints all over it.

"And why would Jacob do this, sir?" The droid posed the question without sarcasm.

"Who knows?" He tapped his chin. "We've got to put a stop to this."

Eb dug through the desk drawer, scrawled a string of letters across a sticky note and shoved it at the droid.

"You've heard this, right?"

"Well, it—"

"It sounds just like them, don't pretend. That's their secret little language, and guess where I found it. Huh? Guess."

"It was part of the code, sir."

"How'd you know?"

"You just told me, sir."

"I didn't say it was the code."

The droid took the sticky note. "I think rest would do you good, sir. Perhaps a little fresh air. I know where we could find a friendly snowball fight. I think you would enjoy it."

"You think I'm crazy, don't you? I'm making all this up. Wake up and listen. Facts are facts. There is a mysterious program; I am having nightmares at exactly the same time that program starts. *The same program with redundant code that sounds exactly like the girls he sent to my house!*"

Eb pointed up then around the room. His sense of direction, of where the front door was located, was upside down.

"They just make sounds, sir. It doesn't always mean something."

"Don't make excuses!"

"They're seven-year-old girls, sir. Not spies."

"You're biased. You like them."

"You don't, sir?"

A strange sound escaped his gaping mouth. The sound that would escape a frog if a curious little boy picked it up. He was supposed to like them. He was their legal guardian. He did like them.

But they also scared him.

"Will you be staying here, sir?"

"For now. I need to think."

"Do you still want me to acquire medicine, sir?"

"No, no, aren't you listening? This isn't about me anymore, dummy. I want you to analyze the house. Reboot the security system, scan for viruses, reset the passwords, and shut down anything that looks suspicious."

Eb made a shaky, chin-tapping loop around the room.

"Contact Avocado. Have them do the same thing."

"On Christmas, sir?"

"Yes, on Christmas. Have you not heard a single thing I've said? We can't be too careful. My... my life is on the line here."

The eye roll was back, a deep sigh escaping the droid.

"You think I'm joking?"

"I think you need to give the therapist another chance, sir."

"Not in a million years. No one can know about this, you understand? No one." Eb grabbed a handful of the droid's baggy sweatshirt and tried to shake some sense into the synthetic dimwit. "We need to find out who's in on this."

"Besides the girls, sir?"

"Yeah, besides the girls," Eb whined. "I know the program is behind the madness. We need to stop it. And then we need to find out why he's doing it."

"You believe there are others, sir? Besides Jacob?"

"There has to be."

The droid patted his shoulder before turning for the exit. The doorway popped on its hinges, cool air sucking through the sealed opening.

"You're the only one I can trust," Eb said.

The droid paused in the doorway, gray hand gripping the edge. A twist of compassion turned the corner of his mouth. He cocked his head.

"I'm here to help you, sir."

With a slight nod, he pulled the door closed behind him. The lock clicked into place. Eb warmed his backside at the fire. He didn't really trust the droid, but it was better he said *that* than what initially came to mind.

You're the only one I have.

22

4:20 p.m.
The droid filled Natty's mug. It was her third cup of cocoa. She leaned against the kitchen table with a chocolatey smile.

Addy was still working on her first. Half of it went down in short slurps and long giggles. Upon request, the droid had filled the mug with miniature marshmallows. Addy stirred the sugary muck until the droid began dancing a silly dance—upon Natty's request. A fountain of cocoa erupted between Addy's lips then her fingers, spraying the dolls sitting in the bowl of bananas.

Cursed dolls.

Such simple toys. They could have anything they wanted and they chose those little tokens of voodoo. If the droids weren't spying, Eb would switch the big-eyed, ragged gingers out with something a little less germ-ridden. The arms were gray, the legs discolored from sleeping drool and now freckled with hot cocoa.

Natty whispered behind her hand. Sludgy cocoa dripped from Addy's chin, spotting the floor. Despite the secretive tone, the words transcribed across Eb's monitor.

Gubbubbgubbuh.

Another line of gibberish was captured through the droid's amplified auditory system and piped directly to Eb's monitor. From there, it would go to IT for analysis.

Their little language would be decoded. No more secrets. No more program.

No more dreams.

The droid chased the girls with a pair of banana tusks. Eb muted the squealing. After three laps around the kitchen island, he snapped the monitor off and returned to the recent analysis.

The house was clean. All scans reported no anomalies. A second scan confirmed it. The only thing to do now was build a bigger and better firewall around the house system. He could always unplug from the world, but how would he communicate with Avocado?

He wasn't going out in public.

The safe room sofa was reasonably comfortable. Depending on what happened, the little room might become long term. The ache in his back hoped it wouldn't.

The newsfeeds blathered from flat-screen monitors. Eb propped a tablet on his belly, dragging data with his fingertip. He missed his rings already.

"You rang, sir?" The droid's dull gray head appeared on the tablet.

"Any news?"

"You mean since you called five minutes ago, sir?"

"The girls blabbered all through your cocoa party. What did IT say about it?"

"They're analyzing, sir."

That was his fibbing tone. How long did they expect Eb to wait? He couldn't live in the safe room forever.

"Would you care for something to eat, sir?"

"Have they been acting differently? Did they ask about me? Did they say anything about dreams? Are they getting weird?"

"If little girls are weird, sir, then yes."

"What about the dolls?"

"What about them, sir?"

"Are they... doing stuff with them?"

"I don't know what you mean, sir."

"Just... they're creepy. I don't get it. What's the deal?"

"I'm not taking away their dolls, sir."

"How did Natty get that doll back anyway?"

"You asked me this already, sir. Are you lonely?"

"No, I'm fine. I just want this to be over."

"Your dreams didn't say to hide from the world, sir. Quite the opposite, in fact. They want you to be in the world."

"How do you know that?" he snapped.

"You told me, sir."

"They're not dreams, let's be clear. This is sabotage. Harassment. Someone will pay for my pain and suffering."

The droid's expression drooped. "I won't be a part of this, sir."

"Of what?"

"You're shrinking from the world, sir. Running away. I can't support that."

He placed the tablet facedown. His gray face was more condescending than his voice.

"I beg your pardon, but I am running *at* the problem. We're investigating this invasion. You can't torture people in their sleep, you know. It's against the law."

"Will you have your subconscious arrested, sir?"

"Just shut up."

"And what if these... *dreams*... were real, sir? Would that make it any different?"

"They're not real, so no."

"Let's say they're accurate, sir. If they really are your future and present life, would you still be doing this, sir?"

"Yep."

Eb flipped through the newsfeeds while the droid reasoned with him. Any other time he would have shut him off. He needed to hear a voice, even if it annoyed him.

He settled on the gossip newsfeed. One of the fashionistas appeared. Pink Stripe was long gone, and the second one, the one with the piercings, disappeared shortly after her. Eb liked the third one, the baldy with tiny glasses. He was fair.

"And you're satisfied with that, sir?" the droid said for the third time.

"Happy as a clam."

"I see, sir. The caterpillar is content until it sees the butterfly soar."

"You're not making any sense."

"I'm making..."

His voice faded from Eb's attention. An avocado appeared on the gossip newsfeed. With a hand gesture, he upped the volume.

"Jerri called again, sir. It's the fifth time this afternoon. I really think you should talk to her—"

"Shhhh."

"She's at the office, sir. She's concerned about the recent activity..."

He crossed the room in three steps. The monitor loomed over him, flickering images of mountain ranges and sweeping hilltops. The view was familiar. The footage zoomed through valleys, between dense forests and above whitewater rapids. It passed between massive tree trunks and squeezed between rocks until it emerged onto an open plain.

The Castle was on the far side.

It closed the distance while the fashionista with the tiny glasses commented on the stealth drone video.

"You need to see this," he said, "before it gets taken down."

The room swayed with the view, the ground tipping in gut-liquefying turns on a crash course. It reached the foot of the cliff. The view turned up and soared in front of the castle. The image of a drone sped past mirrored windows.

"The *mysterious* uploader," Tiny Glasses said, "managed to steer a drone through security to get a close-up of Ebenezer Scrooge's ridiculous mansion."

Ridiculous? Eb cringed.

The snarky tone gave him away. Tiny Glasses knew who the mystery uploader was. It wasn't him, but he knew.

The drone looped around for another pass. The droids were on both sides of the driveway, in the middle of their snowball fight. Addy and Natty must've been in their snow forts, hidden from view.

The drone slowed at the Castle's second floor and turned at the corner where long expanses of mirrored windows covered the building. The quadcopter's reflection hovered in front of it, the view coming into focus.

Then it blurred.

"You see that?" Tiny Glasses said.

"Is that what I think it is?" someone answered.

A vague blob was behind the glass. Both of them played along like they didn't know.

"A little digital enhancement," Tiny Glasses said, "and look at that."

The mirror pixelated.

The edges of the amorphous shadow sharpened. A pear-shaped figure was staring back. It lifted its arm and appeared to dig a finger into its nostril.

"Oh God," Eb muttered.

"Behold," Tiny Glasses announced, "the great Loch Ness of shut-ins, the Sasquatch of the rich and cranky, the man unseen by the world in almost a decade."

"Is that who I think it is?" the cohost chortled.

"We can't say. Legal reasons, you know."

Eb teetered backwards and fell on the sofa, his head thumping the wall.

"We *can* say that we think it is a male that does very well in the technology industry," Tiny Glasses said.

"Interesting."

"And there's more, the mystery uploader promised."

The view jerked upside down. In a tumbling freefall, the drone crashed to the ground, shattering on the boulders below.

Eb windmilled his arms but couldn't wave his body off the sofa. "Are you watching this? Dum-dum! Are you watching?"

There was a pause. "Yes, sir."

"What am I seeing? What am I watching?"

An audible sigh escaped the tablet. "The drone was intercepted but not before it neared the Castle, sir. I didn't expect much to come of it and didn't want to worry you."

"Did you see what they did?"

That was Eb behind the glass. That was his unmistakable grotesque body. He knew it. Thanks to Tiny Glasses and the mysterious uploader, the world would know it, too.

"It's speculation, sir."

"Speculation? It was me!"

"It is you, sir."

"I don't like it." Eb held the tablet with stiff arms, the droid's pallid face looking back. "I don't like!"

"The legal team, sir?"

"Now!"

"The lawyers are rather tied up, sir. You may have to hire more."

"I don't care if we have to buy the Supreme Court, get that video off the Internet and start suing."

A slimy spring of fear oozed from his mid-region. He was ill with grossness. His privacy had been violated. They almost saw him. The real him! It was only an outline, but close enough.

"Jerri's calling, sir. Do you want to take it?"

"I want someone to murder that footage." The view was starting over. "And send down food."

"In that order, sir?"

"Do it at the same time. There are seven of you."

Eb slammed the tablet off the cushion. It bounced onto the floor. The droid's face fractured. Eb kicked it across the room and cursed the stinging pain in his big toe.

The weight of his stupid mountain was crushing him.

23

A block of meat loaf sat on the table. The mixture of cold meat and perspiration made for a peculiar scent. Bluish light strobed across the left side of Eb's face; a variety of entertainment gossip overlapped with current events and political forecasting.

Occasionally, a word or statement yanked him away from the document on his tablet. If his name was mentioned, heart palpitations followed. The rogue video footage hadn't appeared on any newsfeeds since 5:25 p.m.

It was now 6:45 p.m.

His team aggressively wiped out the uploads and threatened newsfeeds that were showing it. Nothing they could do about the talking heads, no way to wipe them out or make them forget. Eb, neither.

That enormous, disgusting shadow was me.

There were ways to scrub his memory. Avocado had experimented with technology to whitewash traumatizing experiences in the brain. Jacob envisioned it helping victims of childhood abuse, those suffering from post-traumatic stress disorder or schizophrenia. Trials were indefinitely suspended when the

American Psychological Association vehemently opposed the practice.

The technology was still at Avocado. He'd have to go there or have it shipped. Option one was never going to happen. Option two would take too long.

Eb broke a bite off the meat loaf. He pecked at the tablet, dabbing the cracked glass with greasy fingerprints, and typed corrections to the public statement. This was the third round of edits. He wanted it out by 10:00 p.m. The PR rep told him to wait a week. She also told him to stay off the newsfeeds, that this would all blow over. And whatever he did, do not even think of making a public appearance.

She didn't have to worry about the last part.

He wasn't leaving the safe room. Maybe ever.

But how could she expect him to ignore the newsfeeds? Seriously. They were talking about him. *We have it under control,* she said. *Just get some rest. Let us spin this.*

That wasn't how he rolled.

The tablet whooshed the corrected statement into cyberspace. More angry vinegar needed drizzled into the wording.

You're the victim, the PR rep said. *They invaded your privacy, remember that. We want the public on your side.*

There was no *they* out there. Eb knew exactly who the mysterious uploader was. So did Tiny Glasses.

Pink Stripe.

That paint-face had it in for Eb ever since he got her sacked. It wasn't his fault she was incompetent. Why take it out on him?

I am the victim.

The verbal chaos suddenly faded beneath the echo of a water droplet. The monitors rippled. The droid's face appeared. His coarse-textured brow furrowed.

"Watching the newsfeeds is not helping, sir."

"Neither is that meat loaf."

"Jerri is calling, sir. It's the tenth time. I'm just guessing here, but I believe it's urgent."

Eb snapped the tablet shut. He couldn't avoid her forever. She'd been at the plant most of the day. He needed her to take care of things while he mopped up this mess but didn't want her to hear the quiver in his voice. *Did she see the blob?*

"Take the call, sir."

"She can't see me, right?"

"No one can, sir."

"You can."

"Of course I can, sir. No one else, I promise."

After a short pace, Eb fell on the couch and hugged a cushion. It wasn't enough cover. He pulled the blanket over him. He couldn't be too careful.

"Perfect, sir." The droid raised his brows. "I'll put her through."

The monitors blinked.

A cluttered desk appeared. A woman stood at a glass wall overlooking the plant. The avocado glowed in the distance. She turned and stopped, eyes darting over the desk.

"Eb? Is that you?"

The frayed ends of the blanket tickled his cheeks. His breath was hot.

"I can hear you breathing." She approached the desk. "Did he take the call, Jenks?"

"Who's Jenks?" Eb said.

"Eb? The picture's black. Is that you?"

"Who were you talking to?"

Jerri leaned on the desk. Her face was without makeup, her gray hair held back with a black band. Her eyes held a thousand questions and a load of concern.

"Are you all right?" she said.

"Technical issue," Eb said. "Security. Can't be too careful. Who's Jenks?"

"Sorry. Your droid reminded me of another project. I saw the footage," she said. "How are you doing?"

"Everything I love has been taken from me. Other than that, I'm good."

"I know how much your privacy means to you and how hard Christmas is."

Eb lowered the blanket. "Why are you at the plant?"

"Kyle called. I thought I should come in and supervise. This is a big deal, Eb. This mystery program is some sort of viral infection; I think it needs to be taken seriously."

"What... what did he tell you?"

"I thought *you* were running the program, Eb. I didn't know it was... I-I'm sorry. Kyle told me about the dataflow and the strange patterns connected with your house."

"What else?"

"It's under control, Eb. The program has been sequestered. He wants to bring in some outside contractors to look at it."

"He can't do that." The blanket fell on the floor.

"Don't worry. I told him not to. We need to keep this in-house until we know more." She pulled the hair band out and fixed it back in place. "You had a rough night, huh?"

"How do you know?"

"Your droid said you didn't sleep much. Want to talk about it?"

"What did he tell you?"

"He just said it was a long night."

"Why are you there, Jerri?"

"This is urgent, Eb. Why do you think?"

"It's Christmas. Don't you have family?"

"This coming from the man who dismantled holiday spirit at the plant? I'm surprised you didn't call for all hands on deck."

A small part of his brain considered turning on his video so she could see his leer. Hearing him just didn't have the same effect. Everyone was suspect. Anything out of the ordinary was to be examined. And Jerri coming in on Christmas?

Top of the list.

"A herd of reindeer couldn't drag you in on Christmas and you come dancing in like eight maids a-milking?"

"Last night," she said with a heavy sigh, "I was with some friends—"

"No, no. No, no. Don't want to know about last night."

His sanity was too thin to support any corroboration with the dream. *Because it was a dream. A dream manufactured by that dreaded program.* That was the only fact that kept the ground from crumbling beneath him.

"Just tell me why you're there," he said. "What are you up to, Jerri?"

"What am I...? There's a program running incognito in the Avocado mainframe that's feeding your castle and you're building a public relations nuclear bomb and I'm supposed to do nothing? I understand you're hurt, Eb; you feel victimized, but you can't order the PR team to seed the newsfeeds with juicier rumors about fabricated celebrity double murders so they'll forget about you."

She snatched a page from her desk.

"You want to spread rumors that the president has a glass eye that can shoot a laser, that the Canadian prime minister has a secret puppet fetish, and the head of a major motion picture company is really a droid? This is your answer?"

She wadded her notes. They thudded in an empty trash can.

"You can't do that, Eb. You can't have our entire legal department prepare subpoenas for every newsfeed that ran the story. You can't sue the world, Eb. So why am I in here? To keep you from burning down the entire company!"

Eb grabbed the couch cushion. "You want me to just do nothing?"

She pinched the bridge of her nose. "Yes, Eb. I want you to sit there and do nothing. That's exactly what you need to be doing right now. Listen to the people around you."

Listening to others didn't make him a mountain of cash. Eb followed his own instinct, made his own decisions. He got to where he was by listening to his own thoughts and no one else's.

It also occurred to him that he was currently hiding in a basement.

"I'm worried about you, Eb. Your droid—"

"Dum-dum. His name is Dum-dum, not Jenks."

She chuckled briefly. It took a moment for her thoughts to gather. "That's part of the problem, the way you treat others. Even a droid."

"He's a machine. He's not real, Jerri. You do know that."

She stepped back from the cluttered desk. Had she aged in the twenty minutes they'd been talking? She looked so tired.

"Rick's leaving, Eb."

"Leaving what?"

"He took another offer. We need to start looking for his replacement. I don't think I need to tell you how important he is to Avocado, do I?"

The cushion collapsed in Eb's grasp. He clawed the fabric like a crumbling ledge. Feet dangling. A high-pitched whine rang in his ears, the sound that follows a swift knock between the eyes.

"Eb?"

He cleared his throat.

"This is a big loss," she said.

"Uh-huh."

"We're going to need everyone on their game going into the New Year. Including you. Do you hear what I'm saying?"

He wasn't in the mood for a pitch for the medical program again. This was DEFCON 1, not what side dish to bring to the company picnic. Eb was already spinning as many dishes as a human could balance.

The sound of breaking china was all around.

"There's a..." He took his glasses off and wiped them with his shirt. "He's got a... the non-compete clause in his contract. He can't just go anywhere."

"That's not going to make him stay, Eb. He doesn't want to work here anymore. Do you know why?"

Eb swallowed. The answer was coming. The itch was too tempting, the ache too deep. The dots were connecting.

Because it has to be a dream.

"Did he... tell you?" Eb said. "Like at his house or something?"

"There's an email." She exhaled. "You obviously haven't read yours."

There was a soft knock. Jerri held up a finger and opened the door. There was a mumbling conversation about operations and protocol. With Jerri there, the fire was under control. Eb released the headlock on the cushion, wondering if he was more relieved that she was handling the crisis or that Rick had sent her an email.

Where would Avocado be without her? Where would he be? She was efficient, lovely and loyal beyond reason. Despite being an office hoarder—she threw away nothing, not even a paperclip—she was always Jacob's favorite.

For good reason.

Someone from IT came into her office and showed her something on a second monitor. It was tilted at an angle so Eb could see the messages. He nudged Jerri's clutter aside to make room for a notepad. Pens and folders and books spilled over the edge. Jerri picked up the mess without taking her eyes off the monitor, stacking the office debris on the corner.

She placed two little gifts on top.

"Let me know when you find out." She walked him to the door and leaned against the glass wall. Eb's office was on the other side of the floor, the lights off. The desk empty.

Arms crossed, she stared.

Eb breathed into the cushion again, eyes perched just above the frilly trim, fixated on the corner of her desk. The gifts hung over the edge.

"Take some time, Eb," she said. "Take a vacation; let PR handle the chaos. I'll handle the rest. Okay?"

He began to rock.

"Eb?"

She sat down. The wheels squeaked forward. "I know some good people to talk to, help manage the stress. I do the same; it keeps me sane. Jacob, too. I'd really like to see you come down here to the plant sometime. Not your projection."

She sat back, pointing at his darkened office across the floor.

"I can't remember the last time I saw you," she said. "Just something to think about, okay? This will be waiting for you when you get here."

Her chair protested the forward lean. She bulldozed the office debris off the corner and grabbed both gifts. Eb followed them with his eyes. She held one in the palm of her hand, the shiny ribbon red. The green wrapping paper. The little tag hanging off the corner, sparkly gold ink.

"Merry Christmas," she said. "This one's for you. We all got one."

He didn't need to ask from whom.

24

Flames roared up the flue, yellow tongues darting through the screen, baking the room with a fierce, dry heat. If a goose lay on the hearth, it would've been well done.

Clothing lay like shed skin. Damp socks balled up, a pit-stained shirt wadded in the corner. Only a pair of boxers covered Eb's glossy body—the elastic band biting the flesh beneath his overlapping stomach, a dark V of perspiration pointing at the floor.

Sweat dripped from his chins, rivulets puddling around his elbows, finding a crooked path to his fingertips, where they clung momentarily. His glasses slid down his nose until they teetered on the bulbous knob. He pushed them up, ignoring the flashing light recording his madness.

He ignored the time, the schedule.

"Oh my, sir." The droid entered, waving his hand.

Eb licked the sweat from his lip.

"The fire has been turned up dangerously high, sir. Perhaps we should extinguish it for inspection."

It was indeed dangerous. The gas key had been maxed out. The room was nearly an oven, a bakery to incinerate guilt and fear and confusion, to cremate the delusions.

He was free falling.

"Your call with Jerri did not go well, sir?"

The droid pretended not to know what happened, pretended the gift that Jerri presented to Eb was the exact same gift Rick had passed out before leaving. It was a gift that revealed the true nature of his delusion, that the dreadlock man was real. That it was not a dream.

That ground below him was crumbling.

"It's late, sir. Christmas is almost over, you'll be happy to know. We can put this year behind us and start a new year very soon. And you haven't touched your food." Dishes clattered, a knife fell. "Perhaps we can move back into the house now. I have taken the liberty of pulling all the shades and curtains. There are no views left open, I assure you. You will not be able to see out, and no one will see inside. Shall I draw you a bath?"

"Have you been watching?" Eb said.

Thoughts swirled through him, a blizzard of embers streaking across his mind, twirling and clashing, searing his soul, eating the pit of his stomach. The depths of despair had no bottom. His feet dangled above a hungry pit, black and toothy.

"Would you care to talk about it, sir?"

Care to talk about it? No one could swim through a riptide of insanity and talk about it. He would inhale the foul current should he open his mouth, would sink to the very bottom.

Those were not dreams.

Despite the impending madness, he knew what to do. When he was trapped in fear, when hurt and confusion fell like stones, he reverted to coping skills he'd learned as a child and did what he always did to survive.

He took that hurt and sculpted a stone to hurl.

"Perhaps I can get you something fresh to wear, sir?"

Eb ignored the droid and pulled on the sour clothing that was more than damp. The shirt stuck to his back, the pant legs clung to his thighs. The droid helped him pull on the socks and held the robe for him to thread his arms. Damp footsteps marked his exit.

"It's a bit drafty, sir." The droid rushed ahead of him. "If you wait a moment, I can have—"

Eb mounted the Segway and sped through the study. The hallway was indeed drafty, the cool air quickly turning into an icy breath. Sweat stung his eyes, blurring the lamps into streaky stars. He sped past the turn that would take him into the house. Lamps flashed awake ahead of him.

"Sir?" The droid's harried footsteps were gaining. "The elevator is in need of repair. I don't think this is a wise route."

It wasn't the elevator he sought.

I don't understand.

That was at the root of the falling, the sinking. Why had his world flipped so quickly, the snow globe of reality shaken so violently? The ice had broken, the water cold and numbing. He sought warmth to make things right.

The world above. Fear below.

The gift. Rick had left the gifts in their desks. Jerri had gone over to their house. Carol confessed he was leaving.

It happened. It all had happened. And I was there.

The hallway hairpinned left. The floor descended toward the lower level—a level that hung off the bottom of the Castle like a hive. There was a heavy door at the bottom.

The cold bit harder. Deeper.

Why am I like this?

The thick door began sliding open. Mechanical noises echoed toward him, the clashing of hard surfaces, the wet slap of fluids. His robe brushed the doorway on the way inside.

A metal tang coated his throat. Hydraulic fumes filled his sinuses.

Why am I... me?

The basement level was narrow and deep. Tubes lit up the ceiling, the far wall too distant to see through an array of mechanical arms, slack bundles of hydraulic tubing and rigid conduit.

An elaborate laboratory surrounded him, shelves arranged with spare parts—dismembered gray arms and legs, decapitated heads with sealed lips. A rack of transparent caskets was set into the wall, the gray skinwrapped bodies of the droids docked snugly inside each one, hands at their sides, eyes closed.

There were operating tables, too.

One of the droids lay prostrate, the midsection splayed open like a feasted sow. Mechanical arms extended from the ceiling to poke inside his split belly, the sound of hot sparks and whirring equipment spilling out.

"Is everything all right, sir?" The droid on the operating table turned his head.

Dusty keyboards were neatly arranged on a long workspace. The inset monitors were dark. The lab was fully automated. The droid didn't just occupy the bodies—he was the Castle, the appliances and communications, the walls and lights. His artificially spawned awareness filled the fiber optics.

His quantum existence was everywhere. He knew everything.

Eb sat on the only chair, his damp clothing pressing against his thighs and back. He pulled off his glasses and wiped his eyes. A red laser passed over his face.

"Verified," the station reported.

The monitors came to life. Data clogged the interface, most of which Eb did not understand. He pecked a few keys, but his fingers were slow and shaky. He switched to verbal.

"Cognition core."

"What are you doing, sir?" The droid had arrived from the hallway.

"Get back," Eb said.

"It's unwise to change—"

"I said get back!"

The droid took a step back. Something clicked over Eb's other shoulder. The other droids had dislodged from their docking stations, heads turned curiously.

"Don't." Eb spun in the chair. "Get back in there."

They blinked, confused. The one on the operating table pushed onto his elbows. They watched but didn't speak.

"Cognition core," he repeated.

The monitors responded with an array of data and graphs, subdirectories that led to various elements of sensory input that allowed the droids' artificial intelligence to function on a humanlike level. A team of Avocado engineers had spent years constructing the droids' personality matrix.

A team led by Jacob.

Sweat stung his eyes. He leered at the avalanche of numbers and code. Without the droid, Eb was helpless. He needed him to take care of the Castle, to monitor the property, to attend to his needs. To care for the girls. He needed the droid.

But not all of him.

"Personality."

The dataflow changed direction. The droid shuffled behind him but didn't come closer. Did not utter a word.

A subdirectory to the droid's personality opened. More algorithms and graphical interfaces. This was Jacob's personal touch—a droid that didn't just walk and serve, but one that presented the human attributes of sarcasm and humor, wit and charm. An intelligence that destroyed the Turing Test.

You won't be lonely, Ebenezer.

"Jenks. Find Jenks."

A shift in data. A root directory appeared. It opened with file headings. Jerri had made an honest mistake. Or had she mistakenly been honest?

Eb faced his droid. "You're Jenks."

"I am a shared personality, sir."

"You serve Jacob."

"Jacob is no longer living, sir. He directed me to help you."

"To help me."

"To help you, sir."

His thoughts continued to blow stinging waves of sleet, blurring clarity and purpose. No one could be trusted.

Even the ones he trusted.

"Consolidate all data and executable files associated with the personality program referred to as Jenks."

Light strobed across the droid's face as the monitors changed directive. The droid's eyes widened, lips pursed. When the light dimmed, Eb turned to face the monitors.

A folder was positioned in the middle. It was labeled Jenks.

A word swelled in his throat, burning in his eyes. He would have to push it over his tongue to get it out.

"Please, sir." The droid shuffled a step. "Reconsider."

Eb swallowed. *Why do I hurt others?*

It was all he knew. But he had to survive. When trapped, he fought. He had been shoved into the corner, ground beneath a heel, flattened nearly lifeless. And very little fight remained.

But he'd been a fighter all his life.

He needed to clean the slate. His life was unrecognizable, his schedule a disaster. All the moving parts needed to stop—just for a second, just one second—so he could think clearly, so he could figure them out and make sense.

He needed space. No one was going to give it to him. He would have to take it.

This was the only way he knew.

"Terminate."

Servers hummed in another room. The monitors asked for confirmation. Eb had to say it again. He bowed his head and listened to the digital grind plow through multiple servers, the command removing all traces. The docking stations clicked. When all was quiet, he removed his glasses to wipe his eyes.

He turned.

The droid stood at attention. The others had locked themselves back into the docking stations. The one on the table was staring at the ceiling. Eyes ahead, arms at the sides. Heels locked. None of them smiled. Their eyes would not widen, their heads would not cock to the side.

No more Jenks.

Why do I hurt others?

"Go," Eb said.

The droid blinked. "I do not understand."

"Go! Get out of here! All of you, leave me alone. Now!"

The request was assimilated. The droids popped out of the docking stations and filed out of the lab. Even the one on the table exited, his midsection still surgically open, the silvery network of gel lines glistening.

Eb slammed the door behind them and slid down the wall. Knees folded against his stomach, he shook violently. His eyes burned. Sobs erupted in his chest.

Had the future been altered? Would the cursed dreadlock man forget him next year? Would life make sense again?

Those questions flitted in a blizzard of thoughts. But one question hovered out of the storm, one that brightly demanded attention. One he rarely asked himself but now was impossible to avoid. A question he pondered deeply.

Why do I hurt?

25

1 2:00 a.m.
The lab door swung open. It was not the soft-heeled cadence of gray feet that approached but the clack of hard soles. The girls were outlined in the soft glow of sleeping computer monitors.

Their dresses were pressed.

Ribbons curled.

"Girls." Eb cleared his throat. "What are you doing down here?"

Lips grim, they stared with oversized pupils. Dolls dangling from one hand, they reached out with their empty hand.

"It's late," he said. "You should be in bed. Where's the droid?"

He choked on the last word. *The droid.*

The girls took his hands. He could hardly feel them. They were tiny, no bigger than the day they had arrived, as if their stunted growth mirrored his own.

His joints ached; his knees refused to move easily. In a series of aborted attempts, he made it to his feet.

Hand in hand, they walked him up the ramp.

He returned to the Castle.

PART IV

THE GHOST OF CHRISTMAS PAST

26

2:55 a.m.
Only the Segway was whirring.
The wheels gripped the hard floor. A mounted flashlight illuminated the way, briefly catching the crinkled reflection of a candy wrapper.

The windows were shuttered and shades pulled. During the day, sunlight streamed through the outer seams in bright thin lines, blotting out the outer world and curious eyes.

Wind rushed into Eb's robe, his heart fluttering anxiously. He leaned into the final turn and sped down a hallway. The projection room was open, a doorway waiting with open arms, a welcome sight to a pounding heart.

He entered at 3:00 a.m. On the button.

A starry sky greeted him. The horizon was lined with rusting canyon rims. A trace of a recent thunderstorm hung thickly, the modified air, clean and fresh, smelled vaguely of wet pavement.

Eb closed his eyes, inhaling the misty fragrance.

This was the projection room, not the Rocky Mountains. This was a small space, a safe space. A security blanket.

Every day for the past year, he had lived beneath the illusion and the comforting embrace of the curved walls. Some days he was greeted by the watery roadways of Sicily or the crowded streets of Broadway or the wide open plains of Wyoming. He experienced the world without being in it.

In the world, not of it. Isn't that what the sages preach?

At 3:05 a.m., he parked the Segway at the foot of a king-sized bed. The ledge upon which it was perched was an illusion, but not the bed and neither was the hook on which he hung his robe. The projection room was cluttered with the essentials of an efficiency apartment.

He walked across the room in striped boxers and black socks. His belly hung in flaps; his knobby knees bulged on chicken legs. For the first time since college, he could count his ribs.

At 4:00 a.m., he slid the rings onto his fingers and waved his hands. A series of holos opened, views from around the house. The kitchen was clean, the halls polished, the furniture dusted. He uploaded the location of the candy wrapper he had seen on the ride in before switching the view to the basement lab, where seven skin-wrapped droids slept in docking stations.

He was back from his shower, safe in the projection room. Eb snapped his fingers. They could wake now.

Quickly, he switched the view before they opened their eyes. He preferred not to see them snap out of their constraints to begin the daily prowl. They would move fluidly yet mechanically, eyes ahead, orders accepted. The floors would be cleaned, the walls wiped, the tables shined. He inspected their work, but had not watched them do it.

Not since last Christmas.

He made his bed—snapping the sheet tight, tucking the corners properly—and slid into his walking shoes. A treadmill was in the center of the room. Red light danced on the control panel as he began his daily pace.

At 5:00 a.m., he called up a view of Avocado, Inc. The plant was sparsely lit, janitorial droids moving in the dark. Office cubicles glittered with tinsel and tiny Christmas trees. His chest fluttered again.

A reminder.

This day had arrived. He had put last Christmas behind him and had carved a corner of sanity out of the reoccurring nightmare. Yes, a nightmare. A dream, nothing more. The mystery program clearly saw what was happening in the plant; it saw Rick place those gifts, it knew what they looked like. They simply transferred real-time information into the dream. He had convinced himself it didn't happen, it couldn't have happened.

For the sake of sanity.

At 6:00 a.m., he counted his medication.

The bathroom was a small construction that contained enough plumbing to do his duty. He steam showered upstairs at 2:30 a.m., that he could schedule. His bowels, however, weren't always cooperative.

Nature got its way.

There was a plastic container on a little shelf above the sink, with tiny compartments, each labelled with the days of the week. A blank wall was above that.

No mirror to be found.

The medication organizer rattled. He unloaded three pills and lined them on the edge of the sink. One at a time, they stuck to his tongue and were chased with exactly one swallow of water.

One for clarity.

One for alertness.

And one for serenity.

At 6:30 a.m., there was a tap at the door. Eb waited two minutes before opening it. A tray lay on the floor, cloth napkin draped over the top. He ate the grapefruit and yogurt while walking the treadmill.

At 7:00 a.m., he watched the newsfeeds, checking the stock market and financial reports. The gossip newsfeeds would be turned on at 7:00 p.m., a guilty pleasure he still indulged.

Moderation required discipline.

He couldn't trust the world. But he could control his reality.

The newsfeeds were off at 7:45 a.m. The treadmill reverberated in the room, punctuated by the heavy clops of his methodic stride. His faint musky odor mixed with various lotions from inside his baggy shirt.

A drip of water echoed from above. Waves retreated around him. He adjusted his glasses, the recording light in one corner, the time in the other. It was 8:00 a.m.

"Yes."

A wide holo stretched across the wall and appeared to hover in the open space of the snow-painted canyon. Jerri's cluttered desk blotted out the lower half, a sight that shot a shiver through his heart. That was where he saw the gift—Rick's gift. The one he had given everyone as a thank you for working with him; they were all excellent employees and wonderful people.

And then he left.

His leaving wasn't what kicked Eb into the downward spiral, wasn't what flipped him into paranoia or compelled him to hunt down Jenks's personality. The dream wasn't a dream after all.

Yes. Yes, it was.

Jerri stood at the glass wall, oversized coffee mug in a crooked arm. Across the plant, Eb's office was dark. The blinds were drawn.

"What's wrong?" Eb called.

She half-turned and shook her head. Their weekly conference calls had been getting distant since Halloween. Her monitor was still blank. She had refused to look at his square-chinned projection, and he refused to let her see him.

Stalemate.

"It's been a long week." She rubbed her face. "How are you?"

He hesitated. She hadn't slept much, if at all. He'd seen that expression before, the dark circles, the droopy cheeks and red eyes.

"Clockwork," Eb said. "Everything like clockwork."

"Good for you," she deadpanned.

Structure was the key to good living. It took a year for Eb to learn that lesson. He was an organized man, but structure kept his mind from wandering. Kept memories in their rightful spots.

In the dark.

"Beautiful day," Eb announced. "The newsfeeds speak kindly of Avocado; strong financial reports are optimistic. What else could I ask for?"

She smirked behind her coffee mug. "Colorado is buried in a blizzard, Eb."

That could be true. The projection room was an exaggeration of the view outside the castle. He saw the bright sun and blue sky; a glittering blanket of white diamonds stretched across the valley. There could be a nuclear holocaust and he wouldn't know it.

The way he liked it.

"Let's talk about today," he said. "We'll be disconnecting the Castle from the plant at noon. I'd like to run another analysis before that so I can see the results."

"Nothing's changed, Eb."

All analytics indicated the mystery program had been purged. Not a trace, not a byte, not a single line of nonsense code existed. Still, he would disconnect from the plant so that no dataflow would reach him.

His sanity was a delicate snowflake, after all.

"Humor me," he said.

"You'll have to work with Jared, then. I'll be gone the rest of the day."

"No. No, no, no… you can't do this. It's… it's Christmas Eve, Jerri."

He pressed his palms together and pleaded. She couldn't see him, but she'd hear the anxiety tainting every word.

"You'll be fine, Eb." She looked directly at the camera. "Everything is on track. If anything changes, you'll be alerted. Just… trust me, Eb. You'll be all right."

"Why'd you even come in?" he asked.

"To take care of a few things. And to hear your muddled voice."

"No, you didn't."

She chuckled. "I was following up with the medical team. We're behind schedule."

She updated him with problems, the legal issues that kept cropping up, the ethical ramifications continuing to loom. She needed more money but didn't ask for it. She smiled through the weariness, hiding what was really on her mind.

Eb had allowed her to crank up the money pit of medical

research, giving her what she wanted. Maybe he was desperate; maybe she was taking advantage of him.

Once again, Avocado was burning money faster than dry kindling.

Six months ago, a company released a groundbreaking discovery of artificial stem cells, the exact innovation Jacob had envisioned. Jerri reminded him of that. They were showing promise to rebuild failed organs or damaged limbs. Three-dimensional printers were already fabricating organic organs. The use of synthetic stem cells called biomites would enhance the replication process.

We need to catch up, Jerri said. *It's now or never.*

It was 8:28 a.m. "Is that all?" Eb said.

She sat back, cradling the mug. No attempt to kill the connection, the pause stretched out. Those were the moments he considered inviting her to the Castle.

She would have to see him then. She wouldn't recognize him if she did. And she wasn't going to wear a blindfold, either.

"We need to talk, Eb."

"Okay." It was 8:29 a.m. "Tomorrow."

She was nodding but not in agreement. Perhaps she recognized the strain in his voice. Or maybe it just wasn't a conversation she wanted to have on Christmas Eve.

"Merry Christmas, Eb."

"Yes. Okay."

He didn't like the way that ended, but it was 8:30 a.m. The meeting was over. A blank holo hung in space.

He wound the timeline back to a still frame of Jerri with her coffee. He stared at it until 8:35 a.m.—five minutes too long—wondering what she was thinking.

27

Another breakfast arrived at 9:00 a.m.

A marble countertop was between the treadmill and bed, a miniature version of what was in the kitchen. He centered the tray, placed the cloth napkin on his lap and smoothed out the wrinkles.

At 9:15 a.m., the projection room view shifted.

Pots and pans appeared over him. An industrial refrigerator was to the right with an apron hanging on the handle—an apron that was probably still warm. Natty and Addy sat at the island, their black shoes kicking the elevated stools.

"Good morning, girls."

"Good morning, Uncle Scrooge."

They grabbed their forks, the starter pistol having been fired, and stabbed the yellow pile of eggs. Natty was on the left, her green ribbon drooping over her forehead. Addy was on the right, the loops of her red ribbon tight and shiny. Their dolls lay on the counter. The girls would wipe down the counter when they were finished.

That was the deal.

A relationship was happening, a slow build that took a year. They ate meals together (sort of). They talked (kind of).

Eb cut his muffin in half. "Have you finished your chores?"

"Yes, sir."

"And you have finished your studies?"

"No, sir."

A fleck of buttered egg shot from Addy's lips. She covered her mouth but only laughed harder. Natty joined her.

"Girls."

It was best to nip the laughing fits before they started. No one was there to calm them down. Natty leaned over until their foreheads were touching. She whispered behind her hand. Addy stopped laughing, like a button had been pushed.

"Natty?" Eb dabbed his mouth. "What did you say?"

"I asked Addy to stop laughing."

"Are you sure?"

"Yes, sir."

They ate quietly again, the tom-tom of their shoes banging against the stools.

Eb would rewind the incident when breakfast ended. The secret language had vanished. Not a single cryptic syllable since last Christmas. They spoke impeccable English. But Eb still listened.

Another Christmas Eve had arrived, after all.

He sipped his spinach-infused smoothie and wiped the green mustache from his lip but not before the girls giggled at his silly face. This got them every time. *Uncle Scrooge has a mustache. Shave it*, they sometimes exclaimed. And he would wipe it with the napkin.

"What will you do today?" he asked.

"Color," they said. "Play."

Very few things escaped Eb's paranoid eye, but it never occurred to him that the girls were eight years old. They had birthdays every year. He watched them blow out the candles, he counted the number of smoldering wicks, watched them open practical gifts like toothbrushes and washcloths. He knew their age.

But he didn't notice they were still quite young.

If he wound back the memories to the day they arrived, he might notice very little had changed about them. But he never did; he just accepted what was presented to him.

A peripheral holo popped open as he finished the smoothie. A box truck was approaching the front gate. This was a live view, a bleak outlook of a blizzard-ravaged mountainside road that, despite being cleared that morning, was already drifting.

It was 9:33 a.m.

"What is that?"

"Hash browns," the girls said.

"I'm not talking to you." He looked at the ceiling, where the illusion of pots and pans dangled. "There is a truck at the front gate. Report."

A droid marched into the foul weather, the exposed skinwrap gray and dull. Icy pellets bounced off his head. The gates began to swing open.

"What is happening?" Eb said. "Who is this?"

"A delivery." The echoing voice was tinny and flat.

"What delivery?"

The box truck swung around and a very large man opened the back door. The droid stood back.

"A tree," the voice said.

The girls threw up their hands and cheered, yellow chunks of egg falling on their laps.

"I didn't approve," Eb said.

A small holo lit in front of him, a document with his approval and date stamp. *Last July.* Those were the foggy days. He was still adjusting to a change in medication. It was before he confined himself to the projection room, before he established the schedule. The structure.

"I said they could have an ornament," Eb said.

"That is the ornament."

The girls had been so good. So smart. He wanted to reward them despite his lifelong creed of not rewarding employees for behavior they were already being paid to do. He saw no logic in paying someone beyond what was already agreed upon. What use was a contract, then?

"Send it back," Eb said.

"Unacceptable."

The very large man jumped into the truck and started for the road before he could argue. Another droid joined the first one. Together, they dragged it toward the house.

"Leave it on the front porch." Eb clutched the napkin, pulling it taut across his thighs. "And don't decorate it."

An image rose from the foggy past, stepping into the spotlight of his awareness. A tree on a front porch. Decorated. Lit.

He attempted to look away, to sweep it back to where he kept those memories forgotten—the dreadlock man and the children, the kitchen where Jerri and Carol discussed Rick leaving Avocado.

The stools tipped over. The girls ran toward the front door, the counter littered with eggs.

"Girls! Clean up! Come back, clean up."

They arrived at the front door still celebrating. The droid opened the door, a gust of biting snow blowing across the foyer. They pressed their faces against the narrow windows, smudging the glass with lip marks. They would discuss this later.

Eb finished his muffin at 9:45 a.m. He returned the projection room's view to the tranquil scene of a crystal mountaintop and quiet valleys.

He didn't notice the girls whispering.

28

Water droplets woke him at 10:40 a.m. Groggy, Eb pried the black band from his eyes. "Who is it?"

A holo hovered above his feet. A very young man was looking at him. His cheeks were acne scarred, the pockmarks rolling beneath flexing muscles as he viciously chewed gum. Long cabinets lined the wall behind him, the depths of IT.

"Hello?" Freddy said.

Eb fixed his glasses in place. "You were supposed to call at noon."

"Sorry, Mr. Scrooge."

"What is it?"

"There's nothing wrong."

Eb paused. "Then what?"

"We're going to initiate the disconnection in ten minutes." He cleared his throat. "The, um, dataflow has started."

"The what?"

"The dataflow, Mr. Scrooge."

"The program... is back?" Eb sat up and pulled a blanket around him. He was suddenly chilled.

"It showed up about half an hour ago." The gum snapped inside his left cheek. "As far as we can tell, something signaled the initiation from outside the plant. It appears to be dormant code that woke up and began a self-replicating cycle."

"What's it doing?"

"Nothing right now, Mr. Scrooge."

"Well, what is it doing exactly? Is it juggling numbers or playing tic-tac-toe?"

"Redundant actions, Mr. Scrooge. We did identify similar code from last year, though." He squinted at something on the desk.

"What is it?"

"More of that strange code. I can send it if you want, but I wouldn't worry. It's contained, Mr. Scrooge. We have it quarantined and we're already analyzing it." He cleared his throat. "We're going to cut the connection to your castle."

"If it's nothing to worry about," Eb said, "why are we breaking the connection early?"

"Just playing it safe, that's all."

The gum was getting murdered by his back molars. Freddy wasn't confident, not like Kyle was. But even Kyle couldn't handle the pressure and left Avocado last February. This guy and his team, they were supposed to be the best in Silicon Valley and even they didn't know what the program was, where it came from or where it went.

If they did, Eb wouldn't be staring at a face full of pimple scars.

"Don't disconnect just yet," Eb said. "I need to scrape the newsfeeds."

"You haven't been watching..." He wiped his forehead with his sleeve. The pitch of his voice went up. "You haven't seen the newsfeeds yet today?"

"No. I do that in the evening." He didn't want to share his obsessive dedication to the schedule.

"Okay," the kid said. "You'll be in total isolation once we cut the cord. Castle Grayskull will be on lockdown."

"Castle what?"

He swallowed. "Just the... sorry, sir. I was thinking of something else. Go ahead and scrape the feeds for later, just let me know when you're ready."

Eb went to the treadmill. He would walk until 11:30 a.m. to get back on track. His legs were already tired. He'd lost twenty minutes of his nap. When he stepped off, little jolts of energy twitched at the corners of his mouth. He sensed an oncoming train.

And he was tied to the tracks.

29

A marching band stomped through his head.

He had been dreaming of a plank. It was the width of a sidewalk but made of wood. Sky was all around, thick billowy clouds below. Occasionally, cotton candy would swirl over the edges, foggy fingers streaming in front of him. It seemed he'd been walking this board for a long time.

He shaded his eyes.

The end of the plank was buried in a storm cloud, bruised edges swirling at the perimeter, flashes of lightning in the belly. That was when the marching band woke him.

Or was it thunder?

Eb opened his eyes. Clouds were above him, but not from the dream. These were projected across the domed ceiling. He was clutching his mattress, sheets damp with sweat.

More thunder.

It was outside the door, footsteps pounding the floor.

His head was a sandbag. Arms molten lead. Legs steel beams.

The air was fluid, slightly sour. It took a long minute to sit on the edge of the bed, rubbery sensations returning to his face. He shuffled to the sink. A dose of cold water washed away a heavy layer of slumber and dripped from his chin.

The stomping parade passed outside the projection room again. He fixed his glasses.

9:00 p.m.

That wasn't the plan. His early evening nap was supposed to end at 7:00 p.m, at which time he would eat a snack while he watched the newsfeeds. His empty stomach confirmed it.

Eb opened a holo as he changed into dry clothing. The hallway was empty. The droid must've retrieved the 6:00 p.m. tray when he overslept. He could use a shower, but it was still early. Best to wait until the girls were asleep.

Why aren't they in their room?

"Girls?"

Holos dialed views through the Castle, following footsteps and cascading laughter.

"Girls, it's time for bed." He called to the sky, "Why aren't they in bed?"

The droid didn't answer. The entire schedule was off. Maybe the disconnection from Avocado was making a mess, but that didn't make sense. The droid wasn't connected to Avocado. He was integrated with the Castle.

The stampede passed outside the door.

Eb spun with surprise, but when he lit up a view, the hallway was empty. He jumped the view to the foyer and was distracted by a red glow around the front door.

The Christmas tree.

It was wrapped in lights that twinkled in rhythm to silent carols. Tinsel and ornaments were draped over the branches that swayed in a gusting wind. A few of the ornaments were nestled in the snow like decorative eggs. Another storm was approaching.

Below the lower branches, partially buried in a drift, the lights reflected off shiny paper.

A gift.

"Schedule," he muttered. "Get back to the schedule."

Eb brushed his teeth and washed his face. Clean, dry and refreshed, he went to the treadmill to step back into rhythm. There would be no sleeping until midnight had passed. This was a bad night to get off schedule, but it wasn't impossible. It was only 9:45 p.m. *Just stay the course, keep steady.*

He fell into the rhythm of walking meditation.

Step.

Step.

Step.

The room projected a peaceful valley and majestic mountains. The air felt crackly. His skin was dry and itchy. He wanted to crawl out of his body and wash it down the drain.

A shower couldn't come soon enough.

He pulled open a holo of the girls' bedroom. Two lumps were beneath the comforter, their hair splayed on the pillows, foreheads together. Arms out. The droids must've corralled their late night run.

He sighed. *So far, so good.*

At 10:30 p.m., he pulled up the newsfeeds scraped from earlier in the day. Without a connection, the reports were slightly stale. The disconnection bothered him. On top of everything else, knowing he was cut off from the world was frightening. What if something happened? No one would hear him call for help.

The isolation was palpable, a thick blanket thrown over the Castle. The atmosphere was dense and stagnant, scratching his throat like wool.

He called up Beethoven's *Moonlight Sonata, 1st Movement*, a piece that never failed. Though he knew nothing about conducting, his hands flitted sharply. He pretended there was a crowd behind him that was awestruck with his instinct for music.

When the air ceased to itch his throat, he sank into his beloved newsfeeds and no longer felt alone. The talking heads rattled off their stories. Their lips were moving, but the words were buried beneath Beethoven.

Christmas carolers sang at shopping malls.

Children cried on Santa's lap.

People hustled into snow-driven homes, fires in the hearths, stockings flat and wanting.

It was 11:00 p.m. His hands stopped.

He was midway through Vivaldi's *Winter* when the Castle appeared. It was a distant view from across the valley. It zoomed low to the ground, buzzing around trees and, temporarily, hiding in the hollow of large stones, eluding the patrolling drones.

Captivated, catatonic, Eb watched this one soar beneath the Castle and hover at the front door. The blinds were pulled tight. It attempted to peek through the seams, searching for a forgotten window or a crooked slat. It crossed over the top of the castle, almost colliding with the Skeye™ dome.

A shiver stiffened his legs. *The Skeye™ dome.*

Neglected, the miniature forest had dried up, the needles brown. Limbs barren.

The music continued.

The suspicions of a missing tycoon, the shuttered castle and absent leadership of Avocado, a company that seemed to be doing just fine without him. The rumors spanned all the way to last Christmas Eve, the last time he'd been seen in public, the last interview he did.

He'd fallen victim to Grinch syndrome.

He'd gone crazy.

Jerri had assured the media that he was doing just fine, that he was stepping back from the company to enjoy his life with the girls, that he was still involved with the company and valued his privacy. The world seemed to forget about him.

So why are they reporting it now?

He would expect it on the entertainment newsfeed, but not a legitimate newsfeed. Earlier footage replayed of the first drone intrusion—the Loch Ness moment in the exercise room. The view zoomed past the snowball fight and slowed. The music drowned out the reporters. Whatever they were discussing didn't reach him.

Something was off.

The droids were packing snowballs and hurling them across the driveway, standing guard at the entrances of snow caves.

Where are the girls?

They were out there that day. Eb had seen them, their floppy stocking caps, the fuzzy balls, their cheerful laughter, snotty lips and cherub cheeks.

They weren't hiding.

Before he could freeze the feed, Jerri's face appeared between the talking heads. She was smiling, a touch of makeup softening her features. This was her headshot, the one they showed whenever they were reporting financials. Rick's picture was next to it.

The Avocado logo between them.

Rick had left a year ago. He'd been out of the industry since then, sitting fat and happy with compensation from a non-compete clause.

Words crawled across the bottom.

Eb tripped on his own feet. He caught himself on the machine's arms, but the conveyor belt carried his feet from beneath him, dragging his lower body off the back end. He clung to the console. Fingers slick with sweat, he slammed off the belt and was dumped into a heap.

Glasses askew, he looked up.

To the lovely sounds of Bach's cello, the words crawled through his eyes and stabbed his brain.

It was 11:15 p.m.

"A massive blow to the company. It's been three years since the unexpected death of one of the company's founders, Jacob Marley, followed by the erratic behavior of his co-founder, Ebenezer Scrooge. And now the interim CEO is rumored to be leaving."

Lightning flashed in the belly of the storm, clouds unfurling.

You haven't seen the newsfeeds? That was what Freddy had said when Eb was going to scrape them for later. He'd assumed Eb had seen them, that he knew the news. The rumor had gotten out. She wasn't planning to release a statement; she was waiting until after Christmas.

Jerri is leaving.

She would be joining Biogenetics, a medical technology company that specialized in organ regeneration and biological fabrication. No official word, but rumor said she would be heading up the biomite division that produced synthetic stem cells. The potential of perfect stem cells would advance medicine by light-years.

The room was a plastic bag.

Each breath was longer and hotter. He'd had plenty of the breath-stealing episodes following last Christmas, those moments when the sky slowly dropped like a steel plate and his world became smaller. Tighter.

"Jerri." He waved his hands, the rings tingling. "Jerri, call Jerri."

A blank holo appeared but refused to cooperate. There was no connection. No way in or out. He was isolated. She was leaving and there was nothing he could do about it.

I'm alone.

The projection room flipped to another newsfeed. The illusion of a peaceful world was replaced by real time. Black wind hammered the mountain. Hail pummeled the Castle.

He had to get out.

It didn't matter if a droid was out there or the girls were sleepwalking, he had to escape. He pulled open a holo and checked the hall. Empty. Quiet.

He yanked open the door like he'd emerged from the deep end of the pool, eyes watering. Cooler air rushed past him. He took a step and kicked a platter.

What's food doing here?

No one had delivered anything. And he had yet to see a droid or hear from one. Were they sprawled in the basement or caught outside, having powered down during some power failure?

But food didn't spill on the floor. It was a tightly wrapped gift. Snowflakes melted on the edges, the wrapping paper damp and spotted.

The gift from the front porch.

His limbs were as cold as the floor beneath his feet. There was doubt he could bend at the knee to pick it up. Doubt he could stand up if he did.

His breathing slowed.

A gift from the girls asleep in their bed, sugar plums all fancy and dancing in their heads. Wishing for a present, wanting something pleasant.

"What is this?" he heard himself say.

One hand out, he braced against the wall. He bent at the waist and dangled his free hand, a mechanical claw brushing the shiny bow. He stood up, the gift sitting in his palm like a treasure to be royally presented.

It was lovingly wrapped, expertly taped. There was no name. He tugged at the corner. The sound of ripping paper raced down the hall. Slowly, he pried off the lid. There was a thatch of white cotton, and for a moment his lungs collapsed. Resting in the center, its mass pressing down, was a smooth stone.

Another paperweight.

Exactly like the others. "What does this mean?" he whispered.

Two years ago, he would've skipped it down the hall, bounced it around the corner until it came to rest somewhere in the foyer. He would've shouted for the droid to find it, to dispose of it.

Because it meant nothing.

It was 11:45 p.m. And there was laughter.

"Girls?"

He stopped, rubbing his hands, looking down the hall and back again. He had to stick to the plan.

"Girls!" he shouted. "Come here!"

The laughter suddenly came from another direction. It was interrupted by gobbledygook. The gibberish was back, a string of nonsense shooting through the Castle, pelting the walls. The mountain shook, the haunting all around.

Gubbagubbagubbah.

Gubbagubbagubbah.

Gubbagubbagubbah.

The storm battered the outer walls, the mountain groaning.

The nonsense was familiar. He'd heard it before.

He clapped his hands, the metal rings striking each other. He stretched open a holo. A gray square hovered in the dark. Eb searched for the last communication from the outside world, the message sent from IT. Freddy had pulled it from the program just before shutting down the castle.

The strange code. The string he couldn't pronounce.

Gubbah.

Eb reached for the corner of the holo. The gray square responded to his imaginary touch and began to swivel. It turned on a center pivot, a slow-moving spinner. The word remained lit, bright white letters in a gray void. The letters flipped and the word read backwards.

It wasn't spelled perfect, but sounded close enough.

Eb followed the footsteps.

30

The girls were no longer laughing.

He followed the sound of their hard-soled shoes past the front door, where the glow of the Christmas tree leaked past the blinds, where sleet battered the windows. He went through the kitchen and down the deep hall and into the center of the Castle.

Ahead, the wide double doors of the Great Room were thrown open. Golden light poured into the hallway, an effervescent promise in the hollow darkness. He covered his eyes. It was never that bright.

Never that golden.

The Great Room seemed lit from within. No light source above, no fixtures on the curved walls or the marble pillars. The room was empty—no chairs or sofas or televisions to watch.

Something lay in the center.

His steps shortened as he neared the limp objects, stopped so abruptly that he teetered. His breathing was raspy, desperate. He took a knee.

The dolls.

The seams were frayed. The button eyes empty. The red yarn hair and mitten hands. Threaded smiles pulling apart.

"Hello, sir."

The room was empty when Eb had arrived. The droid was now at the far end. His hands were folded in front of him, tucked inside long white sleeves. Long, loose pants of the same color bunched over his feet.

He cocked his head.

"You," Eb croaked. "You are the..."

The last word was too big. Once it was out, it would be true. But there was no going back. And not uttering the truth would not make it so. The wet carpet in the girls' room, melting snow in the tracks. He was there when Jacob appeared. There when the thing had arrived. There when the dreadlock man left him in the Skeye™ dome.

And now it struck midnight. And the droid was there.

"Humbug," Eb said. "You are the humbug."

"Yes, sir. I am."

"You're Jenks. I turned you off."

"It seemed that way, sir."

A year passed with stiff droids crawling through the Castle. Was it all an act?

"Why?" Eb adjusted his glasses. "Why would you do this?"

"I am here to help you, sir."

"Is this what you call it? Years of torture and deceit, a sad spiral of despair and grief and loneliness... you call that help?"

"I did nothing to you, sir."

"Then who? Jacob is dead and you are here."

"You did this, sir."

Eb crushed the dolls in each hand. The stuffing flattened. He held them to his face and breathed the musty fabric. Memories of dusty rooms and petrified fear swirled in his head. He clutched the dolls harder as if they would make everything all right.

"Where are they?" Eb said. "Where are the girls?"

"I think you know, sir."

He pressed the dolls against his eyes. Of course he knew. The empty snowball fight. The empty bedrooms. The sudden appearance.

And they never aged.

They had been five years old when they arrived. He was too

caught up in his own self-centered world to notice they never seemed to get older. Or care.

"I'm insane," he whispered.

"Understanding is your path, sir. You know your future. You know your present."

The droid traced a circle as he spoke. And as he did, his body shifted into the gangly form of the thing and then the dreadlock man before resuming the white-clad droid.

"What are you?"

"Does it matter what I am, sir?"

"Yes! Yes, it matters! I don't understand how you're doing this? You... you act as if you're helping me. There is no path of understanding here."

"*You,* sir, are the path. I am simply helping you see that. You live in a false reality. I am pulling back the curtain."

The castle rumbled. The storm battered the walls. Something fell in the hallway.

"I never meant to frighten you, sir."

"Just drive me to madness."

"The path is difficult, sir."

"Says a droid. That's what you are, a droid. You're a fabrication of artificial intelligence. How would you know difficulty? What do you know about change?"

"I am not suggesting change, sir."

"Then what?"

"The caterpillar does not change, sir. It transforms."

Eb fell hard on his knees.

He didn't have the strength to stand. His knees broken, his shoulders wilted. His will drained. If his heart gave up its last beat, he would fondly bid it farewell.

He had seen his future.

He had seen the present.

"I know my past." His voice was muffled in the dolls. "I know who I am."

"To go forward, sir, you must know where you've been."

"I know my past," Eb whispered.

Pliable steps neared him. A dull gray foot protruded from beneath a flared pant leg. The droid gently squeezed his shoulder.

"You've been crawling for quite some time, sir." The walls rumbled. "It's time to fly."

The floor opened below him, a trapdoor that swung on hinges. Eb fell into an endless black night.

31

Arms flailing. A scream trailing.

The gentle hand never left his shoulder.

Deeper he went, further back in time they travelled, where Christmas music called and sugar cookies tempted.

Jingle bells, jingle bells.

"Jingle all the way." A guttural humming followed.

It was a small warehouse with open shelving and black pipes along the ceiling. Three metal desks were pushed together, a rectangle of manila folders and twisty lamps, pencils and notes. A red velvet bag sat on one of the cheap chairs.

The song blared from tinny speakers somewhere on the other side of the shelving. A bank of monitors was anchored on the wall. Someone rhythmically tapped a keyboard. He wasn't wearing his typical black beanie. This time of year, he wore a floppy Santa hat.

"Jacob," Eb whispered.

A strand of garland fell off one of the monitors. Jacob replaced it after bringing a folder back from the desks. He looked so young. His cheeks so smooth beneath the stubble, eyes crinkled at the corners.

The studio.

It was their first office, where Avocado got its start, an inexpensive lair buried in an industrial park on the south side of Chicago. They slept on the desks and ate from a mini-fridge. When they had time, they showered at the YMCA.

Jacob hummed along to "Jingle Bells" as he flipped through a report. The bags of a three-nighter were hanging beneath his eyes. *Too much to do,* he would say, *for just one life, Ebby.*

Ebby. That was what he called him in those days. *When did it turn to Ebenezer?*

Jacob slapped the folder closed, folded his arms and sighed. "What do you have for me?" he said to the wall.

The lifeless monitors came alive.

Colors bounced in rhythm to Jacob's words, an auditory response that continued blazing. Blue merging with green giving birth to violet, a swirling, self-perpetuating chaotic pattern as if the computer was breathing a psychedelic experience, each brain wave a lucid dream, each thought a new universe.

"That's how he described it," Eb muttered, watching Jacob begin to smile. "Each brain wave a lucid dream."

"My story begins with a boy, sir," the voice blurted from the monitors, the colors dancing with the cadence.

Jacob laughed above the music, above the computer's response. He shook his fists in celebration and jumped on the desks and sang "Rudolph the Red-Nose Reindeer" while kicking papers on the floor.

The computer's voice.

There was still a hand on his shoulder. Slack-jawed and glassy-eyed, he turned. The droid cocked his head curiously.

Eb didn't agree with the project in the beginning. Too much red tape, too much fear and competition. They didn't have the resources to create a self-aware intelligence that could drive cars or monitor homes or diagnose patients. That was for the big companies. Avocado was still small. They needed to focus on doable entertainment was what Eb preached.

Eventually, they ran low on funding. Jacob had to choose between it and his medical program. The AI project was scrapped.

Not until they patented the malleable skinwrap, an invention

Jacob initially started as a way to synthetically produce skin grafts, did the droid project take off and the AI project returned. But that was years later, too many years for Eb to remember.

"That's you," he said.

"This is my birthday, sir," he said. "The day I was born."

"Jacob? You ready?" Jerri emerged from the storeroom with a floppy Santa hat. "What are you doing?"

"It's alive!" Jacob cried. "It's alive!"

In Frankensteinian fashion, he laughed manically and swept her into a torrid fox trot around the littered floor, trampling documents and folders like nothing else mattered. She laughed, pulled away and forced him to explain. He wiped tears from his cheeks and described the creative process that the AI project just completed.

The colors were brainwaves.

"It doesn't just think," he said. "It *creates*."

Jerri saw the monitors respond. Eb watched the colors dance in her eyes. They were bluer than he remembered. Her hair was chestnut brown; her cheeks dimpled when she smiled.

"We have to tell Eb," she said, and called his name.

"I don't think he'll care," Jacob said.

"Of course he will."

He joined her. "Ebby! Get over here! Ebby!"

"Where'd he go?" she asked.

Eb remembered them calling his name, hearing their exuberance beneath the jolly cheer of Christmas music. He remembered the dancing, the celebration, the hoots and hollers.

Jerri's disappointment.

"I'm worried about him," Jacob said. "I think Eb needs help."

Their backs were to the monitors. They didn't see the colors splatter from frame to frame, the jagged lines that responded to what he said.

Jenks heard him.

He didn't forget.

I think Eb needs help.

"We're going to be late," Jerri said.

Jacob went to a set of lockers and stepped into a pair of fuzzy red pants with suspenders, wore a thick red coat with white trim, and fastened a white beard to his stubbly chin. The African American Santa Claus bellowed *ho-ho-ho* as he slung the velvet bag of stuffed animals over his shoulder.

Jerri called for Eb one last time, but they were already running late. They were due at St. Mary's Children's Hospital in ten minutes. She would be the elf that helped him deliver the tigers and lions and bears to the children on Christmas Eve.

It came so easy to Jacob. He loved so easily. He gave so effortlessly. It wasn't fair. Eb struggled to be in the room with people. It just wasn't fair.

They turned the music off.

In silence, Eb stood beneath the bank of monitors; colors breathed across the black screens.

"You heard him," Eb said.

"I did, sir."

I am here to help you, sir.

That was the moment the droid was seeded with his first directive —to help Ebenezer Scrooge. To truly help him. To understand his life. To know his true self. That was the conclusion that the droid had come to. The only way to truly help him was to show him how to help himself. Whether he wanted to or not.

When the lights went down, the colorful monitors painted the desks and the paper trail on the floor. Something moved behind the shelves.

A younger Eb came out of hiding.

He turned on a desk lamp and began picking up papers, began reorganizing the residue of Jacob's celebration before sitting at one of the desks. Dutifully, mechanically, he typed at his computer.

He would work through Christmas Eve.

He would wake Christmas morning and work on the fumes of coffee until Jacob found him hunched over his keyboard, bleary-eyed and irritable. He would try to celebrate, but Eb would only remind him of everything that could go wrong.

They did this all beneath the colorful monitors.

The droid dropped his gentle hand on Eb's shoulder and began to turn an imaginary dial. The walls began to spin.

A kaleidoscope of color turned.

Eb's stomach fell through his feet. The droid squeezed his shoulder. Colors bled into each other, water running over wet paint in a turning carnival ride—red bleeding into blue into green into yellow into violet. They blended into white streaks and crystalized.

And began to fall.

Snowflakes.

Footsteps crunched in fresh snow. Eb saw a pair of sharply pressed navy blue trousers. Snow cascaded over shiny black shoes, blotting the dress socks a darker shade.

Eb tripped on broad steps. The droid helped him lean against one of the many garland-wrapped columns that framed a festive set of doors. Crisp winter air cleansed his sinuses.

He wiped his eyes and looked over a stretch of land he hadn't seen in forty years. The great lawn of Millar Academy Prep, lush and swamped with lounging students in the springtime, was buried in snow. Tracks were carved from building to building.

The young man on the steps could've been mistaken for a Swiss guard, standing resolute with a bag slung over his shoulder. Steam rose from his cleanly parted hair, still damp with comb tracks.

"How old are you there, sir?"

Eb peeled himself off the pillar and journeyed to the bottom step just below the eye line of his younger self.

"Eighteen," Eb said. "I'm eighteen, I think. I... I remember the briefcase."

Young Ebenezer clutched a J.W. Hulme briefcase, distressed leather with gold buckles. His father gave it to him his senior year. Large flakes of snow clung to the sides and stuck to the shoulders of young Ebenezer's wool overcoat.

Clouds streamed from his nostrils.

"What were you doing, sir?" the droid asked. "Standing in the cold?"

"I was... waiting."

Young Ebenezer held out his hand. Snowflakes gently settled in the palm of his leather glove, dissolving into the creases at first but eventually holding their form.

Waiting.

This was standard procedure for young Ebenezer, from the day he was sent to Millar Academy Prep. He was the first to arrive for semester and last to leave. One by one, his classmates would climb into cars for the Christmas holiday. Young Ebenezer would watch them from his room until his ride would arrive. He would stand on the steps with perfect form and wait.

Occasionally, no one would arrive. He would have to come back the next day.

"Not this time." Eb stood behind his younger self. "We were flying out for the holiday."

There was no joy in Eb's revelation, unlike young Ebenezer sticking out his tongue, a large snowflake melting on the tip. He remained resolute, at attention and mindful, but a tiny smile dimpled his ruddy cheeks.

A trio of students came from around the corner. They were lobbing snowballs at each other. Young Ebenezer did not move.

"Handler." Eb recognized the boys and fumbled down the steps. "Ericson and Peters."

The boys wrestled each other to the ground, snow packing into their stocking caps, pouring down the backs of their powdered overcoats. The scene lifted Eb from the spiraling fear and confusion, absorbing him in the memory. A smile defrosted the tension on his forehead, melting his ridged brows.

A laugh escaped him when Handler dusted Ericson with a two-handed snowball. Young Ebenezer, however, held his ground.

"Hey," Peters said, "what're you still doing here, Ebby?"

"Parents running a bit behind," young Ebenezer said.

"Why you leaving so early?" Ericson said from the ground. "Exams are tomorrow. And then a party, son. You running out on us?"

Young Ebenezer shrugged.

The snowball fight continued and he was caught in the cross fire. He dropped his bags and fired back, catching Peters square in the ear.

"I took exams early that year," Eb said distantly. "We were going to Aspen. Just Mom, Dad and me."

"Your first vacation, sir?" the droid asked.

"On holiday, it was."

Eb had planned the trip. He'd been forwarding emails and links ever since Peters told him about the same trip he took with his family. Peters had two brothers and a sister. They skied all day and played games with their parents at night. Eb imagined a blazing fire in a cobblestone hearth and a view of a lighted ski slope. The laughter, the fun.

So he planned it. After months of begging, his mother agreed and his father went along with it.

Young Ebenezer yanked a phone from his pocket. Mildly panicked, he brushed the snow off his overcoat and patted down his hair. His good humor drained away.

A black car approached the turnabout.

"Watch the trees," Peters shouted. "Remember… snow plow!"

The boys laughed. Young Ebenezer climbed into the backseat. Eb watched the car pull away.

There was no reason to get in the car with young Ebenezer. The ride would be the same as always. The Uber driver would ask what music he liked, did he like going to Millar Academy Prep, was Devetta Scrooge really his mom?

Devetta Scrooge wasn't his mom, he would answer. Even though she was. If he didn't deny it, the driver would ask questions all the way home. It didn't matter if the driver was male or female, they wanted to know if Devetta Scrooge was really like that because no one was really like that.

But she was.

Eb watched the Uber drive out of the circle, left blinker at the four-way, where he would ask about the music.

"Just leave it off," Eb said, mouthing the words young Ebenezer would say.

Millar Academy Prep was the best part of his life. And it wasn't all that great.

The droid reached out and, once more, turned the invisible crank. The streets and buildings, the snow and clouds began to grind around them, the universe spinning slow at first.

Then faster.

Until it blurred.

Bull-nosed marble steps appeared below their feet. The black Uber pulled into a driveway, the pavers cleared of snow. It circled around a three-tiered fountain, icicles draped over scalloped lips.

The Scrooge name had not been painted on the mailbox. There was no point. They never lived in a house long enough for it to matter. By the time the paint dried, they would already be building a bigger and better house.

"We never stayed long," Ebenezer said, "but never left the neighborhood. We just kept building. My father said we were bringing up the value of the neighborhood one house at a time. Everyone should thank him."

The shrubs were sheared perfectly square, the windows clean, the drapery hung just so. Not a single light twinkled nor ornament hung. Across the street was a modest house in comparison. It was a two-story home with inflated snowmen and jolly fat men and strands of white lights that coiled up tree trunks. Evergreen wreaths blotted out the windows.

Young Ebenezer climbed out of the backseat.

The droid stepped aside, hands tucked into his sagging sleeves, to let him pass. Young Ebenezer wiped his feet before opening the door. High-pitched laughter rang somewhere in the house, the hysterical kind that came with a knee slap and a long sigh.

Amazon boxes were stacked at the foot of the stairwell, some with the tops cut open. Inside were brand-new ornaments and a fourteen-foot artificial tree.

"Never opened," Eb said. "Every year, she ordered new ornaments. Some years they made it out of the package." Eb peeled back a flap. "It all ended up in the garbage. Every year."

Young Ebenezer didn't bother dropping his bags. He toted them down a long hallway and stopped where the laughter was loudest. He watched with the fascination of a young kid seeing his first circus, a bearded lady perhaps or a parade of clowns.

"Yes, of course," Devetta Scrooge crooned. "I will call as soon as I land and you take care. And James? I want to thank you from the bottom of my heart. I can't tell you how much this means to me."

Eb remembered the way his mother would put her hand over her heart, her thick eyelashes fluttering as she half bowed, her way of giving thanks in a meaningful, ancient way. *The Buddhists do that,* she once said.

Without batting their eyes, of course. Or the lipstick.

"You were supposed to pick me up," young Ebenezer said.

"Honey, I had a very important call. How was the trip home?"

He didn't bother describing the awkward silence or the slight nausea he got from riding in the backseat. She had already turned to the computer. If he said anything, she'd interject timely *uh-huhs* while clicking from one tab to another.

Her office was a holy shrine of social media, a monitor for almost every platform. The walls were hardly visible beneath a continuous stream of reality television and status updates. A fog of perfume sent intruders into a coughing fit, a sickly sweet fragrance that attacked the eyes and back of the throat. She could text with her left hand while clicking the mouse with the right.

"Honey." She raised her phone when young Ebenezer started to walk away. "I'll be flying out tonight. Your father wants to talk to you."

"Tonight? I thought we were leaving tomorrow."

"You haven't heard? Silly me. I just got called up for a pilot. Isn't that wonderful?"

She clasped her hands together, the long painted nails folding over the backs of her tanned hands. A wide smile exposed neon white teeth.

"Now?" young Ebenezer said. "I mean, at Christmas?"

"Well, it doesn't start until January."

"Why are you flying out tonight?"

"Honey, I need to get settled and prepared. There's a lot of competition in reality television. You know, I can't just show up and expect them to love me despite all my followers."

The bag sagged on young Ebenezer's shoulder. He hiked it up and started for his room.

"Hey!" Devetta Scrooge shouted. "Aren't you happy for me?"

"There's lipstick on your teeth," young Ebenezer called from the stairs.

She found a mirror and polished her teeth with her finger, mumbling about spoiled brats and a selfish family. "Just once. Can't you be happy for me just once?"

"She never came back," Eb mused. "Met a producer and stayed in California."

"Were you sad, sir?" the droid asked.

The answer was naturally no. An emphatic no. She only left that room to eat or use the bathroom, and she walked hundreds of miles on a treadmill with a Bluetooth in her ear while thumbing a phone and tapping touchscreen monitors. Had she not met the producer in California and divorced his father, she would've knocked out a wall to expand her social media shrine before building another house.

"Your father wants to talk to you!" Devetta Scrooge repainted her lips before taking a call.

On the third floor, young Ebenezer threw his bags on the bed. A mini-fridge hid beneath a wide desk. He flopped on the chair with a bottle of water and went zombie—a faraway place with no thoughts or feelings.

Eb knew the place well.

He'd never seen it from the outside, how vacant his eyes were, how slack his face went. He only knew how empty it felt. A safe house where nothing hurt.

"What's this, sir?" The droid observed the organized desk.

At first, Eb thought he was talking about the old man face carved into a pine branch—a gift from his grandparents. There was a stack of flat stones balanced on the corner of the desk. Black and smooth.

The stones.

Eb plucked one off the top, the remaining stack shimmering in place. He rubbed the smooth edge. He'd forgotten about the stones.

"I got those for him."

"Your father, sir?" the droid added.

Eb nodded.

He'd found them in a stream at camp one summer and kept them in his pockets. That Christmas morning, he stacked them on the coffee table with a little note for his father, something he called natural sculpture. His father looked at them and grunted into his coffee. They stayed on the coffee table until Eb took them to his room.

"Never said thank you," Eb said. "Neither did I."

The girls had given him paperweights since the day they arrived. The fact that he gave them to his father was lost in the zombie fog, a memory he discarded long ago. Even stacked on his desk, young Ebenezer had already banished the memory along with the feelings. Now they were just rocks.

So why did I keep them?

A car door slammed. Young Ebenezer looked out the window. Someone had pulled up to the house across the street. Jacob got out of the passenger side.

Young Ebenezer fumbled for his phone. *What are you doing?* he texted.

You home? Jacob texted on the way inside.

Yeah.

Thought you were gone.

Change of plans. Home for Christmas.

Come over.

"We used to sleep in the treehouse when we were kids." Eb watched the Christmas lights go on at Jacob's house. The trees glittered in the dusky light. "Jacob's mom would call my parents to make sure it was all right. Always had to leave a message. Never got a call back."

Young Ebenezer shoved his bags under the bed. If he left no evidence, his mother might forget he was home. His father would never know.

"What are you doing?" a voice boomed.

A shiver rattled every bone in his body. Eb turned toward the doorway.

His father walked into the room, his steps slow and methodical, the lumbering pace of a calculated thug. The room filled with the smell of an old leather briefcase.

"Unpacking," young Ebenezer said.

"Going somewhere?" his father said.

"Apparently not." Young Ebenezer stood his ground.

His father's eyes darkened beneath hooded brows. A quiver pierced Eb through the stomach. He had the urge to crawl under the desk, roll under the bed next to his luggage. His father wanted his son to be a man, not because that was the right thing for a father to want, not because he wanted the best for his son.

Blake Scrooge liked a challenge.

"You think this is funny?" He held his phone in young Ebenezer's face. "Some sort of joke?"

It took him a minute to read the email. "I can explain," young Ebenezer said.

"No. You can get back to work."

Young Ebenezer pleaded. His father paced the room while his son followed his plodding footsteps.

"I got disciplined," Eb said, his voice as shaky as young Ebenezer's. "We cut class before Thanksgiving, spent the night at a house party. I didn't mean to do it, just one thing led to another. When I woke up, the police were there. I figured the chancellor's email got lost in cyberspace or spam because no one said anything." He clutched both dolls in one hand. He was still carrying them. "He was just waiting for the right time to beat me with it."

"Sit down." His father pointed at the bed.

Eb resisted following the man's order. Young Ebenezer sank on his mattress, head hanging. The sooner he took a submissive position, the shorter the speech. His father knew when every ounce of victory had been wrung from a situation.

"You think this is a joke?" he said.

"No, sir."

"You think I spend all that money to send you to the best school, to hire the best tutors, to provide you with a home and clothing and food and this wonderful life so that you can play grab ass with your buddies? Is that it?"

"No, sir."

"I got news for you, young man. This can all go away in a heartbeat." He snapped his fingers. "Just like that, you're on your own, you understand? I make the calls. I know what's good for you. If you don't want to listen, then you can figure it out on your own."

His father's phone buzzed. He turned away to answer a text. Young Ebenezer deflated, propping his elbows on his knees.

"That was his move," Eb said. "Listen or else. Do what he says or he'd take it all away. He meant it, too."

"He couldn't take it away, sir," the droid said.

Eb turned to the droid. Of course he could. His father had the money, wasn't that obvious? He bought the house and the cars, paid for school and books. Wasn't the droid watching the same thing Eb was? His father could put him on the streets at any moment.

His father was going to take it all away one day. Eb knew that. His father knew the day would come when Eb was capable of being self-sufficient. His father would be watching, he'd see it coming, and he'd snatch it all away, rip the carpet from under his feet just before he got there.

One last victory before manhood.

"He never gave you anything, sir," the droid said. "Nothing that mattered."

Eb swallowed a sudden lump. His bone-crushing fear transformed into something deep and moving, a current of sadness that rushed up his throat and slammed into the back of his brain.

Nothing that mattered.

"Here's what you're going to do," his father said. "The chancellor was kind enough to have your instructor send additional projects."

"But—"

He held up his hand, the fingernails manicured, palms lotioned. "Don't interrupt."

Young Ebenezer went back into hangdog.

"You'll finish them before returning from break. Anything less than an A on one of them, and I'll have another batch sent on top of your schoolwork. You're hanging out with losers, all of them." He pointed out the window. "No son of mine is going to be a no-good loser, you understand?"

Pause. "Yes, sir."

The speech continued. He was extra wound up, probably gamed up at a holiday party that afternoon. A fight was always at the tail end of a good night, his father always said.

He was just getting warmed up.

The lecture came out in clichéd chunks that Eb could recite by memory. If his father wasn't looking, he would mouth along. If he got caught, it would unlock a whole new set of insults. Sometimes it got worse than cursing.

Eb shook his head. He remembered. He knew it well.

Addy and Natty heard them, too.

A bomb detonated in his stomach, a sickening realization that he'd danced the dance his father taught him. He'd towered over employees, shouted at teleconferences, threw insults at everyone that deserved it.

Eb had his own hangdogs.

His father's phone buzzed again. Quietly, he thumbed the screen, his lips moving, a sly smile upon them. His latest mistress needed attention. He hardly tried to hide it anymore and left breadcrumbs as big as sourdough loaves.

"And another thing." His father pointed the phone from the doorway. "Don't plan on going outside or sneaking out to Jacob's house. You are grounded, young man. I will be watching."

Eb fell on the bed next to his younger self. They sat on the bed until night fell. The Christmas lights at Jacob's house cast a red glow on the wall. His phone buzzed with texts from his best friend every once in a while.

Sobs filled Eb's throat. He choked them down and pushed them back. Forced them to stay where young Ebenezer had put them all those years ago, in a locked box deep in the dark.

Eb remembered that Christmas. It was spent in a big lonely house with boxes of unpacked ornaments.

"I never escaped this place." Eb's voice cracked.

"You can leave, sir," the droid said. "The door is open. It always has been."

But it was safer in the house, he wanted to say. *No one could hurt me if I stayed.*

"But no one can see you, either, sir."

The droid turned the unseen crank. The merry-go-round went around. When Eb looked up, the room had changed.

He was still in a bedroom, but this was different. Fat red and green and blue lights slowly alternated on a tree branch outside a window, each casting a different mood across a white comforter.

Red intensity.

Green relaxed.

Blue was… blue.

A lump shifted beneath the covers, a shag of brown hair sunk in the pillow, eyes peeking out. Little Ebenezer stared at the ceiling, clutching the edge of the comforter.

Bing Crosby crooned throughout the thin-walled house.

He was five years old, waiting for the sound of Santa's reindeer on the roof. There were posters of science fiction movies, a shelf with his spelling bee trophy and a bowling medal for perfect attendance. It was the last time his mother let him put posters up because the tape smudged the wall.

A plate of cookies was on his desk. A glass of milk.

He kept them in his room. If Santa was hungry, he'd find them. The year before, he'd heard the fireplace doors squeal, so little Ebenezer had snuck out to see if Santa was delivering the BB gun. The television was blaring, someone complaining about the idiot president.

His father was lying on the couch, eating the cookies.

After that, little Ebenezer snuck them into his room. And Santa never ate them. Not once. Maybe he was mad at his father for eating them. Or maybe he was on the naughty list.

We all were.

"Santa wasn't mad at you, sir," the droid said.

Eb knew that. It was silly to think he was. Eb was a grown man. He didn't believe in fairy tales, didn't believe in a fat man keeping lists or leaving lumps of coal or ignoring plates of cookies.

Nonetheless, guilt had a firm grip on his throat. Because Santa never came back.

The walls rattled as Gene Autry began naming off Santa's reindeer—reindeer that little Ebenezer listened for, reindeer that never landed. Keys jingled on a hook by the front door. The clopping of heavy shoes stopped in the hallway, two long shadows breaking the lighted gap at the bottom of the bedroom door. Little Ebenezer looked up.

Eb's chest fluttered nervously.

His father went back to the kitchen, his steps long and even. Little Ebenezer watched the lighted gap for the shadows to return until the kitchen cabinets opened and closed.

Something is missing.

Little Ebenezer was trembling. He was scared of the shadows, frightened of the voices. Eb could feel it in his own chest as he remembered that night. He was watching it happen again. Something was missing, something that helped little Ebenezer manage the fear, to make it through the night.

"You think this is a joke?"

Eb spun toward the door, his heart thumping. His father's voice was in the kitchen.

"This is funny to you?" his father said.

"It's nothing," his mother replied, dragging slippers over the linoleum.

His father spoke intensely, words with hardened edges so sharp that they cut the ears, imbedded in the brain like slivers that couldn't be surgically removed, where they would root and grow and infect.

Eb clenched his empty fists. He'd dropped the dolls somewhere. They weren't on the floor. Maybe they were back with young Ebenezer.

Something is missing.

"My sister got them for him," his mother said. "He likes them, so what." Ice cubes rattled in a short glass. A long pause, then she said, "You afraid he's going to grow up soft?"

"You see, that's the problem," his father said. "There are no boundaries in this house. No rules, no structure. You let him do whatever he wants like some hippy-dippy ding-dong. You're going to ruin him, Dee."

"Hey, you're welcome to help out. The floor is wide open, honey."

"I'm sure it is."

"What's that supposed to mean?" Her upper lip was tight when she said that. When his mother was backed into a corner, her lips drew into a thin line and cut as sharp as his father's.

Little Ebenezer pulled the blanket over his head. Brown curls were still visible.

"You know exactly what it means," his father said.

"I never should've married you."

"Then what would you do? Huh, Dee? Would you work? Would you do something?"

"I wouldn't be putting up with this crap."

The ice clinked in a now empty glass. A long gap of silence drew out between Christmas songs. And Eb knew what his father was doing, knew he had moved in on his mother, towered over her, looked down on her. She never gave up a step, always stood her ground. But the presence pushed hard on her, bearing down.

"Without me," he said, "you'd be nothing."

She didn't reply.

Blankness entered her. She was staring across the room, wishing for another place, emptying her heart like a vessel that could be tipped over, a cauldron emptied of the boiling contents. All the foulness gone.

She went zombie.

The garbage can lid fell hard. Just before the back door opened, his father delivered parting words. "Ho, ho, ho."

The walls shook again.

Eb watched his father through the bedroom window, stomping holes in the snow. The car fishtailed out of the driveway.

The Christmas music in the house shut off.

"He came back the next morning," Eb said. "Unshaven, bleary-eyed. Sat on the couch and watched me open presents. I gave him a present and..."

He cleared his throat, couldn't say it, not out loud. Even if he could, there was no way he could capture the way his father had laughed when he looked at the smooth rock that little Ebenezer had wrapped.

Blue lights twinkled in his eyes.

It went deep.

"They argued some more. Mom left this time."

"What did you do, sir?" the droid asked.

"He fell asleep, so I went to Jacob's house. My mother came to get me later that night."

It was the only thing that felt special, Jacob's house. The warm candles, the laughter, the hugs, the food. They even gave him a present, a candy necklace. And he had a present for them and no one laughed when they opened it.

It's exactly what I need, Jacob's mother said. *A paperweight.*

And she meant it.

The droid opened the bedroom door. Light from the kitchen flooded the room. Eb backed against the bed. The comforter had fallen away from the mop of brown curls. Little Ebenezer was already sleeping on his side, his arm on the outside like his father had taught him. *This is how you sleep, son,* he would say, creeping in at night to check on him, waking him if he had rolled onto his back.

The droid opened the kitchen trash.

His shadow stretched across the hallway floor. His silhouette stood in the doorway. He was holding something in each hand. What his father had thrown away. What his mother thought would make him soft.

What his father hated.

The dolls.

It was what little Ebenezer was missing. He had come to bed that Christmas Eve and they weren't on the pillow where he placed them every morning, where they would be waiting for him at night, the mops of red yarn, the wide-open eyes. The stitched smiles.

He didn't carry them around the house, but hid them under the cover so his father wouldn't see them. At night, he would squeeze them in the crook of his elbow like a nutcracker, nuzzling his nose into the soft fabric.

They were always there for him. Silly little rag dolls.

The droid put them in his hands. Eb wept softly. *How could I forget?*

"It's easy, sir," the droid said, "to forget who you are."

A blubbering mess on two legs, he pushed the dolls against his cheeks and ran his thumb where the fabric was worn away. He was ashamed of them, of himself.

Of being soft.

He sat on the bed, unfolded little Ebenezer's arm and tucked the dolls in place.

"I don't want to do this anymore. I don't want to be like him." Eb pulled the blankets over little Ebenezer's arm. "I became my father."

"And your father like his, sir."

Eb wanted to stay with his younger self, to tell him that it was all right, it would be all right, that he wasn't what they said he was. He could be exactly who he was.

The droid turned the invisible crank.

The room made a hard spin. The lights streaked momentarily.

A different bed, another boy. His thumb in his mouth, eyes wide with fear. Voices arguing in another room about the thumb-sucker.

Another turn.

Another bed, another boy.

And another. And another. His grandfather, great-grandfather, great-great—

"Where does it end, sir?" the droid asked.

The wheel of time continued to spin backwards. The floor occasionally buckled on speed bumps or air pockets. Red and green and blue lights streaked around him, blurring into each other, the universe whirling, a hurricane turning.

He was in the eye of the storm.

The colors merged until they were bright white and clear. The droid let go of the invisible crank. The wheel was turning on its own now. The force drew on the droid's loose clothing, the sleeves flapping.

He cocked his head curiously.

A cycle of behavior passed down through the generations, culminating in Eb's madness. Whether he had dreamed the dreams or lived them, it did not matter. The result was the same.

He could see it now.

Eb could see who he was. His future couldn't frighten him into changing his path, his guilt couldn't force him to transform. Now he understood.

"I want to fly."

The wall of light sucked the droid out of sight. He was gone, swallowed by a storm that rattled the floor, gone in the howling bright light. The humbug was gone. He wouldn't come back on Christmas, not anymore. Eb didn't need him.

He wasn't afraid anymore.

The wall of light began to slow. The wind grew louder, bits of debris stung his arms, his cheeks. They bit his forearms. He covered his face. The wall of light began to separate into streaks again.

A tree crashed next to him.

The limbs snapped off; dry twigs and soil sprayed his legs. A dark hole had opened above. It looked like the sky had cracked open. Debris was blowing through it; specks of snow and sleet and dead foliage swirled.

There was a hole in the ceiling. It wasn't the sky that had cracked. *The Skeye™ dome.*

The transparent dome had fractured and the ceiling had fallen. Reinforcement rods pointed from chunks of concrete like crooked fingers. Metal beams had pierced the floor.

And the storm outside raged.

Eb was thrown to his knees. The wind whipped in several directions. Another section of the wall collapsed. This time a large chunk caught him square in the butt.

The house moaned.

The mountain coughed.

Furniture moved past him. Eb began sliding toward the back of the room, away from the door.

He dropped on all fours. He didn't want to die. The back wall blew open and the winter sky began inhaling the contents, curtains fluttering into the dark, vases crashing to the ground. Eb lay flat and waited for the end.

Something latched onto him.

Dull gray fingers wrapped around his wrist.

The droid had a firm grip. And the other droids were behind him, each clasping the other's hand, forming a chain that reached back to the doorway. They began to pull.

The floor dropped again and, for a moment, Eb felt the ground fall out, sensed the earth rushing toward him. The droids hung on.

The girls suddenly appeared in the doorway, green dress and red dress. *Addy is for apple, red as can be. And Natty is neither, but green as a tree.*

They seemed unaffected by the wind or the buckling floor. Their ribbons did not waver; dresses did not flutter. They stood holding hands, dolls at their sides. When the house groaned again and the floor dropped suddenly, Eb's round spectacles slid off the end of his nose and clattered out of reach.

When he looked up, the girls were gone.

As the chain of droids pulled him out of the collapsing Great Room, as the house continued to slide out of the mountain, the droids shouted above the storm.

"I'm here to help, sir!"

PART V

THE HAUNTING OF EBENEZER SCROOGE

32

Steam momentarily blotted out the bluegrass music.

Jerri leaned deep into the corner seat and closed her eyes. On the other side of the plant, just below the Avocado logo, a fiddle player sawed into "Jingle Bells."

Eric Thompson, software engineer turned barista, handed a latte to Jamie Lynn, marketing assistant turned gift giver. A roar went up somewhere to Jerri's left where the gingerbread house competition announced a winner. The smell of baked goods rose above the scent of warm plastic.

Jerri hovered over a decaf pumpkin spice.

She was about to melt out of the seat, drain onto the floor and into a sleeping puddle that wouldn't wake until the New Year.

It had been a long year.

The lights were on in her cantilevered office. Someone moved between the blinds, perhaps a secret Santa leaving a gift. The opened slats hid nothing from the plant. They saw her every day, knew what she was doing. Her door always open.

The blinds were drawn on the office opposite hers. Tomorrow would be the one-year anniversary of when it went dark.

The squeal of children and the stampede of tiny feet made her smile. She had never appreciated the weight of running a company until it was fully yoked across her shoulders. Every little fire came across her desk. Sometimes she understood why Eb had withdrawn to his house. There were nights she didn't sleep.

Especially in the beginning.

It was difficult to steer a technology company that was already sinking, one that was licking its wounds from misdirection and confusion. One that lacked an identity. More so, it was difficult to do so with a heavy heart. She had aged ten years over the last year, her hair more white than gray and wrinkles in places she didn't know could wrinkle.

Now she just wanted to enjoy a bluegrass version of "Silent Night."

"Jerri?" Rick must have taken the mic. "We need to get Jerri up here. Somebody find her and get her up here."

She didn't move, even when the crowd started chanting her name and clapping along, calling for a search party to scour the plant.

"Where are you, Jerri?" Rick called. "Front and center, lady."

High-pitched voices of the children cut through the celebration, long drawn-out name calling like they did when hide-and-seek was over.

Ollie ollie oxen free!

"Mom?" Jerri's daughter said. "They want you up front."

Jerri's smile grew wider.

Her son-in-law followed her daughter with a big puffy bag over his shoulder and a six-year-old charging ahead. Jerri threw her arms open and caught her, the little arms clasping and squeezing until she couldn't breathe.

"You all right, Mom?" Jerri's daughter asked.

"I am now."

Her granddaughter bounced up and down, the white fuzzy ball of her Santa hat flipping from one side to the other.

"I like your hat," Jerri said.

"We have one for you," her granddaughter said.

"You do?"

Jerri's son-in-law pulled a fuzzy red hat from the bag. The granddaughter pulled it over Jerri's cropped hair.

"How do I look?"

After another breath-stealing hug, they made their way through the plant, past the deserted Ping-Pong table and odd-shaped furniture.

"Found her!" someone called.

The applause began before she saw the makeshift stage, passing random employees from accounting to IT to engineering and fabrication, all of them wearing Santa hats or foam antlers or horrendously wonderful Christmas sweaters. The celebration reached near chaos when she turned the corner.

A ten-foot Christmas tree glittered beneath the Avocado.

A heaping pile of gifts was off to the side. Jennifer Canton from HR had gone full elven with green stripes and curly-toe shoes and pointed ears. Carl Pendleton from accounting didn't need a fake beard or pillow stuffed beneath his shirt to play Santa.

Carol helped her onto the platform while Rick playfully bowed. Jerri smacked him on the back to stop. Everyone was filling in the empty space where tables and furniture had been pushed aside for the dance floor.

"All right, all right," Rick called into the mic. "Anyone else back there?"

Some stragglers made their way up front. Her granddaughter hid her face on Jerri's shoulder.

"You want me to take her?" Jerri's daughter asked.

Jerri shook her head. *Not in a million years.*

"I'm not going to take long," Rick said. The crowd settled. "I just want to say a few things about this incredible person with the child surgically implanted on her chest."

Laughter.

"I think I speak for everyone when I say there is not another human being on this planet that could've done what you have done in the past year. You took a floundering company and made it into a family again. When I wake up in the morning, I can honestly say I can't wait to get to work."

Applause. Cheers.

"Calling it work just isn't fair, Jerri. Everyone should be so lucky to have an extended family that is changing the world. I want to thank you, personally, for bringing me back to be part of it."

He gave up the mic to applause. They hugged with a six-year-old child between them. Carol helped Jennifer the elf from HR slide a giant gift-wrapped boxed front and center.

"It's just a little something," Rick said. "From all of us. You've been all over this plant, sometimes running. We thought this might help."

Jerri knelt down to unload her precious cargo. Her granddaughter reluctantly let go, clinging to her leg and staring at Santa Claus.

Jerri didn't see this coming.

A gift, sure. But this was heavy and bulky and as tall as her. Had they packed a smart car?

"Thank you," Jerri said into the mic. "Before we open this... this most generous gift, I, uh, just want to say it has been a pleasure to be part of Avocado."

She wasn't a magician, not the messiah like the media had anointed her. In fact, if not for the sudden financial infusion from investors, some that remained anonymous, she could have easily watched the company implode.

"This is hard for me because this is not my company. It's all of our company."

She waited for the applause to settle.

"Before that, it was Jacob Marley and Ebenezer Scrooge's company. It was their vision, their hard work that made any of this possible."

Quiet spread throughout the plant. A few nodded. A few frowned. Jerri looked around at the different faces, the varied expressions. The deep-set opinions. She took in the hanging garland and papercut snowflakes and dangling ornaments. She smiled.

"God, he would hate this."

And the crowd fell out. They knew exactly what she meant—a period of time that would forever be known as Avocado's dark years.

"Merry Christmas, everyone. Happy Hanukah, happy festivus and happy holidays. Thank you for changing the world!"

Hugs went around. First Rick, next Carol, then others. She was facing the monstrous gift, the fat red ribbon shiny and perfect.

Jerri knelt down and whispered to her granddaughter, "Do you want to help?"

The little girl nodded. Jerri tore a hole in the wrapping. Her granddaughter took it from there, ripping it around all four corners. The crowd pushed toward the front, some with no idea what was inside the box.

"Oh my..." Jerri stood back, covered her face and began laughing hysterically.

"Don't let this change you," Rick shouted. "We just thought you could save some energy."

Coffee fueled Jerri's powerwalking stride across the plant, from meeting to meeting. There was no problem sleeping at night when any horizontal surface would do, but her knees ached and a noticeable limp had everyone's attention.

Rick and Carol pushed the gift out of the pile of wrapping. Secretly, Jerri had hoped to never see another one of these things again, but her knees and back cheered. Two wheels. Handlebars.

A Segway.

"I don't think I can do it." She giggled.

"Don't resist," Rick said. "You'll be hooked after the first round."

He demonstrated instant mastery by driving in a circle then off the platform and around the crowd to rhythmic clapping.

The gift-giving began, Santa made room for adult or child on his knee, his ho-ho-ho ringing around the plant, gifts handed out to everyone. Jerri remained on the stage until someone tugged on her arm.

"I think you need to see this," Freddy from IT said.

❄

"Why didn't you tell me?" Jerri said.

"It was over before we could get word to you." Freddy ran his fingers through his hair.

Jerri sat at the monitor. She didn't know what she was looking at. She wasn't versed in the backroom language of the IT vault or the coded messages that computers spoke. It wasn't much different than lifting the hood of her car. All she could do was trust the mechanic.

"The program showed up just like it did last year and the year before that." He ran his hand through his hair again. "The redundant code and everything, like the system was triggered to install it. We started quarantine, but before I could pick up the phone, it just... it was gone."

"You mean dormant?"

"No, I mean gone."

"It disappeared?"

"More like... *left*."

Jerri faced him with a hardened expression she'd honed over the past year, one that cut through hesitancy and demanded progress. "Where did it go?" she asked slowly.

"Best we can tell, it shipped itself out, like an email. We attempted to track it, but the IP addresses were all over the world. It fragmented and just disappeared in cyberspace."

Jerri sat back and tapped her chin, aware that tapping her chin was Eb's thoughtful move, something that seemed to organically grow on her as if the mannerism occupied the job description.

"Is this a problem?" she asked.

Freddy shrugged. "You tell me."

He wasn't at the company when the mystery program first started hitting all the alarms. After contracting the best IT companies to analyze their system, the best explanation was an anomaly that operated like a benign tumor.

It wants to live, the consultant said.

"But why on Christmas Eve?" Jerri had asked.

He shrugged again.

It didn't make sense for it to come back two days out of the year and then go to sleep, disappearing from sight. Jerri wasn't satisfied, but what could you do when every mechanic that looked at your car said the noise was nothing really?

"I don't know if this matters," Freddy said, "but I couldn't find any evidence of this from earlier episodes. The program seemed to have parallels with an already existing project called Jenks."

"Jenks?"

"Yeah. You heard of it?"

She dipped her head. A distant memory pushed into her awareness of a time when dusty shelves and a drafty warehouse was a makeshift home. That was Jacob's project. And the sound of Eb's droids, the cadence in which they spoke, reminded her of that initial success, the day Jacob referred to as Jenks's birth.

Christmas Eve.

"It was the, uh, prototype for artificial intelligence. But that was a long time ago. How is it still in our system?"

"Here's the thing," Freddy said. "I know this sounds weird, but something on the outside seems to be visiting it. All the earlier analysis looked like it was coming from Mr. Scrooge's castle, like something was using the plant to run a full-scale operation, but what, I don't know."

"What do you mean *something*? You mean like the house system?"

"That could be it, yeah. Definitely something artificially intelligent."

"Why do you say that?"

"Because it was like a conversation in code. We can't even follow it."

Jerri couldn't help but think of Eb's servant droids. They were found in the aftermath with nothing to be recovered as to what caused the collapse. *And they sounded just like Jenks.*

"Keep an eye on it." She pushed away. "I don't want to hear that we've unleashed a cyber storm on the world."

She hurried to exit. This would be exactly the reason people didn't want artificial intelligence. An awareness that could travel through a wireless network and inhabit remote bodies simultaneously. Christmas just got a little less merry.

But why only Eb's house?

"One more thing."

Freddy leaned over the keyboard. The data streamed in gibberish code. He tapped the space bar and dragged the cursor over a line buried in the cryptic mess. Jerri leaned forward.

"What do you think that means?" he asked.

She shook her head.

Humbug, it said.

"SAMANTHA," Jerri said, "did someone come up to my office?"

She had snuck up to her office, tempted to pull the blinds so that no one would see her sleeping—a nap perhaps the greatest Christmas gift ever—when something caught her eye. Jerri stared like a snake had coiled on her desk. Perched on top of a pile of papers were bent frames and broken lenses.

Round-spectacled glasses.

Samantha wasn't at the front desk, so Jerri left a message—a message her office assistant might not get until after the holidays.

The last time she'd seen these glasses—maybe not these exact glasses—were on Ebenezer Scrooge exactly a year ago when she spoke to him. He had stopped projecting that silly image and forced her to look at a blank screen. Little did he know that she posted a photo of him to look at when they spoke. It was better than talking to an empty monitor.

She wanted to tell him about her decision to leave Avocado but decided to wait until the New Year. She never had a chance to tell him.

As it turned out, she never left.

The remains of the Castle were all over the newsfeeds. The debris was half-buried in snow beneath a hole in the mountain. News drones descended on the wreckage, a complete architectural failure.

The following investigation exonerated the architects and construction company. Eb had added onto to the structure, built his giant-sized snow globe on top, something he called *Skeye dome*. The droids did much of the work, although some contractors were brought in to help. There were records that warned Eb that the expansion could affect the Castle's stability, but apparently he didn't get that warning. Or he didn't care.

The Castle wasn't meant to support the additional weight in a storm like that.

He had no extended family to press further or stop the rumors of self-destruction, which some suggested was really at fault. The storm was faulted, along with a tremor that fractured the mountain. Or perhaps something caused the tremor. Nonetheless, there was no insurance claim.

No bodies found. Not Ebenezer. Not the girls.

Just lifeless droids.

That alone did not prove self-destruction. It didn't help, especially when word got out that many of Eb's personal financial accounts had been moved offshore the day before.

To complicate matters, no evidence of the girls' adoption could be found. Jacob had either destroyed or hidden the legal papers. Whether he was hiding something or protecting the girls, it didn't make sense. There was no trail, not a single thread of evidence that they had lived with him. Or Eb.

It made for strange thoughts.

Jerri didn't like to poke the evidence too long. If she did, she'd have to shine a light on where Avocado's anonymous cash infusions were coming from. Considered legal, their source was well camouflaged. And they specifically requested the medical research division return to full capacity.

It's not too late, the anonymous donor had said.

This coincided with a major donation to the MPS foundation, the rare disease that afflicted her granddaughter. So no, she didn't want to investigate too closely.

Throw the glasses away. Don't look, just throw them away and give thanks. What good can come of it?

Jerri picked the glasses up as if they were wired to explode. The gold rims were askew, the lenses—what was left of them—scuffed. A miniature camera, the size of a pinhead, winked.

For the first time, Jerri closed the blinds.

In the neon computer light, she opened a Bluetooth connection on her computer. The miniature camera glowed. It took her to a cloud account, the password automatically uploaded from the glasses.

She pushed back. "Oh my..."

It was a video journal that dated back ten years. Screen shots of Eb sitting in a chair, varied expressions, most of them distorted versions of irritation or anger. That wasn't what shocked her.

He was hardly recognizable.

He had used a projected image—the chiseled chin and buff torso and daring eyes—for so long that she didn't know what he really looked like. As she scrolled through them, coming closer to the present date, he grew larger, his color pastier, bags under his eyes.

His complexion splotchy.

She clicked on one and nothing happened. A padlock icon in the bottom right corner indicated it was locked. Only Eb's screen shot mocked her—his mouth contorted, eyes hooded. All of them were unavailable.

Except the last one.

Christmas Eve.

It was last year, a day before the accident. The screen shot showed a much different man. This version of Ebenezer Scrooge was emaciated, a yellowish tinge to the previously pallid complexion. Dark eyes behind the always-present round-spectacled glasses and a slack mouth. His head slouched with effort. He had shed at least a hundred pounds.

Do I want to see this?

Jerri's finger hovered over the mouse. She clicked.

Eb folded his hands on his lap, staring at them as if deciphering a hidden message. He sighed several times, pulling long breaths that didn't seem to contain enough oxygen. Sometimes he shuddered.

He cleared his throat. "There's nothing left to say."

Another long pause was followed by a protracted sigh.

"The dream is coming. I can feel it, if I'm honest. It'll be here shortly and drag me to whatever is next. I... I don't think I'll come back. And I have to admit... I'm looking forward to it. I'm..." He swallowed a sudden lump. "I just want this to be over."

Dreams.

Jerri didn't know the full extent of his problems with Christmas, but something had been happening. It had something to do with the mystery program, something that shook him up, turned him inside out.

How could I be so blind?

"I'm a stranger," he said. "To the world. To myself. And everyone hates me, but..."

He shook his head, twisting his fingers.

"I don't care if the world hates me. It's just... I do, too."

Always a curmudgeon, but the pain that powered his irritability, the suffering that kept the world at an arm's length was now fully exposed. He was looking at himself, not a reflection or a projection, but the raw essence that was Ebenezer Scrooge.

And so was Jerri.

Like Jacob, he was a visionary. He had so much potential. But whatever was ticking inside him had detonated long ago, had driven him into isolation, where he created his own reality with the projection room. He saw the world through the glasses, saw what he wanted to see, created the person he wanted to be.

But it was false.

Everything was a lie. Nothing he experienced was real, and it had driven him to what was sitting in that chair.

"I tried to go outside," he said. "I haven't been out of the Castle in... I don't know. I just thought... I opened the door and stood there. The world was cold. It was so beautiful, and I swear I wanted to take that one step out, just feel the snow under my foot, but..."

He wiped his eyes. Cleared his throat.

"I couldn't do it," he said with new resolve. "I just couldn't. I can't leave, I admit it. I'm trapped in a world that I created and I don't know the way out. But it's my fault. It's all my fault. And that's why…"

He took a deep breath, ran his fingers through his thinning hair and looked directly at Jerri.

"I *want* to change."

It was the look of a tired man. He wasn't beaten, wasn't giving up. He had found the bottom, had looked around, and for the first time in his life wanted it to be different. Ebenezer Scrooge lived life the only way he knew how. But now it didn't make sense.

He wanted it to be different.

He was ready to change.

"And he never got the chance," Jerri whispered.

She thought the journal entry had ended. He sat back and hadn't moved but occasionally blinked or shook his head. She reached for the mouse and was about to close it when he jerked his head to the side.

"Hey," he said. "No, no, no… not in here, girls. You're not allowed in here, you know that. Where's the droid?"

The girls were off to the left, just out of the camera's range.

"Shh-shh-shh," Eb urged. "Stop, settle down. I need you to listen."

There was no volume on the girls for some reason. They must've opened the door but stayed in the hall. Eb looked distressed.

Then he looked around the room and finally stood up, ushering them to come closer while shouting for his droid. But the girls still didn't cross into view. And they weren't making a sound.

Jerri grabbed the armrests.

A lightness swirled in her head, a sudden drop in air pressure, that surge of surprise when you miss the bottom step. Eb held his arms out like he was holding a little girl on each knee.

Only there was no one there.

"What did we talk about?" he said. "This is Uncle Scrooge's private room. You're only allowed up here whenever the droid brings you. Do you understand?"

He paused.

"Okay, good. Now, it's almost time for dinner. Have you done your homework?"

Pause.

"Then why don't you wash up and get ready to eat so Uncle Scrooge can finish his work."

The droid entered the room. Another one followed. They walked stiffly to the chair, their expressions vacant and calculated, and pretended to lift the imaginary girls from his lap.

Eb pushed his glasses up and watched them with a fragile smile.

"Oh my God," Jerri finally said. "Oh my God."

"Jerri?"

Jerri jumped at the sudden announcement. She sat back and clutched her chest. She punched the flashing button on her phone. "Yes, Samantha."

"I missed your call. Did you need something?"

"Um, yes." She took several moments to allow her heart to settle. She had just witnessed the unwinding of Ebenezer Scrooge, the imaginary projection of two little girls that, as far as she could tell, he thought were real. And the droids did, too.

Were they helping him?

"Jerri?"

"Yes. Um, did you send someone up to my office?"

"A delivery droid was here earlier and dropped off a package for you."

"A package?"

"Well, it wasn't a package, more like a pair of broken glasses. He said it was very important, that you would want them. I escorted him to your office and put them on your desk. Why, is something missing?"

"No, no. I just... who are they from?"

"He didn't say, just that they were important."

"Okay. Thank you, Samantha."

The video journal had ended. Eb looked a bit more at ease, the round-spectacled glasses propped on his nose. The very same glasses that were now on her desk. Maybe he was relieved that he'd finally hit bottom. Or the girls brought a trace of satisfaction.

The imaginary girls.

"Jerri?" Samantha called.

"Yes?"

"I don't know if this helps, but the delivery droid left contact information."

"Where did he come from?"

"St. Mary's Children's Hospital."

33

"Can I help you?" The nurse looked up from a wide desk cluttered with candy canes, cookies and a Santa Claus bobblehead that went ho-ho-ho when you tapped it.

"The receptionist said you might be able to help," Jerri said. "I'm from Avocado, down the street." She pointed as if someone might need clarification of what Avocado was. "We received a delivery from the hospital earlier today. It was dropped off by a droid but didn't have an explanation or contact person."

"Okay. What was it?"

"It was a, uh, pair of glasses."

"Did you lose them?"

"No. They belonged to a friend."

"Did he leave them here on accident?"

"I don't believe so."

"Can I see them?"

"I'm sorry. I didn't bring them. I know it's an odd request, I just wanted to thank whoever sent them. That's all."

The nurse picked up the phone and pressed a few buttons. Santa began laughing. At first, Jerri thought it was the bobblehead, but it was followed by children's laughter.

The double doors led to a large room that could be separated by curtains. Children were often hooked up to tubes, lying in beds or pushed around in wheelchairs.

"Howard will be up in a minute," the nurse said.

"Thank you."

Jerri leaned an elbow on the counter and watched the double doors. A cheer rose up and more laughter followed. Perhaps the most wonderful sound in the world.

"I used to come here," Jerri said.

"Oh, yes?" The nurse was busy at the computer. "Your child?"

"No. Well, yes, my granddaughter. But I was thinking of something else. I used to come with Jacob Marley when he delivered presents."

She spotted one of the dogs on the corner of the desk. It was nestled into a crowd of various stuffed animals.

"There, that one. That was from Jacob."

The nurse looked over. "Ah, yes. That was before my time. The others said he was a very nice man. Is that who the glasses belong to?"

"No." Jerri went over to the pack of stuff animals. "Do you mind?"

"Go ahead."

She picked up the dog. Several of the animals fell behind the desk. The nurse slid her chair over to pick them up.

Howard arrived.

He was a tall gentleman, not a wrinkle in his shirt, but his tie slightly undone. He smiled often. Jerri had no idea what his connection to the delivery was. Howard was polite, but assured her there had been no deliveries to Avocado.

What did she expect?

Part of her hoped the past four years had been a hoax, or a dream, or whatever could explain the death of Jacob Marley and the demise of Ebenezer Scrooge, that both of the men she met thirty some years ago would jump out from behind a tree and shout Merry Christmas.

At least, Jacob would.

He would be dressed in his Santa outfit, a bag over his shoulder. And Eb would be his elf.

"Everything all right?" the nurse asked.

Jerri realized she was smiling at the stuffed dog. "Yes. Of course. Thanks for your help. Merry Christmas."

She handed the dog back. The nurse placed it with the collection she had picked up. Jerri started to turn. Something was out of place.

"Is that new?" she asked.

The nurse took a moment. "The doll?"

"I haven't seen that before." Jerri was reluctant to pull it out of the pile and cause another avalanche. It didn't belong with the others. For starters, it was a doll instead of a stuffed animal. One of those old-fashioned rag dolls with bright red hair and button eyes.

Secondly, it was new.

"We just got it," the nurse said. "Santa Claus is handing them out to the children."

A buzz rode up Jerri's backbone. "Now?"

"Yes, he's in there."

"Can I...?"

The nurse tapped the keyboard before leading her to the double doors. Jerri knotted her fingers together. The covers were pulled off dusty memories as the nurse slowly pushed open one of the doors. They crept inside and stopped against the wall.

Children were in wheelchairs or propped on crutches. Some were bald or very skinny, slightly off-color. Santa Claus was on one knee, a big bag by his side. He was walking a redheaded doll up a little girl's leg. When it reached her lap, she throttled it against her chest.

From the back, the beard appeared to be real, a kinky mix of gray and white whiskers spread across white fluffy lapels. His laugh came from the belly and ran down the hall.

"Isn't he wonderful?" the nurse said quietly.

"Who is he?"

"He showed up unannounced."

Santa Claus heaved himself onto his feet and dragged his bag to the next child. His belly might've been stuffing, but he moved like a very large, very jolly St. Nick.

Jerri wanted to come closer.

She wanted to help him pull another doll from the bag, to lighten the load from another child shouldering a difficult, unfair disease. What if this was a stranger doing a good deed? She had gotten too many thoughts mixed with wishful thinking already.

But when Santa Claus bellowed another laugh, he threw his head back and, for a brief second, turned his head. Jerri found the courage to take a step. Santa had moved to a bedside where a young man was propped up with pillows, a tube taped to his arm.

Jerri reached into Santa's bag and handed him a doll with red yarn for hair and button eyes. An old-fashioned doll that under normal circumstances wouldn't stand a chance in a technology world. But these circumstances weren't normal.

The dolls were anything but ordinary.

"Do you get scared?" the boy asked.

"Me?" Santa stood up. "Of course I get scared. Because some things are scary. And do you know what I do?"

The boy shook his head. Santa took the doll from Jerri and tucked it under his chin.

"I hug this." He touched the boy's nose. "And remember someone cares."

Santa started for the next child, a young girl as pale as her sheets, and turned into Jerri. The stuffing shifted under the coat. His breath caught somewhere in his beard. He stood up, hands on his stuffed belly, eyes unblinking.

Jerri wiped her cheeks, a smile that beamed brighter than every child in a room. She put a pair of glasses in his gloved hand. He stared at the broken spectacles. She was certain that he had sent them to her, that he wanted her to find him. He appeared as surprised as her, caught in a stretching moment.

If he didn't send them, who did?

"Is that Mrs. Claus?" the girl asked.

Santa looked up. He grabbed Jerri and squeezed her long and

hard. Only her granddaughter could hug her like that. When he pulled away, he wiped his eyes. A grin crawled beneath his whiskers.

"I hope so," Santa said.

He bellowed jolly laughter, his cheeks rosy. Jerri played the elf, carried the bag for him and handed out stuffed dolls. It was an old-fashioned gift that the children would cherish in their times of need. It was something they could hug. Something that reminded them.

Someone cares.

Much later, Jerri would understand what the dolls meant to a little boy.

She left the hospital with Santa. They would return to the hospital the next year and the next. In the meantime, they would talk. They would laugh. They would share their lives out of the public eye.

Eventually, she would secretly become Mrs. Claus.

While they never learned who sent the glasses that led her back to him, Jerri always suspected Santa knew. Someone knew his heart belonged to her. He was too frightened to give it. Someone knew that, deep down, Santa believed in her. He had always believed in her. And she had always believed in him.

And he didn't need the glasses anymore. Glasses that once hid a blue eye.

And a green eye.

EPILOGUE

Hannah hated waiting.

Even Keurigs were too slow. She wanted her coffee now, not in two minutes.

She rubbed her face. The squabble from the next room was already climbing on her nerves. If she didn't pour some caffeine through her system, she'd shut it down. She hated Christmas.

The longest day of the year.

This year, though, was slightly different, she had to admit. Not the screaming and the fighting of the children or the excess presents from the grandparents. That was exactly the same.

Hannah was actually looking forward to Christmas for the first time since she'd become an adult with adult responsibilities.

She was fourteen years old when that happened. Her parents died and she started caring for her younger siblings along with her aunt. She'd done such a spectacular job of raising them that they were all in prison. Well, technically not all of them. The youngest was on house arrest. It was only a matter of time.

Hannah turned out better than them. She was smart.

She married an older man. He was overweight and short-tempered, prone to angry outbursts and dangerous tantrums. It was no accident she chose him. He was a mirror image of her father, so there was that. Unlike his bank account, his health wasn't built for the long run.

The end struck him in a restaurant on his sixty-fourth birthday.

Hannah received a lump sum settlement and four children that were currently throwing something in the front room. The littlest one began crying. Sometimes she wondered if he got a better deal.

This Christmas would be different.

Her late husband's will promised help in the New Year. She wasn't sure what that meant, but even if it was part-time, she might burst into tears. If it was a live-in sort of maid or butler, which she dared to dream, she might actually pass out when all the blood rushed to her head from prolonged celebration, after which she would pack her bags for a long-deserved vacation that didn't include children.

She pulled her robe tight and sipped half the cup of hazelnut before braving the front room.

Wrapping paper was everywhere. Boxes were crushed, bows torn, toys still trapped in wire ties, their limbs twisted in attempts to free them. The two girls were under the tree, ripping open the remaining presents regardless of whose name was on the label.

The boys were playing tug-of-war with a lifelike gun.

Like throwing meat to the lions.

"Stop!" Hannah screamed. "Put it down, now!"

She threatened to haul it out to the backyard and have a Christmas bonfire, tree included. It would be fueled by their tears and last for days. The boys cheered. Nothing would make them happier than to burn something.

She fell on the couch and let the destruction continue. All the gifts were stripped apart by the second cup of hazelnut. They were already on their phones, the festive aftermath nothing more than a discarded pile of faded desires.

Hannah was waiting on her third cup when the doorbell rang.

"Someone answer that!" she shouted. When the doorbell sounded off a second time, she added, "It's your grandparents!"

"Presents!" they exclaimed.

Her caffeine kick had already peaked, but she still hit the third cup, hoping the surge would carry her through the afternoon when her in-laws would take the kids off her hands.

That would be her Christmas present.

"What's that?"

The kids were prying at the front of an eight-foot-tall crate, shreds of brown paper hanging from the sides.

"A box," the youngest said.

"Where's your grandparents?" Hannah asked.

She didn't get a response. It would be much later that she discovered the shipment had arrived special delivery. It was supposed to arrive Christmas Eve but had instead been dropped off Christmas morning.

She tore a card off the front.

A little help, it said. *Especially for you.*

When the front of the box popped open, a flood of packing peanuts poured across the floor. The children tossed and rolled in them like snow, pulling the packaging out like endless snakes.

A hand was uncovered.

They stood back. Hannah with her coffee, the kids with handfuls of peanuts. She pulled on a pad of foam packing. A face, a bald head, a torso and fully developed biceps were revealed. All of them dull gray.

The eyebrows arched up. The eyelids fluttered.

The droid pushed his shoulders out of the custom-formed foam packing. The kids and Hannah took a step back. He looked at each of them, eyes glittering.

"Merry Christmas," the droid said.

The children took the crazed celebration to new heights. The boys smashed ornaments; the girls kicked boxes. Hannah was struck numb.

The droid remained in the crate and offered her a small gift. Hannah put down her coffee and opened it. The children angrily shouted for their gifts. Hannah pulled out an odd little gift.

A pair of round-spectacled glasses.
"I am here to help you," the droid said.
And cocked his head to the side.

CLAUS: RISE OF THE MISER (BOOK 5)

Get the Claus Universe at:
BERTAUSKI.COM/CLAUS

Claus: Rise of the Miser (Book 5)

CHAPTER 1

It started with a letter.

The boy who wrote it wasn't much different than other little boys, full of hopes and dreams and puppy dog tails. He took a blank piece of paper and a pencil and, with his tongue between his teeth, wrote in very neat cursive.

Dear Santa, it started. All letters to the North Pole start that way, sure. It's what followed that made all the difference.

Dear Santa, I hope you are warm. I will leave you a blanket when you stop by my house. I do not want anything for Christmas. Can you bring my mother something? And if it is not too much, could you maybe give me a ride on your sleigh? I understand if you can't.

Seriously, he wrote that. If I could cry, I would.

How many seven-year-olds don't want anything for Christmas except for their mom to be happy? I'll tell you, none. That's how many.

He wrote that letter in looping cursive letters and sealed it in an envelope before taking it to his mom because he didn't want her to read it. Not that he was embarrassed. He believed letters to Santa were like birthday wishes. If you told someone, they didn't come true.

Precious.

Santa Claus, North Pole, he addressed it, because everyone knew where Santa lived. He gave it to his mom and she put a stamp on it. The next day, they took it to the post office. And that was it.

Well, not entirely.

His mom actually opened it before they mailed it. It wasn't just her curiosity that got the best of her. He wouldn't tell her what he wanted for Christmas, so you know what she was thinking.

She ended up bawling.

Of course, Santa didn't wake him up when he stopped by on Christmas. There were no magic sleigh rides, but his mom did seem happier in the morning, so the boy got what he wanted. Minus the sleigh ride.

I wasn't around when all of this happened. In fact, I wasn't anywhere. But I have a copy of the letter. I know what he did and what she did, the details of their memories, the way he sealed the envelope, how he tried to stay awake on Christmas Eve, and how his mother cried.

But like any good iceberg, there's way more to the story beneath the surface. It started with the letter, but it has a lot to do with a mother's love.

And a very fat man.

Click here to get Claus: Rise of the Miser (Book 5)

YOU DONATED TO A WORTHY CAUSE!

By purchasing this book, you have donated to the development of mental health since 10% of the profits is annually donated to the National MPS Society.

Supports research, supports families, and increases public and professional awareness of MPS and related diseases.

ABOUT THE AUTHOR

My grandpa never graduated high school. He retired from a steel mill in the mid-70s. He was uneducated, but a voracious reader. As a kid, I'd go through his bookshelves of musty paperback novels, pulling Piers Anthony and Isaac Asimov off the shelf and promising to bring them back. I was fascinated by robots that could think and act like people. What happened when they died?

Writing is sort of a thought experiment to explore human nature and possibilities. What makes us human? What is true nature?

I'm also a big fan of plot twists.

Printed in Great Britain
by Amazon